Forlorn River

Forlorn River

ZANE GREY

SAGEBRUSH
Large Print Westerns

First published in Great Britain by Hodder & Stoughton
First published in the United States by Harper & Bros

Published in Large Print 2005 by ISIS Publishing Ltd.,
7 Centremead, Osney Mead, Oxford OX2 0ES
United Kingdom
by arrangement with
Golden West Literary Agency

British Library Cataloguing in Publication Data
Grey, Zane, 1872–1939
    Forlorn River. – Large print ed. –
    (Sagebrush western series)
    1. Western stories
    2. Large type books
    I. Title
    813.5'2 [F]

ISBN 0–7531–7297–6 (hb)

Printed and bound in Great Britain by
T. J. International Ltd., Padstow, Cornwall

CHAPTER
ONE

Ben Ide named this lonely wandering stream Forlorn River because it was like his life.

Ben was well-born and had attended school until sixteen years of age, but from the time he had given up to his passion for the open country and the chase of wild horses he had gotten nowhere. That seemed the way of Forlorn River. It had its beginning in Clear Lake, a large body of surface water lying amid the Sage Mountains of northwestern California. It had begun well enough at its source under the beautiful rounded bare mountains of gray sage, and flowed bravely on for a few miles, then suddenly it became a lost river. That was what it was called by the Indians.

It meandered around under the foothills with their black fringe of juniper, into the wide gray valleys where thousands of wild horses roamed; to and fro across the open country as if seeking escape, on toward the dark pine-timbered ranges of Nevada; and back again, a barren little stream without creeks or springs to freshen it, a wilderness waterway, dear to the Indian and horse-hunter and cowboy; slackened by the thirsty Clay Flats to the west, and crowded away on the north by the huge red bluff that blocked entrance into Wild

Goose Basin, forced at last to describe a wandering hundred-mile circle and find on the other side of the sage-hills, not far from its source, a miserable sand-choked outlet into the vast level ranch and pasture-land which had once been the bottom of Tule Lake.

Ben's gray weather-beaten cabin partook somewhat of the melancholy austerity of the country, yet it was most picturesquely located on the south shore of the big lake, on the only elevated and wooded cape that jutted out into the wind-ruffed waters. Forlorn River was born just under his door, for his cabin did not face the lake, but the river and the west. Ben could watch the aimless windings of the stream for many a mile. Scattered juniper trees saved this slight eminence of land from the baldness of the irregular shore line. Clear Lake was ten miles round, and everywhere but at this point the gray sage reached down to the white high-water line. Back from the cabin where the cape widened stood a large well-built barn, which adjoined an enormous corral. Spirited horses kicked up the dust, and whistled, perhaps to their wild kindred in plain sight on the distant gray slopes, swelling toward the blue sky. Barn and corral, presenting such marked contrast to the little gray cabin, might have told an observant eye that Ben Ide loved horses and thought little of himself.

Spring had come late, the dryest of six successive dry springs. Clear Lake was lower than ever before in the memory of the Modoc Indians, who had lived there always. The white baked earth spread a long distance down from the sage line to the water. Flocks of ducks dotted the yellow surface of the lake. Wild geese tarried here on the way north, and every hour of day or night Ben heard their resonant and melodious honk, honk, honk. It was high country. Frost glistened on the roof of the barn and ice glinted along the shores of Forlorn River. Snow peaks notched the blue sky above the black-timbered range of Nevada mountains. The air was cold and crisp, fragrant with the scent of sage.

Ben Ide came out on the porch to gaze across the river and the long gray slope that led up to a pass between two of the Sage Mountains. His keen eye followed the winding thread that was a trail disappearing over the notch.

"No use to worry. But they ought to have got back last night," he muttered, as he again scanned the trail.

Then from force of habit he looked on up the vast heave and bulge of the mountain, so softly and beautifully gray and purple in the morning sunlight. Here he did not meet with disappointment. Nine wild horses were in sight, two pure white that shone wonderfully in the clear air, and the rest all black. They lived on that mountain-top. They had been there all the four years Ben had lived at Forlorn River. During the first year of his sojourn there he had often chased them, as much for sport as for profit. But the advantage had always been theirs, and as they could not be driven from the great dome of this mountain, he let them alone, and came at last to watch for them in pleasure and love. When there was snow on the slopes they never left the mountain, and in summer, when they ventured down to the lake to drink, it was always at night. They never raised a colt and never took a strange horse into their band.

Just the mere sight of them had power to thrill Ben Ide. He hailed them gayly, as if they were as near as his own whistling horses in the corral. He gloried in their beauty, freedom, and self-sufficiency. He understood them. They were like eagles. They could look far away and down, and see their kindred, and their enemy, man. Years had taught them wisdom.

"Oh, you wild horses, just how long will you last up there?" he cried, poignantly. "Another dry year means your doom! Nothing to eat but sage, and the water going fast!"

That reminded Ben of his own long-unrealized hopes. If he were ever to catch a valuable string of wild horses and prove to his father that wild-horse hunting was not profitless, not the calling of a wanderer and outlaw, he must do it this year. If he were ever to catch California Red, the sorrel stallion that more than anything had lured him into this wild lonely life, he must accomplish the almost hopeless task before another dry season killed all the horses or drove them far out of the country.

Fifteen thousand wild horses grazed in that sage country between the gray California mountains and the Nevada ranges. They were the bane of the cattlemen who had begun to work back into the wild country. Horses were so plentiful and cheap in Oregon and California that there was no sale for any except good stock. Ben Ide was chasing a rainbow and he knew it.

4

Yet something irresistible bound him. He would rather catch one beautiful wild mustang and keep it for himself than sell a hundred common horses at a profit. That very failing had ruined him. Ranchers had made attractive deals with Ben Ide, deals calculated to earn him money and free their ranges from these pests of wild horses, but Ben had always fallen short of success. At the crucial times he had loved the horses, not the money. He could not be brutal to the fiercest stallion, and he could not kill the meanest mustang.

Along the winding trail below the notch between the Sage Mountains appeared low rolling clouds of yellow dust.

"Nevada and Modoc. Good!" ejaculated Ben, as he watched with squinting eyes. "Traveling along right pert, too. That means they've sold my horses . . . Wonder if I'll hear from home."

Ben Ide had never failed to look and hope for some word from home, though seldom indeed did he get any. Sometimes his sister Hettie, who alone remained true to him, contrived to send him a letter. The last one had been received six months ago. With the return of spring dormant feelings seemed to revive in Ben. During the long cold winter he had lived somewhat like a hibernating bear. The honk of the wild geese and the new fragrance of sage, the gray slopes coming out of the snow, and the roving bands of wild horses — these stirred in his heart the old wandering urge to get into the hills, and along with it awakened keener memories of mother and sister, of his stern father, of the old ranch home and spring school days.

He sat on the porch, bareheaded, and watched the moving clouds of dust come down to a level and fade into the gray sage along the lake. Black dots appeared and grew in size, and at length took the shape of horses. Watching them, Ben experienced a familiar old thrill — the vague boyish emotion he had learned to associate with sight of the wild lonely country and the smell of sage and whistle of mustangs, sunrise and the long day ahead. But happiness no more attended this fleeting state. He had thought too much; he had grown older; he had realized that he must find something more significant to live for. Not that the wild open country did not suffice! But he was unsatisfied and could not divine why.

Horsemen and pack-horses wound along the gray sage-slope shore line, splashed through the shallow mouth of Forlorn River, and climbed to the level shady patch in front of the cabin.

A stout square-faced Indian, dressed like a cowboy and wearing his hair short, was in the lead. The other rider was a striking figure. He sat his saddle as if he had grown there. His hair was long and black, showing under a dilapidated old sombrero. He had a lean face, clean and brown, a long nose, and piercing dark eyes, and an expression of reckless good nature. He wore a checkered blouse, a flowing scarf of red, a silver-buckled belt about his lean waist, and rough leather chaps. From a pocket of these, low down, protruded the brown handle of a heavy gun.

"Howdy, Ben!" he called, as he slid out of his saddle. "Made a jim-dandy deal with the hosses. Paid all your debts an' got six months' grub. How about that, old timer?"

"Nevada, if you're not lying, it's sure great," replied Ben, heartily.

"It's true, Ben, I'm darn glad to say," said Nevada. "An' here's a letter from your sister. I just rode over to the ranch, sent a kid in to tell Hettie, an' waited."

"Oh, but you're a life-saver!" declared Ben, as he eagerly grasped the thick envelope Nevada held out. "I was feeling pretty blue."

"We had supper in town, an' have been ridin' ever since," returned Nevada, wearily.

"Say, you must be tired and hungry . . . And how're you, Modoc?"

"Bad. Town no good for Indian," replied the Modoc, with a grin.

"Ben, I wouldn't trade this camp for any town on earth," declared Nevada.

"Neither would I, if you and Modoc were here. It's been lonesome," said Ben, as he set to the task of unpacking the three laden horses. Presently Modoc led away the smoking wet animals.

"Nevada, this is an awful lot of stuff," continued Ben, surveying the large assortment of boxes, bags, and bales.

"Bought every darn thing I could think of," rejoined Nevada, mildly.

"First time I've felt rich for years. Now I'll pack this outfit inside and then get some breakfast."

It took all of the small storeroom, the kitchen shelves, and half of the loft of Ben's cabin to hold the

7

new supplies. While Ben worked at this task Nevada lay on one of the narrow red-blanketed couches and talked.

"Got an all-fired lot of news," he said, complacently, "if I can only remember. Reckon though it won't make any difference how it comes . . . Ben, your dad has made a pile of money. Sold two thousand acres that used to be under water, they said. The drainin' of Tule Lake made your dad rich. But he ain't the only one. Hart Blaine had the most of that low land. I loafed around Hammell in the saloons an' stores, waitin' for it to get dark, so's I could sneak over to your dad's ranch. An' I shore asked questions. All the ranchers livin' away from Tule Lake drains have been hard hit by the drought. Stock poor an' grass scarce. It's an ill wind that blows nobody good. This dry spell hasn't hurt your dad or Blaine, or any of them farmers in the middle of the basin. But if Forlorn River dries up this summer they're goin' to be in the same boat with the others . . . I run into that McAdam guy an' he wasn't overly civil askin' about you. I strung him good an' plenty when all the time I wanted to slam him on his slick jaw. One of the waitresses told me he had a cinch on the Blaine girl — I forgot her name — the one that's been away to school. An' —"

"Was it Ina?" interrupted Ben, quickly.

"Yep, shore was. Sort of pretty little handle to Blaine, huh?"

"Ina Blaine," said Ben, dreamily, pausing in his task. "She ought to be nineteen now."

8

"Pard, was this Ina Blaine an old girl of yours?" queried Nevada, with great interest. But as there was no reply forthcoming he went on: "Reckon she was only a kid when you left home . . . Well, to resoom, I hired a lad to take me over to your dad's place, while Modoc rode on with the pack outfit. Smart little fellar, keen about wild-hoss huntin'. No use talkin', Ben, there's somethin' about a wild hoss that gets even a boy. He rode behind me an' we got to the ranch before dark. I hid outside in a grove of trees an' sent the kid in. It was just a gamble, you know, because there was ten to one he'd run into somebody else beside Hettie. But, by golly! she came to the door, he said, an' we waited. Hettie slipped out with the letter I gave you . . . Ben, she's grown up. I couldn't see her as well as I'd have liked, but it was enough. She was nice, Ben, soft-voiced an' sweet — an' it got me. Reckon I'd better not pull this letter stunt for you again. But she asked me to come an' I was fool enough to promise . . . So I took the kid back to Hammell, an' hung around some more . . . Ben, there's an outfit of wild-hoss hunters over here between Silver Meadow an' the Nevada line that's takin' to stealin' cattle."

"Who said so?" demanded Ben, suspiciously.

"Common gossip round Hammell," continued Nevada. "But after buyin' some drinks for two cowboys I got a hunch who'd branded wild-hoss hunters as cattle thieves. Nobody else but Less Setter. You know we run into some of his deals last summer, an' he rode right in here one day when you was away. Ben, I'm tellin' you Less Setter is not on the level."

"How do you know?" queried Ben, sharply.

"How do you know a hoss that's thoroughbred from one that ain't? But it's only fair for me to admit that I knowed Less Setter before he came to California."

"Ahuh!" ejaculated Ben, with intent gaze on his friend's masklike face. That statement of Nevada's was absolutely the first he had ever made in reference to his past. Years before, one night back in the sage hills, Nevada had ridden up to Ben's lonely campfire. He had a wound in his arm; he was exhausted and almost starved; his horse limped. Ben expressed himself twice: "Get down and come in, stranger," and, "Where are you from?" The answer had been, "Nevada." Ben had succored this rider and had never asked another question. Nevada had become attached to Ben and had never mentioned his past.

"What's more to the point," went on Nevada, calmly, "Less Setter knowed me. An' it's a good bet he has never gabbed about me. If he had — your folks might reckon I wasn't fit company for you."

"Ha! Ha!" laughed Ben, bitterly. "Nevada, don't talk in riddles. Tell me anything or not, just as you like. I love you for what you *are*, not what you might have been."

"Ben, you're talkin' strong," said Nevada, with his piercing eyes softening. "Reckon no one ever loved me in all my life till now — if you really do. I wouldn't want you to throw around such talk careless, you know."

"Well, I do," declared Ben, stoutly.

10

"All right, pard," replied Nevada, and there was a beautiful light in the gaze he bent on Ben. "We make a good or bad pair to draw to, accordin' to the draw . . . I get queer hunches sometimes. Not many, but when I get one I can tie to it. An' I've had a hunch your bad luck has changed. It came to me when Hettie put that letter in my hands. Funny feelin', Ben. It's not a thought. It just comes from somewhere outside."

At this moment the Indian entered with his slow silent tread and taking up the water pails he went out. Ben replenished the fire in the wide stone fireplace, and then set swiftly to the preparation of biscuits, coffee, bacon. His mind worked as swiftly as his hands.

"I'd like to believe the tide of my fortune has turned," he said, seriously. "It sure was lucky I sent you. I'm no fellow to sell or buy, to make deals and carry them out. But you're as smart as a whip, Nevada, and for me at least you drive good bargains."

"Ben, have you noticed anythin' particular about me?" inquired Nevada, complacently.

"Can't say I do," returned Ben, looking up from his work. "You've got a nice clean shave an' a new scarf."

"No good. You lose. Ben, I didn't have one single solitaree drink at Klamath or Hammell. The reason was I had a hunch I might see your sister Hettie, an' I didn't want her to smell whisky on me."

"That's to your credit, Nevada. I'll bet it would please Hettie . . . But what about it?"

"Nothin', only I feel better. Reckon I'll quit drinkin'," rejoined Nevada, thoughtfully. "Ben, if I ketch California Red for you —"

"What?" shouted Ben, jumping as if he had been struck.

"Excoose *me*, pard. I meant if I help you ketch that darned wild stallion you're so dotty about will you listen to some sense?"

"Yes, Nevada. I'll listen to that right now. But see here, you've heard something about California Red."

"Sure have an' it'll keep. I want some breakfast an' if I told you where that red hoss is you'd chuck everythin' an' run."

Ben thrilled at the words and at the bright light in Nevada's eyes, but he smothered his burning eagerness.

"Reckon I don't know whether this is sense or the hunch I mentioned," said Nevada. "But it's got me, pard. Now listen. We've homesteaded three hundred an' twenty acres of this sage. There are three homesteads we can buy for almost nothin'. That acreage takes in the best of Forlorn River Valley an' gives control of the range beyond. Right here under our noses is a big cattle country. Let's go in for cattle, Ben . . . Damn! Don't look like that. I tell you I've had a hunch. Now's the time to buy cattle, when there's no water or grass. Let's make up our minds an' get the money afterwards. When the rains come this Clear Lake country is goin' to boom. The wild hosses have got to go. You admit that, Ben. Well, let's ketch California Red an' a thousand head, an' *keep* them for ourselves, an' settle down to ranchin' on a big scale."

"Nevada, you said you didn't have one drink."

"I swear I hadn't."

"What's got into you then?"

"Sense an' hunch."

"Nevada, how long did you talk to my sister?" queried Ben, gravely.

"It seemed like a few swift seconds, but I reckon it might have been longer," replied Nevada, with unconscious revelation of enchantment.

"What did Hettie say?" continued Ben, hungrily.

"She remembered me, but all the same she asks, 'You're Ben's friend, Nevada?' an' I answers I was. Then she fired a beltful of questions at me, all about how you were, an' I shore answered quick. After that she looked square up at me — reckon it was then I fell — an' she asks, 'Nevada, if you're Ben's friend you're *mine*, too. Tell the truth. Are you an' Ben livin' honest?' An' I says, 'Miss Hettie, I wouldn't lie to no girl, let alone you. Me an' Ben are shore livin' honest!' . . . She squeezed my hands an' cried. It was awful for me. Then she fired up. 'Aren't you two boys ashamed to be thought — what you are? This is a new country. It'll be big. You're young, strong. You're great riders. Why don't you *do somethin'*? Chase wild hosses, if you must, but *ketch* them. Sell them. Buy cattle. Homestead land. Study an' think an' plan, an' *work*. Fool these hard-shelled old people! Make big ranchmen out of yourselves.' . . . Pard Ben, you could have roped me with a cobweb. An' there I stood, burstin' to talk, but couldn't say a word. She told me how to fetch word from you an' then she ran off."

"Hettie! God bless her!" exclaimed Ben, heartily. "I'm not surprised. Even as a kid she was big-hearted.

Hettie has grown up. She's sixteen. And to think I've not seen her for two years!"

Modoc returned with the pails of water. Ben soon had breakfast ready, and when his companions sat down at the rude table he went outside to read Hettie's letter. He threw himself in the shade and with trembling fingers tried to open the envelope quickly yet not tear it.

THE RANCH.

Dearest Ben:

I'm in a terrible rush and won't be able to write half what I want to, as the little boy said "Nevada" is waiting for me outside and I must hurry. Oh, how I wish it were you!

Dad is away. He went to Klamath Falls with Mr. Setter. They're making big cattle deals. So many poor ranchers are failing on account of the dry season. I think it'd be more to Dad's credit if he helped some of these little fellows, instead of taking advantage of their bad luck. I don't like Mr. Setter, and when I see you I'll tell *you* why.

Ben, it's a long time since I wrote you last. Nearly a year. I'm through high school. Dad wants me to go to college and Mother wants me to stay home. Dad and Mr. Blaine and several more of the old lake pioneers have made an awful lot of money since the government drained Tule Lake. I don't know whether it's good or not. In a few ways it's nice, but there's something gone. Dad always was hard, you know, and now he has gotten "stuck up". And I'm afraid I must tell you that your brothers and sisters (except me) are almost as bad. I'd like to write you just what they do, but you must wait until I can tell you. And that brings me to the important thing in this letter.

Mother is not well, Ben. There's no use to dodge the truth. She's failing. It breaks my heart. You were her favorite, Ben, and she has pined in secret. I believe Dad's bitter hardness about you, his injustice to you, has broken Mother. Anyway, she is ailing and I know longs to see you. She'd obey Dad, of course, and not ask you to come. But you can surprise her. And, Ben, dearest, if you could *only* prove to mother that you were not wasting your life — that these vile things Mr. Setter and others have told Dad are lies — I think she might improve. So the day you get this ride in to the ranch. I'll be looking for you down the lane just about dusk. You can see Mother for a little, and then you and I will go out in the grove and have a long, long talk.

I've a lot to tell you, Ben, about what's going on here. And I'm going to put some pretty plain questions to you. Dare say you'll know some of them before you see me, because if I have a minute with this "Nevada" I'll sure put some to him.

Ben, I mustn't end this without a word about Ina Blaine. She's home from school. I was afraid to meet her, but, oh! Ben, she's as sweet and nice as ever she was when you and she were kid sweethearts and I was forever pestering you. And she's lovely. School has improved *her*, that's certain, and if it weren't for mother I'd grasp my opportunity and go.

I've seen Ina three times. I believe we're going to be friends. We think the same about a lot of things. Ina isn't crazy about money, and I'll miss my guess if she goes in for the town gaiety that has struck the Blaine family.

Ben, she remembers you. I'm not in her confidence yet, but I can feel how she feels. She *likes you*, Ben. I don't believe the years of school have made any difference in her, except to improve. The difference in her looks, though, is tremendous. You'll not know Ina. Already she's heard this village gossip about you. For she asked me straight out. I told her no, that you had your choice and took it. She wants to help you, and says we are arch plotters. She was awfully curious about that terrible wild horse they say you're mad to catch. Brother, you know I wouldn't mislead you, and I'm telling you I couldn't make a mistake about how I feel — or mother — or Ina Blaine. And if we care for you still you've *got* to do something. She'll be the richest and most popular girl in this whole valley of towns and ranches. Do you imagine that'll ever change her? No! Ben, you've more to catch around these sage hills than a beautiful wild mustang. You've your boyhood's sweetheart, Ina Blaine. So there!

I must close now, but it's hard. Don't let *anything* keep you from coming. I'm quite capable of riding out to Forlorn River.

With love,

Hettie.

When Ben finished the letter his eyes were blurred and he had a hard dry contraction of his throat, a pang deep in his breastbone. Wave after wave of emotion had swept over him. And then he sat there motionless, the open letter in his hands, his gaze across the gray melancholy river to the dim gray hills of sage. He did not see them. The eyes of his mind were fixed on the dear familiar scenes of boyhood, home and Mother, and freckled-faced Hettie with her big loving blue eyes, on the miles of wind-swept swamp land along Tule Lake, on the schoolhouse at Hammell, and the long lane that led from the Ide ranch down to Blaines'. He saw a girl of fourteen with a chestnut braid down her back, a white pearly skin that even the summer sun could not tan, and dark eyes of velvet softness. Then the heart-numbing pictures faded for the stalwart figure of his father, iron of muscle and of mind, the gray clear eye like sunlight on ice, and the weathered wrinkled face, a record of labor and strife.

A second and more thoughtful perusal of Hettie's letter fixed Ben's mind upon the most poignant and unavoidable fact of it — that pertaining to his mother. She was failing. What a terrible sickening shock ran through him! Then he was gripped in the cruel clutches

17

of remorse. It was a bitter moment, but short because his decision to go was almost instantaneous. Folding Hettie's letter, Ben went into the cabin.

"Modoc, saddle the gray," he said, shortly.

The Indian laid down pan and dishcloth and abruptly glided out. Nevada looked up quickly from his task, with swift curious gleam of eyes searching Ben's face.

"Bad news, pard?" he queried.

"Yes. Hettie says Mother is — is failing, and I must come in to see her," returned Ben, getting down his spurs and chaps. "It'd hurt like hell, Nevada, in any case, but to realize I've broken mother's heart — it's — it's —"

With bowed head he slouched to the bed, dragging his chaps and dropping the clinking spurs, and sat down heavily.

"Ben, it's tough news, but don't look on the dark side," said Nevada, with swift hand going to Ben's shoulder. "Your mother's not old. Seein' you will cheer her. She'll get well. Don't be downcast, Ben. That's been your disease as drink was mine. Let's make an end to both of them . . . Shake on it, pard!"

"By Heaven! Nevada, you've got something in your mind that you must drive into mine," replied Ben, rising with violence, and jerking up his head he wrung Nevada's hand. "I've got to get over not caring. Oh, it's not that. It was that I cared too much."

"Ben, you can't care too much," went on Nevada. "When you don't care you're no good. I never cared —

till I rode into your camp on Forlorn River . . . Let's brace up an' fool the whole country."

"If I only had in — in me what Hettie believes — what you believe —" muttered Ben, thickly, struggling for self-control. He flung his chaps on and buckled them with shaking hands. There seemed to be a tight painful knot in his breast that must burst before he could feel relief.

"Ben, I felt this comin' to us six months back," said Nevada, soft-voiced, hovering around Ben like a woman. "Reckon I didn't know what it was. But Hettie gave me the hunch. I tell you our luck has changed . . . Mebbe I'll have to kill Less Setter, but that's neither here nor there . . . You ride in to see your mother an' sister. Make them happy for havin' faith in you. While you're gone I'll do a heap of thinkin'. But come back tomorrow night."

"What'll you think so hard about?" asked Ben, curiously.

"Wal, most about California Red," replied Nevada, with utmost seriousness. "Ben, that red-skinned mustang has wintered over here at Mule Deer Lake."

"Nevada!" expostulated Ben, suddenly transfixed.

"It's a fact, unless all them cowmen was lyin'. An' I don't see why they should lie. Red is pretty darn smart. We thought he was rangin' round the lava beds an' Modoc caves, where there was so many wild hosses, or else over in that big country east of Wild Goose Lake. But the son-of-a-gun wasn't ten miles from here all winter. Nobody chased him. Reckon those who knew didn't think there was any chance. But I say winter's the best time to ketch wild hosses. I'll prove it to you yet."

"Too late now. Here's spring and summer coming fast. You and Modoc ride over to Mule Deer Lake tomorrow."

"Shore will. I hate to tell you, Ben, there'll likely be more'n one outfit after California Red from now on."

"Why now, more than last winter or summer?" queried Ben, sharply.

"Wal, I heard a lot of talk in the saloons," replied Nevada. "One of them new-rich lake ranchers, Blaine it was, has offered three thousand dollars for California Red, sound an' well broke."

"Blaine!" ejaculated Ben, in amaze. "That's Hart Blaine. There's only one. He's neighbor of my father's . . . Three thousand dollars! Why, that's a fortune! He used to be so stingy he wouldn't give a boy an apple out of his orchard. All that money!"

"You ought to be tickled to death," declared Nevada. "For no one else but you will ever ketch Red."

"I didn't think of the money. But what could Blaine want that wild horse for? Sound and well broke!"

"Say, any rancher in northern California would go broke for Red," rejoined Nevada. "Some cowboy said Less Setter offers more than three thousand. If he pays it I'm goin' to think money's comin' easy, an' you can bet I'll look around on the ranges . . . Yes, I mean just that, Ben Ide. But the fellows at Hammell reckon Blaine wants California Red for his daughter."

The idea struck Ben so strangely that he uttered a loud laugh. California Red, that wild fleet sorrel mustang for sweet little Ina Blaine! It seemed so ridiculous. Yet Ina Blaine was the only person Ben could have allowed to possess the great stallion, even in thought. California Red was his, by right of discover — for Ben had been the first to see the red-flashing colt on the sage — and by the years of watching and striving.

CHAPTER
TWO

Honk! honk! honk! The coarse wild notes pierced Ina Blaine's slumbers. She opened her eyes, and in the dim room with cool gray dawn at the window she did not recognize where she was. Honk! honk! honk!

"Oh, wild geese!" she cried out suddenly, with rapturous recognition. "Oh, I'm home — home!"

All the time Ina had been away at school she had never heard the melodious cry of a wild goose. She had forgotten, perhaps, the most significant feature of the wild life about Tule Lake. But once the loved honk penetrated her mind, what hosts of sweet memories, stretching back to childhood! It was a welcome home. The sound offered some little compensation for the loss of the lake. Ina had been astounded and dismayed to see vast green and yellow and brown fields, crisscrossed by irrigation ditches, where once Tule Lake had rippled and smiled, a great shining oval of water lying between the gray sage hills and the black lava beds. Tule Lake was gone. It seemed to change even the towering white glory of Mount Shasta.

Ina lay there watching the dawn brighten through the casement. This large luxurious room was not the one in which she had spent her childhood and girlhood. That had been a tiny one, whitewashed, with a low slanted ceiling and one small window. "The days that are no more," she whispered. That dear room, sacred to her dreams, was gone as Tule Lake was gone. The childhood days, so sweet and stinging now in memory, had passed away forever. Her old home was not the same. Father, mother, sisters, and brothers had changed. She realized all this with sadness. While she had been away at school, growing up, nothing at home had stood still.

The sun rose red over the sage hills and streamed in at her window, gilding the new furniture. A cool breath of morning, with a hint of frost, made her snuggle down under the warm blankets. She had awakened happily, but there had come with memory and thought a check to her joy. She had not anticipated change. Yet all was changed. Even she? Yet the honk of wild geese had found her heart true to the old life, the old order.

Ina Blaine was the third child of a family of four boys and three girls, the favorite of a Kansas farmer who had emigrated to northern California and had taken up a great tract of marshland along Tule Lake. In wet seasons his land was under water. He had labored there, along with several other farsighted pioneers. And when the government drained Tule Lake it was as if their fortunes had been touched by the magic of Aladdin.

But he had sent Ina to a Kansas college long before fortune had smiled upon him. He had a brother at Lawrence, in whose home Ina was welcome during the period of her schooling. It had not been his intention to leave Ina there all this time. But one thing and another, including lack of funds and illness in her uncle's family, had prevented Ina from spending a vacation at home. So she had been away four years, during which wealth had come, as if overnight, to the Blaines.

To revel in being home, to delight in her freedom, to play a little after the long years of study, to put off the inevitable settling down to the serious things of life — these had been Ina's cherished hopes.

"I must see the funny side of it," she soliloquized, with a little laugh. "For it is funny. Dad so important and pompous — Mother fussed over a multitude of new fandangles — Archie impressed with his destiny as the eldest son of a cattle king — Fred and Bob leaning away from farm work to white collars and city girls. Kate engaged to a Klamath lawyer! I really can't savvy her. The kids, though, will make up for much. We'll get along, when once they remember me.

"To begin, then," said Ina, resolutely, and she got up on the right side of the bed. She was home. Whatever had been the changes in country and family, here was where she had longed to be and meant to live and serve. She had spent time in St. Louis, Kansas City, Denver, San Francisco, the last of which she had found most interesting. But she would never be happy in the confines of a city. She loved northern California — the vastness of it, the great white mountains, the ranges of soft round sage hills, lakes and rivers and streams, and in the midst of them the little villages here and there, not too close together, and the green flat ranches, still few in number.

"Last night when I said I'd teach school some day, didn't Dad roar?" she mused. "And Mother looked offended. What has happened to my dear parents? I fear they must suffer for my education. I wonder what they have in mind. Heigho! I feel tremendously old and learned . . . Back to the tomboy days for Ina! I'll slide down the haymow with Dall. I'll fish and ride and swim with Marvie. How keen he was to ask me that! . . . And Ben Ide? . . . Not a letter from him all these years. Dear old Ben! I seem to have forgotten much until now. How time flies! They wrote me Ben had gone to the bad. I never believed it — I think I didn't. Ben was queer, not like the other boys, but he was good . . . Has he forgotten me? Ben was a year younger than Archie. He's twenty-four now. Quite a man! Five years didn't make such difference when I was fifteen."

Ina peeped out of her window. The east above the gray range blazed brightly gold, and the glow of the spring morning shone over the level waving plain where Tule Lake had once shimmered. Flocks of ducks dotted the rosy sky, and a triangle of wild geese headed toward the dim blue swamp land under the black lava mounds. Old Mount Shasta stood up majestically, snow-crowned and sunrise-flushed. The fresh keen air vibrated with sounds — honk of geese, song of spring birds, bawl of calf and low of cow. The pasture was alive with horses, cattle, pigs. Cocks were crowing, and out by the jumble of barns a cowboy whistled merrily.

Ina went downstairs and through the wide new hallway that connected with what had been the old house. Her father had made the mistake of erecting a large frame structure as an addition to the old half-log, half-stone house. It was significant that despite his rise in the ranching world he could not quite forsake his humble abode. And indeed he had his room and office there still. A kitchen had been added to the living room, which evidently, from the long tables and benches, was now a dining room for her father's horde of cowboys.

Ina peeped into this dining room before she ventured farther. It was empty. Then she heard her mother in the kitchen. Ina ran through to surprise Mrs. Blaine helping the man-cook.

"Good morning, Mother. Where's everybody?" cried Ina, gaily.

"Bless your heart, how you scared me!" ejaculated her mother, quite manifestly embarrassed. She was a large woman, gray-haired and somewhat hard-featured. "Nobody's up yet, except me an' your father."

"Well! Why, Mother, Archie used to clean out the horse stalls, and Kate used to milk the cows!" retorted Ina, laughingly.

"They don't any more," replied Mrs. Blaine, shortly.

"I shall try, at least, to milk the cows."

"Ina, your father didn't give you a college education for that," protested her mother, in vague alarm.

"But you used to milk cows and I'd never be above what you did," said Ina, sweetly, and embraced her mother.

"Father has some big hopes for you, Ina," returned Mrs. Blaine, dubiously. She did not quite know this long-lost, grown-up daughter. She seemed bewildered by circumstances of monumental importance, but which were unnatural.

"The cow-hands will be comin' in for breakfast any minute," she said. "You'd better go."

"Why? I'd like to see them."

"Your father said he'd not have any cowboys gallivantin' round after you."

"Indeed! But suppose I *liked* it," retorted Ina, merrily. "You married Dad when he was a cowboy."

"But that was different, Ina."

"I'd like to know how."

"My child, I was a milkmaid on the Kansas farm where Hart Blaine was a hand. You're the daughter of a rancher who will be a millionaire some day."

"Mother, that last is very high-sounding, but it doesn't impress me," returned Ina, with seriousness. "Dad and I are going to have some arguments."

"Ina, you were our most obedient child," said Mrs. Blaine, divided between conjecture and doubt.

"I'll still be, Mother dear — with reservations. And I'll begin now by running off so the interesting cowboys will not get to see me, this time."

Ina returned to the other part of the house, with a thoughtfulness edging into her happy mood. Her mother was plodding amid perplexities and complexities beyond her ken. The old simple hard-working farm life seemed to have been disrupted. Ina went to the sitting room, which she had explored yesterday and had found attractive in spite of its newness. There were some sticks of burning wood in the open fireplace. Ina liked that. A familiar fragrance, not experienced for a long time, assailed her nostrils. How warm and stirring the emotions it roused! Her girlhood again, trails and ponies and camp fires!

Ina curled up in a big chair before the fire, as she had been wont to do as a dreamy child, and was about to give herself up to the pleasure of retrospection when Dall came bounding in, pursued by Marvie. Sight of Ina interrupted hostilities. Dall was a gawky, growing girl of twelve and Marvie a handsome lad of fourteen, tow-headed and blue-eyed, as were all the Blaines except Ina. An animated conversation ensued, in which Dall reverted to her endless queries about college, Kansas, towns, and travel, while Marvie tried to tell about his horse and that on Saturday Ina must ride with him and go fishing.

In due time the oldest girl, Kate, came down wearing a dress rather unsuited to morning, Ina thought, and certainly not becoming. Kate Blaine was twenty-two, tall and spare, resembling her mother somewhat, but sharper of face and eye. She had not manifested any great delight in Ina's return. Yesterday Ina had become aware of Kate's close observance, flattering, yet somehow vaguely disconcerting. Ina's consciousness had never been crossed by a thought other than loving all her people. She had been compelled to thrust something away from her mind.

"Marvie, you an' Dall needn't eat Ina," said Kate, with a sniff. "She's home for good. An' Ma says you're to hurry up with breakfast, or be late for school."

Ina followed them into the dining room, where Mrs. Blaine was waiting. It was a cheerful sunny room, well appointed, though elaborate for a rancher's home.

"Where are Dad and the boys?" asked Ina, as she seated herself.

"Bob an' Fred have early breakfast with the cow-hands," replied Mrs. Blaine, then added, reluctantly, "an' sometimes your father does, too."

Dall and Marvie sat one on each side of Ina, and she felt that they would save any situation for her. They were still too young to be greatly affected by whatever it was that had changed the elder Blaines. Ina sensed happily that she could bring much to her younger sister and brother. As for her mother and Kate, they began to force Ina to face the establishing of ideas that would be far from humorous.

"Ina, we ride in a buggy to school," announced Dall, with just a hint of the importance so obvious in the others.

"I used to have to walk," declared Ina. "Oh, maybe I don't remember that long muddy road in the winter — dusty in summer!"

"Aw, I like the ridin', but I hate the hitchin' up," said Marvie. "Say, Ina, Paw lets me have the horse and buggy on Saturdays. Day after tomorrow is Saturday."

"I'll go anywhere with you," replied Ina. "I want to ride horseback, too, Marvie. Has Dad any saddle horses?"

"Say, where have your eyes been?" demanded the boy. "Pasture's full of horses. So's the corral and barn. An' the cowboys tell me Paw has ranches full of horses.

He's gone in with a big horse dealer, Less Setter, who has outfits all over the country. I've got two horses. Dall has a pony. Bob an' Fred have a whole string. Just you tell Paw you want California Red an' see what happens."

"Who's California Red?" asked Ina, with interest. "Is he a cowboy or a horse?"

"He's a wild stallion, the swiftest an' beautifulest ever heard of. Red as fire! Too smart for all the wild-horse hunters . . . Aw, Ina, I'd sure like to see you get California Red."

"Marvie, you thrill me, but I want a tame horse, one I can saddle myself and ride and pet."

"Wild mustangs make wonderful pets, once they're broke proper."

"Well, then, just for fun I'll tell Dad I want California Red, to see what happens."

It was Kate who broke up this conversation and hurried Marvie and Dall to get ready for school. Ina went out with them, and made them let her ride as far as the end of the lane, to their immense delight.

The long lane had not changed. She remembered it, and the trees and rocks and bushes that bordered it. Facing back, she saw the green grove half hiding the white house, and the cluster of barns, new and old, and all around and beyond the wonderful level ranch land that had once been under water. Spring was keen in the morning air. Flocks of blackbirds swooped low and high. From somewhere came the honk of wild geese. Far beyond the level expanse rose the brown lava mounds, rising to the dignity of hills, step by step, until changed their hard bronze for the green of pine. Above them white Shasta gleamed like a sharp cloud, piercing the blue. To the south and east the soft gray sage mountains barred the way to the wild country beyond. Ina breathed it all in, color and fragrance and music, the sweet freedom of that ranch surrounded by wild mountains. It filled her heart to overflowing. Here she had been born. The dear sad happy memories of childhood flooded her mind. She realized now that she had never changed. All she had learned had only strengthened her hold upon the simple natural things that had come to her first.

Ina lingered long in the grove of pines and maples that, happily for her, had not been touched in the improvement of Tule Lake Ranch. The fork of a gnarled old maple seemed precisely the same as when she had perched there in her bare legs and feet. And the spreading pines gave no hint of the passing of years. It frightened her to realize the growth and change in herself while these beloved trees had remained the same as in her earliest remembrance. How incredible the power of a few years over human life! There was one pine, her favorite, a great old monarch that split just above the ground and rose in separate trunks, sending low branches spreading down, affording the shelter of a natural tent. Many a storm she had weathered there.

Suddenly another memory picture flashed upon her inward eye. She and Ben Ide had quarreled only once and this had been the scene of that youthful difference. What had been the cause? Ina blushed as she leaned between the tree trunks. It had been because of Ben's one and only departure from their tranquil platonic comradeship. The thought held a pervading sweet melancholy, somehow disturbing. She would meet Ben presently, as she expected to meet all her other schoolmates. And she wanted to, yet, as far as Ben was concerned, she guessed she would rather not see him very soon. About the old pine tree clung vague haunting scenes, dim and imperfect, all of which Ben shared.

Ina's prolonged walk brought her at length to the picturesque old corral and barn, which, strange to note, had not been altered with the advent of newer structures. Hart Blaine had, unconsciously perhaps, preserved some of the old atmosphere of Tule Lake Ranch.

She espied her father's tall spare form, not quite familiar in severe shiny black. She remembered him in soiled overalls and top boots. He was bareheaded now and his gray locks waved in the breeze. He was talking to a man seated in a buckboard, holding the reins of a spirited team. They did not observe Ina's approach. The several cowboys nearby, however, were keen to see her, and as she passed them, frankly interested in their presence, they appeared to be strangely disrupted from their work.

". . . tell you, Setter, it's a deal I don't like," her father was saying, impatiently, as Ina approached.

Then the man in the buckboard sat up quickly and Blaine turned to see Ina. His seamed hard face lost its cragginess in a smile of surprise, love, pride. Ina was the apple of his eye.

"Hello, Dad!" she said, gaily. "I'm poking around to see what you've done to my Tule Lake Ranch."

"Mawnin', lass," he replied, extending his long arm. He had big gray eyes, still keen, a hooked nose like the beak of an eagle, and a large mouth, showing under a grizzled mustache.

"Ina, this is one of my pardners, Less Setter, from Nevada," went on Blaine. Then he faced the man, drawing Ina forward with arm round her shoulder. "My blue-ribbon lass, just home from school."

"Proud to meet you, Miss Ina," returned Setter, gallantly, with a gloved hand touching his sombrero. As Ina acknowledged the introduction she looked up into a yellow-bearded mask of a face, with almond-shaped, heavily-lidded eyes that seemed to devour her. Setter did not appear young, yet he looked vigorous, intense, different from men Ina had been in the habit of seeing. Even in that casual moment, when she was not interested, he made such impression upon her that it broke her mood of gaiety. She felt instant distrust of her father's partner, and she had impatiently to force herself from intuitive womanly convictions. Suddenly Marvie's talk about horses flashed into her mind, and she grasped with relief at something to say.

"Dad, I want a saddle horse," she said, brightly, turning to him.

"Lass, you can have a string of horses," he replied. "We've got in a lot of stock. Mr. Setter just sold me a hundred head, all from Nevada, an' some of them are beauties. I've a big order from Seattle, so you must take your pick."

"But, Dad, I always dreamed of a really grand horse," went on Ina, which was telling the truth.

"Lass, I don't recollect you bein' keen over any kind of horses," observed her father.

"We were very poor," she said, softly. "You must recollect that I walked to school, winter and summer."

"Haw! Haw! Yes, Ina, I sure do, an' somehow it's good to think of . . . Wal, my daughter, we're *not* poor now, an' if you want the best hoss in all this country you're only to say so."

"Dad, I want California Red," she rejoined, swiftly.

"What! That wild stallion?" ejaculated Blaine, in amaze. "Why, lass, all the hoss outfits in three States have swallowed the dust of that sorrel."

"Oh, he must be grand!" exclaimed Ina, now thrilled about what had grown out of a joke.

"Miss Ina, he is indeed a grand horse," interposed Setter. "I saw him once, two years ago. He's a racy, fine, clean-limbed animal, red as fire, with a mane like a flame. An' he's not a killer of horses, as so many stallions are. Most of the riders an' hunters think he'd break gentle. So you get your dad to promise . . . I'm witness, Blaine, mind you, of your word."

"California Red is yours, Ina, if he can be caught," replied her father.

"He can be, I reckon," said Setter, meditatively. "There's only a few outfits after him. That is they claim to be wild-horse hunters, but it's only a blind to hide their thieving of cattle and range horses. Hall an' his outfit are workin' close to Silver Meadow now. Probably the only hunters really chasin' Red are this Ide boy an' his pards. They're leanin' to crooked deals, too, but I reckon Ide wants Red so bad —"

"Ide!" interrupted Ina, quickly. "Do you mean Ben Ide?"

"Yes, his name's Ben," replied Setter.

"You lie! Ben Ide is no horse thief," flashed Ina, hotly.

"See here, lass, easy, easy," interposed her father. "You've been away from home a long time. Much has happened to others, as well as to your folks. Bad as well as good!"

Then he addressed Setter.

"You see, Less, it's news to Ina. She an' Ben went to school together. They used to play here as kids. An' I reckon it's a kind of a blow to learn —"

"Dad, I don't believe it," spoke up Ina, still with heat, her voice breaking.

"It's too bad, Miss Ina," said Setter. "I'm sorry I was the one to hurt your feelin's. But it does appear your boy schoolmate has gone to the bad."

Ina turned her back upon Setter, suddenly gripped by an unfamiliar fury and pain. Surprise at these feelings had a part in her agitation.

"Dad," she said, striving to hide it, "has any — any dishonest thing ever been traced to Ben Ide?"

"Lass, there's been a lot of talk," replied her father. "Soon after you left home Ben took to the hills, crazy about wild hosses. Amos Ide, if you remember, was a religious man, an' I reckon Ben represented to him somethin' you do to me. Anyway, Amos couldn't break the boy — make him settle down to work. They had a final quarrel. Ben's been gone ever since. I've never seen him, though others have. Mrs. Ide takes it hard, they say. I drop in to see them now an' then. But Ben's name ain't never mentioned. The last two years we've begun to run cattle out in the valleys an' flat along Forlorn River. Ben lives over there. An' a good many cattle an' hosses have — wal, disappeared. So Ben had worse said about him. But I can't say anythin' has ever been proved."

"It's not easy to fix rustlin' an' hoss stealin' on any one in an unsettled country," cut in the cold voice of Setter, with its note of authority. "Stock missed by your father or other ranchers is never seen again. That means it goes over the line into Nevada or down across the high Sierras."

"All the more reason a young man of good family — once a neighbor and — and friend of ours should not be accused of being a —"

As Ina halted over the unspeakable word Setter flicked the ashes from his cigar and then bent his inscrutable colorless eyes upon her.

"Any man is known by the company he keeps," he asserted. "Young Ide lives with a renegade Modoc Indian, an' a cowboy who was run out of Nevada for bein' a horse thief."

The pointed positiveness of the man struck Ina strangely even while his information made her heart sick. She stared at Setter until his cool assurance seemed slightly to change. Ina caught a glimpse of what

36

hid behind that mask. She was fascinated by something impossible to grasp. Forced to listen to damning statements, she was unconsciously peering, with a woman's strange inconsistency, at a man whose face and voice and look struck antagonism from her. There was no reason in the attitude of her mind.

"Dad, what Mr. Setter said does not strike me quite right," she declared, frankly. "It makes me remember Ben Ide more than I thought I did. Dad, I don't believe Ben would steal to save his life. How could any boy change so in a few years?"

Then she deliberately faced her father's new partner.

"Mr. Setter, if I remember Ben Ide *at all* you will have to prove what you say. I shall certainly see him and tell him."

"Ina, what're you talkin' about?" queried Blaine, impatiently. "That's 'most an insult to Setter. An' you can't hunt up this Ide boy. I wouldn't let you be seen talkin' to him."

"I should think you would take me to see Ben, so I —"

Ina saw the leap of red to her father's craggy face and suddenly remembered his temper; she also saw several cowboys that had edged closer and now stood gaping.

"Girl, you've come back with queer ideas," declared Blaine. "If that's all school's done for you I'm sorry I sent you."

"Dad, I have a mind of my own — I can think," replied Ina, feelingly.

"Wal, you needn't do any thinkin' about seein' Ben Ide, an' that's all there is to that."

"My dear Father, I shall most certainly see Ben Ide," said Ina.

"Go in the house," ordered Blaine, harshly.

Ina strode away with her head high and face burning, and it was certain that she looked straight at the cowboys.

She heard Setter say: "Spunky girl, Hart, an' you have your hands full."

"Why'd you rub it in about young Ide?" demanded her father, angrily. "Seems you're set on it, blowin' at Hammell an' all over —"

Ina passed out of hearing, and when she was also out of sight she slipped through the bars of a gate and went back to the grove. Here she found a seat under the double pine tree, and the act of returning there established a link between the past and the lamentable news she had just heard. Whereupon she went over the whole conversation. It left her with a desire to feel grieved at instantly distrusting a man close to her father, and at the ensuing clash, but she could not feel in the least sorry. Instead, she found she was angry and hurt.

"If it's — true," she faltered, "I'll — I'll — somehow I'll bring Ben back to his old self."

CHAPTER
THREE

Ina spent the rest of the morning under the pine tree in the grove; and after she had recovered her equanimity she applied some solid and tolerant thought to the problem which confronted her.

The complexity of that problem would have to be understood and dealt with as it became obvious. She would not try to cross any bridges before she came to them. Disappointment must not be allowed to get a hold on her.

She had lunch alone with her mother. Kate had gone to Hammell with Mr. Blaine. Ina exerted herself to be amusing and sympathetic, to reach her mother, and was not wholly unsuccessful. She had quickly sensed that if she let herself be guided by the desires and whims of her family there would be no strife. Mrs. Blaine seemed preoccupied with the innumerable duties of a rancher's wife, when these duties had mostly been made impossible for her. For thirty years she had been a slave to labor, early and late, to the imperative need of saving. She now occupied a position where these things, though fixed in habit and mind, must not be thought of at all. It was impossible to forget them, and her trouble rose from the consequent bewilderment.

The truth was, she was a sorely puzzled and unhappy woman because the circumstances of the Blaines had vastly changed. Yet she did not know this. It would have been natural for her to talk to Ina about the past, and their trials and joys, about all the homely tasks that had once been and were now no more, about neighbors as poor as they used to be, gossip, blame, worries, praise, and the possibility of a manly young rancher who might come wooing Ina. But as she had to talk of things relating to this new and different life, she was no longer natural. Ina thought her mother a rather pathetic person, yet recalling the severe toil and endless complaint of earlier years she concluded this was to be preferred.

"Mother, tell me about the Ides," asked Ina, among other casual queries.

"Well, I'm sorry to say the Blaines and the Ides are not the neighbors they used to be," replied Mrs. Blaine, reflectively. "I reckon it's your father's fault. Amos Ide has made money, but it's never got him anywhere. He thinks we're stuck up. Mrs. Ide these late years has kept more to herself. She used to go to church regular. But since the parson preached about prodigal sons she has stayed away. I haven't been over there in ages. But I've seen Hettie. She has grown up. Fred was sweet on her once, but lately he's taken to a town girl."

"How about Ben?" inquired Ina.

"He's a wild-horse hunter now, the cowboys say."

"Sort of a — an outcast, isn't he?" went on Ina.

"The story goes that Amos Ide gave Ben a choice between plowin' fields an' livin' his wild life in the hills.

Ben preferred to leave home. It was hard on his mother."

Ina gained some little grain of comfort from her mother's talk, and she decided to go over and call on Mrs. Ide and Hettie some day. But once the idea had come, it gave her no peace. Ina spent the early part of the afternoon unpacking her belongings and changing her room into a more comfortable and attractive abode. Books, photographs, pennants, served her in good stead, and were reminders of happy college days. While she was thus occupied her mind was busy with the Ides, and when she had finished she decided to go that very afternoon to visit them.

Once upon a time there had been a well-trodden path between Tule Lake Ranch and the farm of the Ides. Ina had observed that it had been plowed up in places, and fenced in others. She would take the lane out to the road, and upon her return wait for Dall and Marvie to pick her up on their way home from school.

While changing her dress Ina suddenly realized that she was being rather particular about her appearance, something which since her arrival home had not caused her concern. She could not deny that she had unconsciously desired to look well for the Ides. "What Ide? Do I mean Mrs. Ide or Hettie?" she asked, gravely, of the dark-eyed, fair-faced girl in the mirror. The answer was a blush. Ina became somewhat resentful with her subtle new self.

It happened that Kate saw Ina come down the front stairs.

"For the land's sake!" she ejaculated, in genuine surprise. "Goin' to a party?" Her hawk eyes swept over Ina from head to toe and a flush and a twinge appeared on her sallow face.

The look and the tone completely inhibited Ina's natural frank impulse, which was to tell where she was going.

"Like my dress, Kate?" she asked, coolly. "Aunt Eleanor got it for me in St. Louis. It's only a simple afternoon dress, but quite up to date."

"I'm not crazy about it," snapped Kate.

Ina laughed and went out. Her elder sister bade fair to be quite amusing. Ina's genuine love of home and family had buried for the whole of her school period certain irritating traits, especially peculiar to Kate. They were recalled.

"It almost looks as if Kate does not like my coming home, and especially my clothes. Wait till she sees my graduation dress!"

There was a clean footpath along one side of the lane, and when Ina started down it she found herself facing the sage mountains, far across the level lake basin land, and the bulge of red rocky ground beyond. The afternoon sun, low in the sky, cast a soft light upon the round gray domes and the beautiful slopes. Suddenly her heart beat quicker and fuller. An old love of the open country, of lonely hills, of the wind in her face and the fragrance of sage revived in her. That was another reason for her inward joy at returning to the scenes of her childhood. Moreover, as she gazed intently, these mountains of gray, with the shadows of purple in the clefts, seemed to call to her. It was a distinct sensation almost like an audible voice. The beckoning hills! Then it occurred to her that beyond them lay Forlorn River. She checked her thought and hurried on, with pensive gaze on the black buttes of lava to the west.

Before she realized it she had come to the Ide farm. The same old barred gate! The untrimmed hedge! The green shady yard and the lane that led into the old house seemed exactly to fit her expectations. Almost she expected to see Rover, Ben's dog, come bounding out to meet her. But Rover did not come. Ina entered the gate, and found that habit led her round to the back door. Yard and house had the homely appearance of use and comfort. Ina crossed the wide porch and knocked on the door.

It opened at once, revealing a pleasant-faced girl with fine blue eyes and curly hair. She had freckles that Ina remembered. She wore a gingham apron; her sleeves were rolled up to firm round elbows; in one hand she held a broom. For a moment she stared at Ina.

"Hettie, don't you know me?" asked Ina.

"I — I do and — I don't," gasped the girl, with her face lighting.

"I'm Ina Blaine."

"Oh — of course — I *knew* you were, but you're so different — so — so changed and lovely," replied Hettie in charming confusion. "We heard you were home. I'm glad to see you. Come in. Mother is here."

"Hettie, you've grown up wonderfully, much more than Dall or Marvie," said Ina, as she entered the big light kitchen that made her remember raids on the cupboard. "And I can return your compliment."

"Thanks," replied Hettie, blushing. "You always used to say nice things, Ina. Come in and see Mother." She led the way into the large sitting room.

"Mother," announced Hettie, to the sad, sweet-faced woman who rose from beside a table, "this is Ina Blaine, come to call on us the very next day after she got home."

"Mrs. Ide, I hope you remember me," said Ina, advancing with a little contraction of her heart. Faintly she grasped at an affinity that brought her close to this woman.

"Ina Blaine!" exclaimed Mrs. Ide, in a slightly quavering voice, making haste to adjust her spectacles. "I ought to remember. That name is almost as familiar as Hettie's . . . So you are Ina! I wouldn't have known you. Welcome home to Tule Lake, my dear. It was like you to come to us at once. I told them last night you'd never change."

"Oh, I'm changed, grown up, Mrs. Ide," replied Ina, taking the proffered hand, and then yielding to a warm impulse she kissed the faded cheek. "But I'm happy to be home, and I — I intend to be as I used to be."

"Of course you will," responded Mrs. Ide. "Even though you are a young woman now. Come, sit here an' tell us all about yourself."

Ina had never before found such inspiring listeners and she talked for an hour, telling all about her school life, and just touching at the end on her arrival home.

44

"It's good to hear you, Ina," murmured Mrs. Ide. "I hope an' pray the changes that have come will not make you unhappy."

"I shall not let myself be unhappy," replied Ina, spiritedly. "I confess I'd have liked to find my home — my people the same as when I left them. But — they're not. I'll adjust myself to it."

"Are you going to come to see us occasionally?" inquired Mrs. Ide, gravely.

"Same as I used to," replied Ina, with feeling.

"Your father will not like that, Ina. He is a hard man, as hard in some ways as Amos Ide."

"We have already clashed," said Ina, naïvely. "To my discomfiture."

"Mother, Ina's as spunky as when she used to quarrel with Ben," spoke up Hettie, impulsively.

Manifestly it was an unfortunate allusion, for the older woman appeared to retreat within herself. Ina regretted the reference to Ben, for she knew she must say something about him, and was at a loss.

"Yes, I remember Ben and our quarrels as well as anything," she replied, simply. "It would be nice to — to talk over old times, but we'll leave that till another day. Good-bye, Mrs. Ide. I shall come to see you often . . . Hettie, will you walk down the lane with me? I'm going to meet Marvie and Dall."

"That I shall," rejoined Hettie, heartily.

But once out of the house, Ina felt the constraint that bound Hettie as well as herself. She would make an end of that. But despite her overtures, it was not until they were well down the lane that she hit upon the right way to reach Hettie.

Suddenly turning to Hettie, she had queried, bluntly: "Now tell me about Ben."

Hettie turned so pale that the freckles stood out prominently upon her face, and her eyes filled with tears.

"You've heard?" she asked, huskily.

"A lot of gossip," replied Ina, swiftly. "I don't believe a single word of it. Hettie, tell me the truth."

"Oh, Ina — that's so good of you," burst out Hettie, almost sobbing, and she seized Ina's hand. "There's not so much to tell. Ben loved the wild country and wild horses. He couldn't help it. Father drove him away from home — made an outcast of him. It broke Mother's heart — and it's breaking mine. All kinds of lies have been flying around about Ben. Of late, since that man Setter came to Tule Lake, they're growing worse."

"I met Setter. I don't like him or trust him, Hettie. He said some hard things about Ben's friend, a cowboy from Nevada."

"I hate him, Ina," flashed Hettie, with a dark flush. "I could tell you a reason outside of his lies about Ben."

"You needn't. I've met and seen many men these four years of my absence . . . Hettie, I just cannot believe Ben would steal. I *can't*."

"Ina, I *know* he wouldn't," rejoined Hettie, eloquently. "It's not easy to tell how I know, but it's in my heart."

"Have your family lost faith in Ben?"

"Yes, all except Mother. But it's hope now, more than real faith. Father has broken her. Ben was his pride, if you remember. The disappointment has made Father old . . . Oh, such a mess to make over a boy's love of horses! I grow sick when I think of it."

"Well, Hettie, it seems we're of the same mind," went on Ina, soberly. "Now it's not *what* we must do, but *how*."

"Ina, I don't — understand you," faltered Hettie.

"We've got to save Ben before it's too late," declared Ina, and the strange sweet warmth that seemed liberated by her conscious words brought the hot blood to her cheeks.

"*We've* got to! You and I?" asked Hettie, in low, wondering voice.

"Yes. You're his sister and I'm — his old playmate. Probably his only friends, except the cowboy from Nevada . . . Hettie, I'm forming impressions of that cowboy Setter claimed was a horse thief. I believe he's someone who's standing by Ben. He has found Ben alone, forsaken, an outcast. Perhaps he too loves wild horses. Hettie, we've got to see these boys, especially Ben, if we have to ride out to Forlorn River."

"I'll go, though Father will half kill me when he finds out," declared Hettie, in awe.

"As a last resort, we'll do it," returned Ina. "But let us wait. Something may happen. We might get word to Ben. He might hear of my return and want to see me."

"He'd want to, Ina, but he'd never come, even if you sent him word," said Hettie, sadly.

"Poor Ben! What a pass he must have come to! . . . Well, here's the end of your lane and I think that's Marvie coming way down the road. I'll see you soon again, Hettie. Meanwhile remember we are arch plotters."

"Oh, Ina Blaine, I could hug you!" cried Hettie, in passionate gratefulness.

"Well, do it!"

But Hettie turned and fled down the lane.

Saturday came and passed. Ina spent it with Marvie out in the open — a long beautiful spring day, full of laughter and excitement, yet with moments for appreciation of the soft gray sage slopes above the brook where Marvie loved to fish, and lonely intervals when she dreamed.

Through some machination of Kate's, that almost roused Ina's temper, Dall was not permitted to accompany them. So Ina, not to disappoint Marvie, had gone alone with him.

It was dark when they drove into the lane of Tule Lake Ranch. Ina, as she shuffled wet and disheveled into the bright kitchen, did not need sister Kate's wry look to appreciate her appearance. She did not care. She was tired, and strangely happy. Her father's displeasure with Marvie, her mother's divided state of mind, Kate's manifest disapproval, had not the least effect upon her. What a day to bring back the past! She hardly remembered even the thrilling incidents, let alone the multitudinous commonplace ones.

Marvie had proved to be such a brother as any sister must love. He made Ina a chum. How little did her dignity and schooling impress him! Ina had shared everything. She had driven, walked, climbed, and waded; she had fallen off a slippery bank into the rushes; she had rowed a boat while Marvie had fished with intense hopefulness; she had helped him fight a fish that got away.

Ina, spurred despite herself by Kate's peremptory call from below, made haste with her bath and change of clothes. Then she hurried down to have late supper alone with Marvie. Someone evidently had crushed the boy's exuberant reminiscences of the day. Ina felt that nothing could crush her remembrance of it nor take from her the nameless joy. She was cheerfully oblivious of Kate, and soon won her mother to keen interest in the adventures of the day.

"Wal," said her father, "reckon it was fun for you. But you're growed up now. Marvie ought to have knowed better than to take you to Forlorn River."

"But we only went to the mouth of the river above Hammell," protested the boy. "Not over the hills."

"Why not over the hills?" queried Ina, quickly. "I want to ride everywhere. Next Saturday we'll go to the lake."

Mr. Blaine shot a significant glance at his wife, as if to remind her of some prediction he had made, and he got up with a little cough that Ina well remembered.

"Marvie, you'd make a wild tomboy out of your sister," he said, severely. "You shan't have no horse an' buggy next Saturday."

"But Paw, Ina can't walk all over," protested Marvie, getting red in the face. "I'd just as lief walk."

"Ina will have someone to drive her around," replied Mr. Blaine.

"Ahuh! That Sewell McAdam fellow, for one, I s'pose," ejaculated Marvie, in imminent disgust.

"Sewell McAdam? Who is he?" inquired Ina, glancing from Marvie to her father.

"Reckon the boy guessed right that time," laughed Mr. Blaine. "I forgot to tell you about Sewell. He's a fine young chap from Klamath. Father's a friend of mine. Owns the big three C stores. You'll meet Sewell. I asked him for Sunday dinner."

"I shall be pleased, of course," said Ina, dubiously, with her eyes on Marvie. The boy did not show that he would share her pleasure. After supper, in the sitting room, when they were alone except for Dall, Ina put a query to him anent this young man who was coming Sunday.

"He's a city fellar, Ina," replied Marvie. "Kind of a willie-boy who puts on style."

"Don't you like him, Marvie?"

"Haven't any reason not to, but you bet I wouldn't take him fishin'."

"That's very conclusive," said Ina, thoughtfully. "I don't remember Dad inviting young men to dinner Sundays."

"Ina, I heard somethin' — if you won't tell," whispered Marvie, swiftly glancing round. "Dall knows, for she was with me."

"Cross my heart," replied Ina, solemnly.

"We heard Paw an' Mr. McAdam talkin' out by the barn. They had some kind of a big deal on. This

50

McAdam man is the father of Sewell, who's comin' Sunday. He's awful rich. Owns stores. He an' Paw are goin' into somethin', an' you figgered in it."

"Marvie! What are you saying?" exclaimed Ina in amaze.

"Ask Dall," returned the boy.

"Ina, I heard Pa say if Sewell got sweet on you pretty quick it'd work out fine," answered Dall, her eyes bright and round with importance.

"Did you tell anyone?" asked Ina.

"I told Mother, an' Kate heard. Mother seemed sort of fussed, like she is so much. Kate chased us out of the kitchen. She was mad as thunder. Kate's city beau is a friend of this Sewell McAdam."

"Don't tell anyone else, please," said Ina, earnestly.

"I promise," rejoined the boy, with loving gaze upon her. "But, Ina, if you let this city fellar come courtin' you, I — I'll never take you fishin' again."

He ended stoutly, though manifestly fearful that he had overstepped his brotherly limit. Ina's heart warmed to him, and she acted upon the feeling by giving him a kiss.

"Don't worry, Marvie. We'll go fishing whenever you'll take me."

They were interrupted then, and Ina had no opportunity to think over this odd gossip until she went to her room. At first the idea seemed ridiculous and she endeavored to dismiss it. But other considerations added their peculiar significance; and it was not long before she confessed the exasperating complexity of the situation. Only for a moment did it dismay her. Ina was

51

dauntless. But to oppose the wills and desires of her people hurt her. That seemed inevitable. She did not determine upon any course of action. It was necessary to await developments. Nevertheless, she looked forward with something of curiosity and humor to the meeting with Mr. Sewell McAdam.

Sunday morning acquainted Ina with the fact that for the Sabbath, at least, much of the old home life of the Blaines had been retained.

There was indeed more elaborate dressing, especially on the part of Kate, than Ina could remember. Her sister showed more than ever that she was a country girl unduly influenced by city associations and ambitions. The boys, it appeared, except Marvie, had their own horses and buggies to drive to church. Mr. Blaine drove the rest of the family in a two-seated vehicle that Ina imagined she recognized. She and Dall rode on the front seat with their father.

The village church, of gray and weather-beaten boards, the young men loitering round the entrance, self-conscious in their shiny clothes, the girls in bright dresses and bonnets, and the horses hitched in the shade — these looked precisely to Ina the same as before she had left home.

As they entered, her father leading up the aisle, very pompous, her mother trying to live up to her part, and Kate proud as a peacock, Ina became aware that they, and particularly herself, were the cynosure of many eyes. This fact did not embarrass her, but it quite prevented a free range to her curiosity and interest. Some time elapsed after they were seated before she recognized anyone. Ina sat between Marvie and Dall, both of whom added not a little to her self-consciousness. Marvie, with his handsome face to the front, serious as was becoming to the occasion, kept slyly pinching her and making slight signs for her to notice some young men in the pew in front. Ina did not look directly, because she felt she was being stared at. Dall was tremendously concerned with what she evidently thought was a sensation Ina was creating.

The preacher was strange to Ina, a plain middle-aged man of serious gentle mien, who had a fine voice and talked simply and earnestly. Ina had listened to poorer preachers in big city churches. After the sermon when all bowed during the prayer Marvie leaned close to Ina and whispered like an imp: "That's Sewell McAdam right in front, settin' with Kate's city beau. Couple of slick ganders! But they ain't foolin' *me*."

Ina hid her face and cautioned Marvie, by both hand and whisper. She found herself, without any apparent justice or reason, quite in accord with Marvie, and she feared he might discover it.

On the moment, however, Ina did not have opportunity to satisfy her lively curiosity. And when the congregation filed out she soon found herself besieged by old acquaintances, schoolmates grown up, as she was, and people who had been neighbors and friends. There were a good many warm welcomes accorded her; yet she did not miss the poisoned honey of some tongues or the expressive glances of many eyes. Ina was quick to grasp that her father's rise in the world of Tule Lake had engendered envy and contempt. She met the

53

keen inquisitive eyes of motherly women who no doubt were wondering if she, too, had been spoiled by education and riches.

She was introduced presently to Kate's *fiancé*, rather a matured man, whose name she did not catch. He had a florid handsome face, and his manner was intended to be suave and elegant, but was neither. Ina did not care for his keen-eyed appraisement of her person.

His companion, a dapper young man, blond, with curling mustache and large, languid, blue eyes, was Mr. Sewell McAdam. He wore gloves and carried a cane. It was plain that Ina was being presented to him, and that the occasion afforded him a gratification he did not intend to betray. Ina's quick ear did not catch any words of pleasure at the meeting.

Gradually the crowd dispersed with groups and couples going toward their conveyances, and others walking down the street. Mr. McAdam quite appropriated Ina, but it pleased her to see that Marvie stayed close beside her.

"I'm having dinner with you," announced her escort. "You can ride home with me. I've a fast little high-stepper."

"Thank you, Mr. McAdam," replied Ina, sweetly, "but I'm afraid of fast horses. I'll ride home with my folks."

The young gentleman appeared surprised and then annoyed. Ina bowed and passed on with Marvie, who was certainly squeezing her hand. They both climbed to the front seat, where Dall was already perched, while

Mr. Blaine untied the horses at the hitching rail. Upon turning, with the reins in his hands, he espied Ina.

"Didn't Sewell ask you to ride home with him?" he queried.

"Yes," replied Ina, smiling.

"What're you doin' in here, then?" he demanded.

"Well, Dad, I'd rather ride home with Marvie and Dall," returned Ina.

The presence of others, no doubt, restrained her father from a sharp retort. Ina saw the jerk of his frame and she heard him mutter as he climbed to the seat. Ina divined there was more here than just casual suggestion of the moment. It made her thoughtful all the way home, gravely anxious to reserve judgments.

Ina's first Sunday dinner at home was saved from being boresome, even irritating, by Marvie and Dall. These youngsters were wise enough to grasp the opportunity company at table afforded. Dall had a secret which she intuitively shared with Ina. Marvie was subtly antagonistic with all the ingenuity and devilishness of a keen boy. Some of his remarks were lost upon his father, whose appetite precluded observation, and his mother, buried in thought. They glanced off Mr. McAdam, too, but Kate's glare was provocative of more, and Ina's kicking him under the table made no impression.

"Mr. McAdam, you must have lots of sweethearts with that fast horse you drive," remarked Marvie, naïvely. "Most girls wouldn't mind anythin' if they could ride behind a horse like yours."

"Not so many, Marvie," replied the young man, blandly.

"Can you drive him with one arm — so you'll have the other one free?" inquired the boy.

"With my little finger."

"Gee!" exclaimed Marvie.

The dinner was a bounteous repast, which it took time to consume. At its conclusion Marvie was dispatched on an errand, invented for the hour, and Dall was sent to her room. Kate paraded away with her *fiancé*, evidently to go out riding, and Mr. and Mrs. Blaine, without any excuses, left Ina alone to entertain their caller. The thing struck Ina as almost barefaced, and but for the pity she felt for her parents and older sister she would have resented it. How childish and silly of them! Ina viewed with augmenting dismay the gulf between her and them, something that could be bridged only by her understanding. Then she addressed herself to the task of entertaining this most eligible young man. Ina commenced amiably enough, but did not progress in a way that she thought flattering to herself. Mr. McAdam first interrupted her to say they would go out for a drive; then when it transpired that she was of different mind he stated he always took a lady out riding on Sunday afternoons.

"That's very nice of you," responded Ina. "It's still early in the afternoon. I'll excuse you."

He stared at Ina as if she were a new species, and when finally it dawned upon him that she actually would not go and was sweetly advising him to hunt up another girl, he betrayed in sulky resentment not only his egotism, but a manifest disillusion. The moment ended Ina's tolerance and desire to do her duty to her father's friends.

"I wanted to drive you over to Lakeville. Told some friends I'd fetch you. Well, next Sunday we'll go," he said, his petulance easing out to words of finality. It did not occur to him that Ina might again refuse.

After conversation had been renewed he began to question Ina about her college life and her relatives in Kansas. Ina replied fluently, for to her it was a pleasant subject; but very quickly she grasped that Mr. McAdam was not interested in anything concerning it except the men she had known. He was not adroit in concealing his jealous curiosity. Ina would have had more respect for him if he had deliberately asked her if she was engaged or had a sweetheart, or if she flirted promiscuously or at all. Promptly then she cut her discourse on college and Kansas, and led him to talk of himself. He required no urging. Suggestion was not imperative. All she needed to do was listen.

Sewell McAdam was a salesman. He sold commodities for money. Stores and people, no credit and quick turnovers of goods, long hours and small wages for employees — of these things he was glibly full. His little leisure he devoted to fast horses, adornment of person, pinochle, and pretty girls. Never had Ina felt so immensely flattered! He had no love for open country. Never had sat round a camp fire in his life! Hunting was too hard work and fishing a dirty waste of time. The draining of Tule Lake was a master stroke of business minds, of whom his father claimed to be one.

He had never seen a wild horse or the purple-gray of the sage hills.

"Let's go out for a little walk in the yard," suggested Ina, rising. So she got him outdoors where there was air, but no escape. They inspected the corrals, sheds, barns, horses, with all of which Mr. McAdam found fault. He hated farm life anyway.

"You'll like living in Klamath Falls," he said, as if inspired.

"Indeed!" murmured Ina, stifling a laugh. If only Marvie would appear to the rescue! But certain it was that this favored suitor from the city had been accorded a fair field.

Then to Ina's dismay the voluble young gentleman spied the grove of large trees far back of the house and desired to go thither. In truth, he was sentimental. Ina suffered herself to be led there. It seemed a sacrilege — something she did not quite understand. But the sympathy and humor with which she had accepted her father's company vanished under the old double pine tree. Here Sewell McAdam possessed himself of her hand, unobtrusively he made it appear on two occasions. On the third, however, Ina had to pull to release it.

"Mr. McAdam, I fear I do understand you," she said. "But you don't understand me. I'm not in the habit of letting young men hold my hand."

"Aw, be sociable, Ina. What's a little hand holding?" he urged.

"It doesn't amount to much, but I haven't any desire for it," she said, edging away.

58

"Say, I may strike you as pretty thick, but I'm not that big a fool," he returned, frowning.

"As what?" queried Ina.

"Why — to believe you're that uppish, when you've been away for years at school among a lot of Tom, Dick and Harrys. Besides, it's a bad start for us if you're to be — if we're — if things are —"

Ina's grave questioning gaze brought him to a floundering halt.

"Mr. McAdam, you are laboring under some mistake," said Ina. "We — if you mean you and I — have not made any kind of a start. Come, let us return to the house."

He accompanied her sulkily. Ina was quick to give him an opportunity to say good-bye and make his departure. But he carried his petulance even into the presence of her father and mother, now sitting on the porch with other visitors, of whom Mr. Setter was one. Ina was relieved to join them. A few minutes later Kate and her escort drove into the yard. Presently Ina excused herself and went to her room.

An hour's pondering alleviated her anger and disgust, but she did not intend to endure any more afternoons like this one. She did not feel sure of her father's motive, but his action had been rather pointed. Ina had dim recollections of the trials of country girls whose fathers' wishes were the law. She saw that the only course for her was to assert herself at once. Accordingly, when the company had departed and she was again in the presence of the family she addressed her father.

"Dad, why did you all leave me alone with that Mr. McAdam?"

"Wha-at!" ejaculated Mr. Blaine, and when she repeated her query he said: "Reckon Sewell was callin' on you."

"But I did not know him; I didn't ask him."

"That makes no difference. I asked him."

Ina saw him then, somehow transformed from the loving though hard parent she had cherished in memory. He had been as powerfully affected by the touch of money and his false position as had her mother, only in a vastly different way.

"Why did you?" went on Ina, aware that her composure and spirit were inimical to her father's temper.

"Sewell's a fine young chap. His father's my friend, an' maybe partner. Reckon I thought you an' Sewell would take a shine to each other."

"Thank you. That explains Mr. McAdam. He seemed pretty sure that I'd take a shine to him, as you call it."

At this juncture Marvie exploded into a rapturous: "Haw! Haw! Haw!"

"Shet up, an' leave the table," ordered Mr. Blaine. Then turning to Ina with face somewhat reddened, he continued: "Ina, I ain't denyin' I told Sewell you'd sure like him."

"I'm sorry, for I don't."

"Wal, that's too bad, but I reckon you will when you get acquainted."

60

"It's quite improbable, Father," returned Ina, unconscious that for the first time she omitted the familiar "Dad".

"Sewell's father an' me are goin' into a big business deal," said Mr. Blaine, laboriously breathing, and his huge hands held up knife and fork. "They're mighty proud folks. If you snubbed Sewell it'd hurt my stand with them."

"I'll not snub him or any of your friends or partners," replied Ina. "I'll be respectful and courteous, as one of your family, when they call here. But I do not want to be left alone again with Mr. Sewell McAdam or any other man. And I won't be, either."

"Paw, Ina is still sweet on Ben Ide," interrupted Kate, spitefully.

All the blood in Ina's heart seemed to burn in her face. The name of Ben Ide, spoken aloud, had inexplicable power to move her. This was so thought-provoking that it rendered her mute.

"You ought to be grateful for the attentions of Sewell McAdam," declared Kate, with a flare in her eyes.

"Listen, Kate, I'm not so susceptible as you are to the blarney of city men," returned Ina, goaded beyond restraint. "They might be actuated by the change in our fortunes."

This precipitated the imminence of a family quarrel, which was checked by Mrs. Blaine's bursting into tears and Marvie's yelling derisively at Kate from the hall. Mr. Blaine stamped after him. Kate, white-faced and shaken, sat there in silence. Ina endeavored to soothe her mother; and presently, when Mr. Blaine returned with fire in his eye muttering, "That damn youngster's goin' to be another Ben Ide!" they all resumed their supper, jointly ashamed of the upset.

That night Ina sat alone in her dark room beside the open window. Spring frogs were piping plaintively. How the sweet notes made Ina shiver! They too flooded her mind with memories of the home she had cherished in her heart, of childhood and youth. Of Ben Ide! She could make out the dim high black hills beyond which lay Forlorn River. Dropping her head on the window sill, she wept.

CHAPTER
FOUR

Ben mounted his gray horse, and splashing across Forlorn River, he headed north, his mind teeming with poignant thoughts. He timed this ride to get him into Hammell late in the afternoon, but the gray was not a slow traveler, and Ben, lost in vain regrets and hopeless longings, forgot to hold him to a walk.

At noon, from the divide between the sage mountains Ben looked back and down at Clear Lake, shining like a green jewel set in the gray-purple of sage, and far across to the dot that was his cabin home. "What a country! I'd hate to see it settled. But that'll come, and my chance to get possession of Forlorn River Valley."

Northward down the other side of the pass spread the vast level range land of California and Oregon, green and gold, square-patched in brown, threaded by bright ribbons of water, bordered by the black lava beds and buttes. Far beyond glittered snow-clad Shasta, solemn and white in the sky. Survey of both east and west was blocked by the bulk of the gray mountains.

It was Ben's habit to look and think while he rode along the trails; and this day his sensorial perceptions were abnormally active while grief, resolve, hope, dream, and doubt possessed his heart in turn. That part of Hettie's letter referring to Ina Blaine recurred and recurred despite stern effort to dismiss it. Hettie was faithful, brother-worshiping, and she had allowed her imagination to run riot. Ben gave no credence to her wild beliefs. Yet what smothering sweetness overcame him! Madness lay in mere dreaming of what Hettie suggested. No, Ina Blaine was not for a poor lonely wild-horse hunter.

Ben rode into Hammell ahead of the hour he had set, and tying the gray to the hitching rail in front of Ketcham's big store he went in. How good to feel free of debt! Ketcham's greeting was cordial enough to please even Ben. He exchanged bits of news with the genial merchant, and then crossed the wide street to the high board-faced saloon. He found welcome here, too, from Smatty McGill and his bartender, to loungers, cowboys, gamblers, most of whom knew Ben.

"Soft drinks only for me, fellows," he said, inviting them all to the bar. "But have what you like on me. And tell me all that's going on around."

He spent an hour there, hearing again all Nevada had told him, and more besides. He had worked with one of the cowboys. When Ben was about through with his pertinent questions, Strobel, the county sheriff, strolled in. Ben knew him well and was sure of his stand with this lean-jawed, narrow-eyed officer.

"Howdy, Ben!" replied Strobel, to Ben's greeting. "Haven't laid eye on you for a year. Tell me aboot yourself."

It was then that Ben realized the subtle transition which had taken place in his affairs. All in one day! Ben had to draw upon Nevada's queer ideas and auguries about the future. When spoken out, frankly, Ben felt that they became fact.

"Wal, Ben, I feel I ought to tell you there's queer talk floatin' around aboot you," drawled Strobel, confidentially, and he proceeded to acquaint Ben with some unsavory gossip.

"Charlie, they're the dirtiest kind of lies," declared Ben, with sincere heat. "You've known me since I was a kid. Don't you ask me to deny I'm a horse thief."

"Wal, I reckon I never took much stock in it, far as you're concerned," went on Strobel. "But how aboot your pards? That Modoc had a bad name before he went to ridin' fer you. An' Less Setter swears Nevada is a thief an' a gun-fighter of note in other parts."

"I knew about Modoc," replied Ben, earnestly. "But I know as little about Nevada before he came to this country as you do. Since they've been with me they've been straight, Charlie. They couldn't do anything crooked without me finding out. What's more, I intend to live this talk down."

"Wal, Ben, I'm dog-gone glad to hear you say that," responded the sheriff. "I always felt close to your father till he fell into a gold mine. It's my idee he was hard on you. Now don't go blowin' aboot it, but you can count on Charlie Strobel."

"You bet that makes me proud, Charlie," responded Ben, feelingly.

"Wal, keep this under your hat. I've been jacked up considerable lately 'cause I can't lay my hands on this thievin' outfit back in the sage hills. An' I'm het up aboot it. Your father an' Hart Blaine both are on the Council. Reckon you know what that means. Now, Ben, come over to my office an' I'll swear you in as a deputy, secret of course. Then you keep your eye peeled out in the hills an' if you run acrost any fellers you're not sure of you can arrest them on the spot."

"Thanks for your trust, Charlie, but I can't bind myself. I'll keep my eye peeled, though, and post you in no time."

"Good. I'll take it as a favor, Ben."

"Wait a minute, Charlie," added Ben, as the sheriff shook hands with him. "Tell me, who is this Less Setter?"

"Wal, come to think of it, darn if I know," rejoined Strobel, musingly. "He hails from east of the range somewhere. Talks big. Spends lots of money. Makin' deals all the time — cattle, hosses, land. Particular friend of Hart Blaine's now."

"Sounds like a whole lot," returned Ben, thoughtfully in turn. "All the same, Charlie, I'm giving you a hunch. Watch this Less Setter. Dig quietly into his deals. It can't do any harm and it may surprise you."

"Ben, you've got your nerve," said Strobel, his narrow eyes like slits over blue fire. "But I'm a son-of-a-gun if you haven't hit me plumb center."

They parted at the door, Strobel plodding thoughtfully down the road, and Ben, wrapped in a profound study, starting to cross to where he had tied his horse. As he approached the hitching rail he saw a buckboard and a spirited team in front of the store. He heard the gay voices of young people. Untying his horse, he was about to step into the saddle when he remembered he wanted matches. So, leading the gray, he walked toward the steps.

Someone, a girl in blue, came tripping down. Ben saw her trim feet halt. Then he looked up into a face that was an older, sweeter image of the one cherished in his heart. Ina Blaine, tall, slim, stood gazing at him with the velvety dark eyes that had been her greatest charm.

After the shock of recognition whirling thoughts and feelings crowded Ben's mind.

"Ben Ide! Don't you know me?" she asked. The gladness, the reproach in look and voice, upheld him from utter confusion. He became aware of people in front of the store, of those in the buckboard. Before them he must not be awkward; and that, with the spur of her undoubted intention to meet him as an old friend, inspired him to cool, easy dignity.

"It's Ina," he said, meeting her outstretched hand.

"Oh, Ben — how you've grown!" she exclaimed, running an appraising glance from his boots to his bare head. "Why, you're a man! . . . Older, Ben, and —" She studied his face with dark eyes growing troubled. "But I knew you. Are you well, Ben, and — and all right?"

"I reckon I was both until about a minute ago," he replied.

"Same old Ben," she said, gaily, yet she blushed.

With that, restraint seemed to seize upon them both. Ben tried to break it. "You look wonderful, Ina. I hope your homecoming made you happy."

"Ben, it did, and then it didn't," she rejoined. "I've so much to tell you. And we can't talk here. When can you see me?"

"That's for you to say, Ina," he answered, his eyes on hers.

She looked away, hesitated, and then as if with a happy thought turned to him: "I'm to meet your sister tonight at eight o'clock, in the lane between the house and the road. Won't you come?"

"Ina, I'm on my way to see Hettie and Mother. I'm afraid you'd risk a good deal, meeting me."

"Risk? In what way, Ben?"

"People would gossip if they saw you with me. Then your father —"

"I'll welcome the risk, Ben. Say you'll come with Hettie to meet me."

"If you really — wish it — yes — I'll —" he replied, thickly, halting over the last words.

"Thank you. Good-bye till eight," said Ina, and turned away.

Ben strode up the steps, passing men whose faces blurred, on into the store where with difficulty he remembered what it was he wanted to purchase. His mind was in a whirl.

"That was young McAdam in the Blaine buckboard," announced Ketcham, confidentially, as he waited for Ben to make known his wants.

"Didn't see him. McAdam? Who's he?" returned Ben.

"Father's a big merchant in Klamath. This boy Sewell is a high-stepper. He's runnin' after Ina pretty keen, an' folks say Hart Blaine would like him as son-in-law."

Ben moved away as quickly as possible from a radius of such gossip. He scouted it with strange savage intensity, but that did not assuage the hurt. Then he recalled what Nevada had said about this fellow McAdam.

Ben, suffering a division of mood, went outside, and led his horse to a livery stable to get him grain and water. Then he bethought himself of his own needs, though hunger seemed far from him. But he headed toward a restaurant. The hour was near sunset. A cool wind came down from the hills. Wild geese were honking overhead.

Dusk had fallen over the Tule Lake basin when Ben Ide rode into the lane that had once known the imprint of his bare feet. Over the distant range a brightness attested to the rising of the moon. Halfway down the lane, in the shadow of a clump of trees, Ben halted his horse and proceeded to walk.

The smell of freshly plowed earth filled the cool air. A sadness, fitting the gloaming hour, pervaded the level land.

All Ben's boyhood flooded back in swift memories. It seemed long past. None of it could ever return. He was an outcast, sneaking home in the absence of his father.

69

Yet with the shame of it burned a righteous wrath. Somehow the fault had not been all his.

As he turned off the lane toward a gate, indistinct in the shade, the figure of a girl approached him noiselessly.

"Ben?" she called, in shrill whisper.

"Yes, I'm here," he replied.

She ran into his arms and held him closely, crying low and incoherently. He returned the embrace instinctively. Of course it was his sister. But she was tall, a woman grown, firm and strong of build, and a stranger, except in her voice.

"Why, Hettie!" he whispered, deeply touched.

"Oh, Ben — I'm just — glad to see you," she replied, moving back from him yet clinging to his arm. "How big you are! It was good of you to come — at once. I owe that Nevada cowboy something. He's nice . . . Ben, I want you to slip in with me and see Mother. She's alone. But somebody might come any minute. You and I can talk afterward. I hope the surprise will not hurt Mother. But I just believe it's what she needs. Come. You're clumsy, Ben, and your spurs jingle."

"Hettie, I can't get over how tall you are," whispered Ben, permitting himself to be led under the dark trees toward the lighted window of the kitchen. They reached the porch. She cautioned him not to make noise. How tightly she gripped his hand! Ben's heart throbbed high. The past flashed back stingingly — the many times he had come home in the dark, after a day of running wild against his father's command, to be protected by his mother. His feet seemed leaden and his spurs clanged. Hettie opened the door. The kitchen was empty. Ben slipped in behind her. Nothing had changed. His father's new riches were not proclaimed in this homely kitchen. The ticking of the old clock suddenly seemed to smother him. It had ticked like that when his little brother Jude lay dying. So many years ago!

Then Hettie turned toward him in the bright light, her face pale, her eyes bright, a prayer on her lips.

"Mother," called Hettie, in a voice low and broken, "here's somebody to see you."

"Well, child, fetch somebody in," replied her mother, complacently, from the sitting room.

"No, you're requested to come out here," returned Hettie.

There was a moment's silence. Ben's heart kept time with the clock. Hettie moved toward the door of the sitting room. Ben heard the sound of a chair pushed back, then slow footsteps, almost feeble, he thought; a shadow crossed the light that shone in this room. Then Ben saw his mother's face and it seemed all the riot of his heart suddenly ceased.

"Mother!" called Ben, unable to keep silent longer. Two strides brought him into the glare of the lamp. She saw him, recognized him. The grief, the care, the age of her sweet face vanished marvelously.

"Ben! My son — oh, my son!" she cried, holding out her arms.

A little while later Hettie led him out through the yard, now moonlit in places, shadowed in others, to the gate.

71

"Let's wait here. I'm expecting someone you *might* like to see," said Hettie, drawing him to a bench in the shade. "Oh, Ben! ... my prayers are answered. Somehow I knew what Mother needed was to see you — and find out what I always felt — that these stories about you are lies. You convinced her. She is a changed woman. Oh, it will all come out well, now. Father can't help coming round."

"Humph! He'd never forgive me in a million years," returned Ben.

"Little you know him! If you made a success of the very thing he hates he'd sing a different tune. Father worships industry, success, money. Too much! Ben, before I forget let me tell you that he and Mr. Setter are going to buy up homesteads out in Forlorn River country. Prick up your ears, Ben. If there's to be a boom in land and cattle out in your wild-horse range get in on it yourself."

"Nevada had the same hunch," replied Ben, thoughtfully. "We each have a homestead, and we can buy up three more. How many acres in five times one sixty?"

"Why, you dunce, eight hundred acres, of course!"

"Whew! That's a lot of land. But I'll risk it. I'll sign up for those three homesteads tomorrow. Moore and Sims are sick of the long dry spell. Want to sell quick and cheap. But I've got mighty little money. It may ruin me."

"It will be the making of you," declared Hettie, vigorously. "Be sure you have those homesteads when Father and Mr. Setter ride out there to buy. I'd like to

72

see their faces ... Ben, I wrote you I didn't like Mr. Setter. He tried to be too — too familiar with me."

"That's something else and worse against Less Setter," muttered Ben, grimly.

"He is to blame for most of this new talk about you, Ben. For the life of me I can't see why he should lie about you. He gives me a creepy feeling. But Father thinks he's a big booster for Tule Lake, and he's thicker than hops with Mr. Blaine."

"Don't bother about Setter, but keep out of his way," said Ben. "I've a hunch this summer will surprise some folks. Hettie, now I've seen you again, it'll go harder with me to lose you for a long time."

"You're not going to lose me," declared Hettie, hugging his arm. "Oh, I'm an arch plotter, and I've got somebody wonderful to help. We're going to keep sight of you and Nevada."

"We! Who's the other arch plotter?"

"Ina Blaine," whispered Hettie.

"You talk — like — like a book," said Ben, incredulously. Yet he thrilled all over. The circumstances of the last twenty-four hours were too much for his hardened bitterness. He had softened. He could not resist Nevada and Hettie and Ina Blaine, if they persisted in this talk.

"Just you wait till you see Ina," went on Hettie, forcibly.

"Hettie, I have seen her. I met her today in Hammell. She asked me to meet her here when she comes to see you."

"Well, I never! Of all the luck! Doesn't it prove what I hinted?"

"Hettie, it proves nothing except that Ina is as sweet, kind, good as ever. She's heard about my downfall. She'd risk her reputation to show she still believed in her old friend."

"Friend, nothing!" scouted Hettie, warmly. "You and Ina were sweethearts. I tell you she loves you, Ben. I know it, if no one else does."

"For Heaven's sake, Hettie, don't talk nonsense!" burst out Ben, passionately. "You'll drive me mad."

"Don't you love Ina still?" queried his sister, inexorably.

"Love her! Never thought — of that," returned Ben, huskily. "No — of course not. How'd I dare? Hettie, you forget I'm a poor horse hunter, disowned by my family, disgraced, branded as an outcast and thief."

"Hush! Here comes Ina now," whispered Hettie. "Marvie is with her. He's true blue, Ben, and worships you. Talk to Ina as you did to Mother."

Rising, she left Ben and went out into the moonlit lane to meet two dark figures approaching. Ben crouched there, fighting a strange wildness that threatened to master him. His mother! Hettie! They had unnerved, uplifted him. And he trembled at the approach of that slim tall figure in the moonlight.

Hettie met Ina and Marvie in the lane and led them through the gate. Ben could see clearly, himself unseen. Ina stood bareheaded, her hair waving in the slight breeze. How fair her face! She seemed intent upon

74

Hettie's whispers. The boy clung to her. Then Hettie said: "Come, Marvie, walk with me a little."

Ina came slowly out of the white moonlight into the black shade. She walked as if into obscurity, holding out her hands. She bumped into the bench.

"Ben," she whispered, breathlessly.

"Ina," he replied.

"I was afraid you might not wait," she went on, seating herself beside him. "I'm late."

She bent closer to look at him, evidently with her eyes still affected by coming suddenly out of the bright moonlight. But Ben saw her eyes clearly enough. Too clearly for the composure he struggled to attain! How dark, eloquent, wonderful they shone out of her white face.

"Hettie said you saw your mother — left her better, happier. Ben, I'm so glad I — I could cry . . . You denied all this vile talk?"

"Yes," muttered Ben.

"You swore it was false? Made her believe you? Vowed you'd outlive it? You *were* honest, you'd *be* honest. You'd work, you'd keep sober, you'd save money, you'd show your hard old father that he'd have to be proud of you in the end. Come to you on his knees!"

"Yes, Ina, I'm afraid I committed myself to all you've mentioned," replied Ben, hoarsely. "But though I meant it all, I'm afraid it's too much. Hettie's faith, Mother's love, made me weak. I'd have sworn anything."

"Ben, it was the best in you speaking. You must live up to it . . . Not Hettie, nor even your mother, believes in you any more than I do."

"Ina! Don't talk — nonsense," stammered Ben. "What do you know of me now — after all my wandering years out there?"

"Has your heart changed?" she asked, softly.

"No, by Heaven! it hasn't," he muttered, dropping his head.

"Have you wronged anyone since you became a wild-horse hunter?"

"No," he declared, "unless it was a wrong to Mother not to obey Father. But, Ina, I couldn't stick to farm work. Father always gave me plowing, milking, digging, fencing, errands — anything except the work of a cowboy or range rider. He wanted to kill my love for the open country. But he only made it worse."

Stirred by these few full utterances, Ben burst into a swift, tense story of his free lonely life on Forlorn River — of his faithful friends and dumb companions, of the wild horses shining on the hills, of the glory of California Red as he raced like a flame through high grass, of the dawns and sunsets at Clear Lake, of the geese and deer and wolves, of all that made his home among the sage slopes something that he could not forsake.

"Ben, if your father was human he'd recognize the opportunity for you in the country you love," replied Ina, gravely. "And he would help you. But he is as hard as the lava out yonder. You must go it alone, Ben . . . My father is more set in his mind than yours. Then wealth and dreams of more have turned his head. I was wildly happy to get home. But gradually it dawned on me that home was not what I had left. It was no longer a home. Mother is out of place and does not understand. She has no sense of humor. She is obsessed with the vast change in our circumstances. She is absent-minded. She forgets that she must not churn butter. Oh, it is pathetic. Kate has been affected differently. She has become a snob, and she's engaged to a city man who I sadly fear has his eye on her prospects. My older brothers are no longer cowboys. They lean cityward, and Tule Lake Ranch will surely lose them. Marvie and Dall are still kids. They are my consolation. I'll stand by them and fight for them. Father and I clash. And the first time, by the way, was through a man named Less Setter, one of Father's stock partners. This Setter accused you of being a horse thief, and I told him he lied. I also told him that if I had not forgotten Ben Ide he would have to prove what he said."

"Ina, you stuck up for me that way, before your father?" queried Ben, huskily.

"I did. And that was the cause of our first quarrel. We've had others since. I believe, though, that after he gets over his anger he has a sneaking admiration for me. I hear him championing me to Kate. My older sister doesn't like my looks, my ideas, my clothes. We don't get along at all. But Mother and I, when we're alone, do better all the time. I'm helping Mother, Ben, and I shall stick for her sake and the youngsters'."

"I never thought you'd have trouble at home. Aw, what a shame! These old farm hands grown rich! . . . But Hart Blaine will marry you to some partner of his, like Setter, or — or that nincompoop McAdam I hear so much about."

Ben's feelings, flowing and augmenting with the outburst of his words, ended in misery. It confounded him with a possible revelation of the true state of his heart, of an appalling trouble that he dared not face.

"You flatter me, Ben," returned Ina, with something keen edging into the softness of her tone. "You've forgotten me — and many things."

"No — no . . . Forgive me, Ina. It's you who forget. I've lived a lonely hard life since we — since you left. Straight, I swear to God, but nothing to help me toward your level . . . Only don't you dare say I've forgotten you."

"I understand you, Ben," she said, in sweet earnestness. "You've suffered. You think you're bitter, hopeless, no good. Oh, Ben, what a blunder! You're hurt because of the infamy which has been heaped upon you. Because you imagine you're an outcast from your father's house. Because you must meet me, your old playmate, in secret. You're proud. I would not have you any different, except to see things clearly."

"I don't understand *you*. I can't follow you, Ina. I'm only a poor stumbling fool. Even your kindness amazes me. We were schoolmates — playmates, childish sweethearts — and I've never had another in any sense, but that's all past. It's over, done, buried. I'm a poor wild-horse hunter, to say the least . . . You've come home a lovely girl, educated. You're the pride of a rich old farmer who wants to hobnob with city folks . . . That's how I see it. And I'd far rather —"

She rose abruptly and standing over him, her face finding a ray of moonlight that penetrated the leafy foliage, she placed a hand on each of his shoulders. Ben's instinct was to sink under that touch, but some magic in it or her look caught his spirit, and he seemed to be uplifted.

Before she could speak Hettie came running to them, panting and excited.

"Ben — Father is driving — down the lane," she said. "I must be with Mother — when he comes. Good-bye. Send Nevada for letters. Good night, Ina. You and Marvie better slip through the field."

Ben had risen while Hettie was speaking, and as she hurried away he noticed a boy standing near.

"Hello, Marvie! Take care my father doesn't see Ina here," he whispered. "Come out to Forlorn River and fish with me."

"You bet I will," replied Marvie.

Above the clatter of rhythmic hoofbeats Ben heard the sound of his father's voice. It turned him cold. Ina stood there calm, white, as if all the cruel fathers in the world could not concern her. Ben felt, as he leaned toward her, that the great dark eyes would haunt him.

"You'll never know my gratitude," he whispered. "I'll try to live up to — try to be . . . Good-bye, Ina."

"Not good-bye, Ben," she returned.

He touched her extended hand, then leaped away into the dark shade of the yard and ran on until he reached the fence that bordered the field. As he paused he heard the clatter of hoofs pass up the driveway to the house.

Like a fugitive Ben stole along the shadow of the fence to where he had tethered his horse, and he rode away from the Ide Ranch as if he were being pursued. He was pursued by remorse, by resolves that mocked him, by an unknown emotion he could not stifle and feared to face.

Clouds covered the moon, and as he began to climb out of the basin he drew away from the pin-pointed lights in farmers' houses and from the barking of dogs. At last he mounted the rough slope of the basin rim, leaving the low country behind out of sight. He felt safer then; he breathed freer; he could think. A terrible sense of havoc confounded him. He rode on through the dark cool spring night, immeasurably glad for the lonely melancholy silence, the smell of sage, the looming domes of the mountains. But would these ever again suffice for his happiness? Happiness was nothing save a dream word. He did not want that or need it, or anything unless it was the something about his wild horses, his little cabin, his Forlorn River that made life there sweet.

Coyotes barked from the sage slopes. Wild geese honked overhead. The rhythmic hoofbeats of the tireless horse thudded softly on the dusty trail. Ben rode round the western bulge of the mountain and soon felt the sweep of wind from the great depression of land from the bottom of which Clear Lake gleamed pale and obscure. Some time after midnight he reached his homestead, and turning the horse into the corral he walked wearily to his cabin. Nevada and Modoc would not have returned from their scouting trip back in the direction of Silver Meadow. Ben sat down on the porch. Sleep seemed to be something impossible.

Hours of intense thought and feeling had followed his first wild state when he had fled from the Ide Ranch. He no longer hated his father. It had come to him how to overcome that dour individual. Remorse for the grief he had caused his mother and Hettie had turned away with the realization that he could make up for it all. As he gazed out over the dark river and lake he grew conscious of how these things pertaining to his family had changed, lessened, faded in the tremendous might of Ina Blaine's place in his life.

He worshiped her. He would never have run away to be a wild-horse hunter if she had stayed at home.

"What did she mean? What was she going to say when she put her hands on my shoulders?" he whispered aloud what he had thought a thousand times in agony during that ride. "I believed it just bighearted Ina's way. She would not forget an old schoolmate. She would never listen to gossip or care what people said . . . But the look of her — those lovely eyes — the tremble in her voice — the straight noble talk! Was that merely friendship? I'd be a fool to think so. She doesn't know yet, but the old feeling has grown along with her to womanhood . . . She didn't know, but she was waiting for me to take her into my arms. My God! If I'd guessed that, no thought of my honor or her good name would have stopped me. But I didn't see . . . Oh, the sweetness of her! Ina, my little sweetheart — a woman, fine, strong, splendid, sensible. Just to think of her raises me out of the dust. But I must not let her go any farther. She would be ruined, disgraced. Her heart would break . . . Yet, it might be that — Oh, it'll take me years to clear my name. Years in which she'd have to wait for me and suffer the scorn of her people, the gibes of friends. And I — consumed by longing, jealousy! No, it can't be. Ina Blaine is not for me. I will not see her again. So best can I prove worthy of her faith."

CHAPTER
FIVE

Ben's restless slumbers were disrupted at dawn by a noisy trampling of boots on the cabin porch. Nevada and Modoc had returned.

"By golly! he's heah in bed!" declared the former, stalking in.

Sitting up abruptly, Ben surveyed the cowboy with magnificent disfavor.

"I've a mind to lick you," he shouted.

"Now, pard, what've I done?" queried Nevada, incredulously.

"You woke me up," yelled Ben.

"Shore. It's time. Was you havin' pleasant dreams?" returned the cowboy, grinning.

"Dreams? No! But I was dead to the world. You tramp in here — wake me up — bring it all back."

"Huh! Bring what back?" flashed Nevada, stung in an instant.

"The cold hard facts," moaned Ben. "I'm the unluckiest poor damn miserable beggar on earth. I want to get a horrible drunk, but I can't — I can't."

Nevada's keen scrutiny lost its edge and something like relief replaced it. For a long moment he gazed down upon Ben.

"Shore you can't get drunk, you locoed fool," he declared, shortly. "That's past for you an' me. What'd you do in town?"

"Aw — it was bad going in but hell coming back," groaned Ben.

"Find your mother — well?" asked Nevada.

"Pretty well. Better than I expected. I cheered her up. Oh, Lord, the things I swore to! Nevada, I'll never be able to live up to them. But I'll *have* to!"

"Shore. I savvy. An' how aboot Hettie?" rejoined the cowboy, eagerly.

"You could have knocked me over with a feather," declared Ben. "She's grown that tall. And a good-looker, too. But what struck me most was her cheerfulness and faith. Why, she seemed almost happy to see me."

"Funny, now, ain't it?" drawled Nevada. "Wal, did you run into the old man?"

"No, thank goodness."

"Or anybody else who thinks you're a low-down hoss thief?"

"No, I was lucky that way. Not even in Hammell. Met Strobel, the sheriff, and I swear I believe he's my friend."

"Good! Wal, then, what's all this hollerin' aboot? Looks to me you've no call to be down in the mouth."

At that Ben dropped his head in shameful recollection. The momentary glow of hope and satisfaction faded away in a mounting tide of incredible disaster. To awaken to that awful trouble, and find that the night had only augmented it, was more than Ben could bear.

"Ben, I reckon you seen your sweetheart," declared Nevada, as if enlightenment had come to him.

"Who — what?" stammered Ben, jerking up.

"Your kid sweetheart, as Hettie called her," drawled Nevada, deliberately. "This young college dame who's goin' to be worth a million dollars. The girl them Hammell cowboys call the peach from Tule Lake Ranch."

"Shut up, or I'll soak you over the head with a chunk of firewood," yelled Ben, frantically.

"Lord! you must have it bad!" ejaculated Nevada, shaking. "You're shore full of gratitude. Say, if you go drivin' me off, who's goin' to handle this heah love affair for you?"

Ben groaned and writhed. "Nevada, it's terrible to hear you speak out — so — so — cold-blooded — as if — as if —"

"But, pard, you're up in the air an' I've got it figgered," declared the cowboy, persuasively. "You did see Ina Blaine? Now confess up."

"Yes. That's what ails me," rejoined Ben, abjectly.

"Aw, she wasn't changed — stuck up like the rest of them Blaines? Don't tell me Hettie made a mistake," implored Nevada.

Ben straightened up suddenly as if goaded to expression of something that it was impossible to place credence in.

"Nevada, I did meet Ina Blaine. Twice, once at Hammell, and last night at home. She greeted me on the main street of Hammell, before her friends and lots of the other people — just as if nothing had happened . . . Then last night when I was with Hettie in the yard Ina came. We were alone — I don't know how long. It seems like a dream. But I'm not quite crazy. I remember facts . . . She was sweet. Oh! she was wonderful! She set me on fire with her faith — her — her — I don't dare think what. But she's on my side, just as Hettie said. She'd already had a fight with her father in front of Less Setter, whom she heard call me a horse thief . . . And, oh, she said so many things. We were interrupted before she'd said all she wanted to. My father came driving in and I had to run . . . But I felt her hands on my shoulders — I saw her eyes in the moonlight . . . and, Nevada, I may be mad, but I believe Ina cares for me still."

"Ahuh! An' you fell in love with her all over again, deeper an' a million times wuss?"

"That must be it," whispered Ben, drawing his breath hard.

Nevada reacted to that confession in a manner totally unfamiliar to Ben. After all, Ben did not know this cowboy so very well. Nevada seemed to be accepting a responsibility that entailed grave things only he could vision.

"Get up, you big baby," he said, coolly, with a light in his eyes not meant for Ben. "You've got a fight on your hands. Cut this misery stuff! You can love your girl as she deserves an' break your heart over her. But that'll only make you more of a man. The hunch I had grows stronger every day. We're goin' to gamble, Ben Ide, with all we've got — with love an' life itself. I know this man Setter. He's got some deep game, an' blackin' your name is part of it. Reckon I've a hunch why, too. Setter wouldn't let anythin' stand in his way, Ben."

"Come to remember, Nevada, I've worse than that against him," asserted Ben, darkly.

Nevada leaned over with quick tense action that thrilled Ben.

"Ahuh! An' what is it?"

"I'm half afraid to tell you."

"But you can't hold it back now."

"Nevada, my sister Hettie confessed that Setter had tried to get too — too familiar with her," rejoined Ben, gravely.

Instantly Ben felt himself clutched by an iron hand and jerked upright off the bed. Nevada glared at him with eyes of black fire.

"Say, have you got that straight?" he queried, in a voice which cut.

"Sure. Hettie can be depended upon, Nevada. She's not given to exaggeration. I didn't ask for any details. She just said he'd tried to get too familiar with her."

"I'll kill him!" rasped out Nevada, letting go of Ben so suddenly that he sat back upon the bed.

"I'm pretty sore myself, Nevada, but it doesn't call for killing. You just cool off. I don't want you going to jail, even for my sister."

"Wal, you'll sing another tune when you know Less Setter as well as I do," returned Nevada, grimly. "Let's eat. Then we've got lots to figger on, pard, an' you shore can bet on that."

★ ★ ★

Ben found that despite the poignancy of his emotional state he was drawn into the current of Nevada's keen energy and spirit. Always Ben had been the dominating factor in this partnership; nevertheless, at this turn of their fortunes Nevada took the upper hand.

"All this talk about buying out Sims and his neighbors, catching another string of wild horses, and Lord knows what else, yet you haven't said a word about what you and Modoc found out," protested Ben.

"Wal, pard, fact is I don't want you to fork your fastest hoss an' leave us heah with all the work," drawled Nevada.

"You don't trust me?"

"When a fellar's in love he ain't reliable."

"See here, Nevada, I believe you're in love, too. With my sister! That's what has changed you from a lazy, good-humored, don't-care cowboy to a regular devil with highfaluting hunches."

Nevada's face turned a dusky red and he halted at his task of packing to bend a piercing dark gaze on Ben. His lean hand shook as he held it out in a gesture of unconscious appeal.

"An' suppose I am in love with Hettie?" he asked, with effort.

"Suppose you are! Why, it's plain as your nose, which is pretty long. What do you mean?"

"Pard, I'm not fit to wipe the dust off Hettie's little boots. I'm tellin' you. But meetin' her has changed me."

"Nevada, I don't believe you've been so darn bad," said Ben, frankly. "Anyway, I'd trust Hettie with you. I told her so."

"You did? My Gawd!" cried Nevada, huskily. "An' what'd she do?"

"Hettie got as red as a rose," laughed Ben. "And she said, 'Why, Ben, I'm only sixteen!' . . . If you want a hunch from me, Nevada, here it is. My sister likes you pretty well. That's sure. We Ides are queer. But if we love anybody it's forever. Of course my father would horsewhip you off the ranch if he caught you hanging round."

"Reckon that'll do. I'll say you're my kind of a man, Ben Ide. I owe you more'n I can ever pay."

"We're square, Nevada."

"Wal, on that we'll never agree. But lookin' things plumb in the face heah we are two ragamuffin hoss-wranglers, outcasts if not outlaws, so all-fired crazy as to love the daughters of the richest an' hard-headedest ranchers in northern California. Funny, ain't it — aboot as funny as gettin' kicked in the gizzard by a mean hoss?"

"Nevada, it'd look funny to other people, especially to guys like Mr. Sewell McAdam. But it's not funny to us. It's great and terrible. Maybe it'll be the saving of us."

"Ahuh! You're comin' around to sense. Cinch that tight, Ben . . . An' now enough of this mushy gab. Shake hands on this, Ben. We'll make good, by Gawd, or die!"

Nevada's ringing harsh words, his lean working white face, the passionate fire in his eyes, swayed Ben utterly. Their hands met in a grip of iron.

"Now, Ben, we're shore goin' to gamble," said Nevada, his cool easy drawl returning.

"Are we?" queried Ben, ironically, yet with a thrill.

"How many hosses have you got in that river pasture?"

"Forty head. What of it?"

"How much are they worth?"

"I wouldn't sell them."

"You shore will. You'll have to. What'll they fetch, quick, at Klamath?"

"A hundred dollars a head, maybe more. Any horse dealer could see they're worth two hundred."

"Good! I reckoned so, but I wasn't shore. Now, Ben, how many haid of that bunch can you let go?"

"Not a darn one!" yelled Ben.

"Boy, calm yourself. Listen. This heah card is the first you're playin' in the deal for Ina Blaine."

Something shot like a bolt through Ben, a sensation that was both thrill and pang. Nevada was inexorable and irresistible. He held the mastery here and he knew it.

"All right, Nevada. How many horses do you want?" returned Ben, as if the words were wrung from him.

"Thirty haid. That'll be three thousand dollars, enough to buy out these three homesteaders an' to spare. I saw Sims yesterday an' asked him if he'd sell. He thought I was razzin' him. He'd almost give that hundred an' sixty acres away, just to get out. He's been there three years, an' this is the sixth dry year. He's ruined, an' so are his neighbors. They can't stick it out. Wal, we'll not drive any hard deals, Ben. It's a cinch Less Setter has his eye on them homesteads. He's buyin' up for Hart Blaine. They aim to buy for a few hundred. I heard at Hammell that Blaine had bought a dozen ranches heahaboots, 'most for nothin'."

"Pretty tough on these little ranches, caught at the end of this long drought. I don't think much of Hart Blaine."

"Wal, Blaine has lost his haid. He was always poor. Then he got rich quick. Like a drunken cowboy with money! An' don't overlook that he's fallen under the influence of Less Setter."

"Heigho! it's a great world," sighed Ben. "Let's get this horse deal over quick, unless you want to kill me. Thirty of my last and best horses! That leaves me ten. Ten! I wonder what ones I'll keep."

"Wal, let me pick out ten for you," suggested Nevada, grinning.

"I should say not. Let's see. Gray and Knockeye, of course, Juniper, Brushy, Modoc Black, Gander. That's my six favorites. I'd starve to death before I'd part with them. Now to choose between Sandy and Bess, Simple Simon and Blue Boy —"

"Aw, say, Ben, you're not hesitatin' aboot Sandy, are you? I love that hoss. Shore you never gave him to me, but —"

"For Heaven's sake, take Sandy now. He's yours," burst out Ben, wildly, stamping up and down the little cabin room. "You see for yourself how hard it is."

"Shore it's hard, Ben. But you mustn't be silly. Keep the hosses you love best. So will I. That'll be aboot a dozen haid in all. An' that's plenty. We've got to ketch another string, an' say, if we happen — excuse me, pard — *when* we happen to ketch California Red, are you goin' to get stuck on him an' keep him?"

"I'll never keep him. I'll *give* him to Ina secretly, then sell him to her dad. That'd tickle her, I'll bet. Oh, she's a thoroughbred."

"Ahuh! I'm shore anxious to get a look at that girl . . . Wal, let's throw these packs on a hoss an' rustle out to the pasture an' get the dirty deed done."

Modoc, the Indian, had been standing outside with two pack animals. When these were ready he led them away toward the barn while Ben and Nevada mounted their horses and rode at brisk trot along the river trail to the pasture.

Ben had fenced about one hundred acres of his land, a long strip five acres deep bordering the river. It was a piece of lowland, covered with sage and grass, and near the edge of the water still fertile enough to take care of his horses.

Never had Forlorn River so deserved its name as now. It appeared to be a pale, discolored, stagnant lane of water, covered with green scum and bordered by sun-dried rushes, winding away between the gray sage hills. Every day the water lowered an inch or two.

"Dryin' up," said Nevada. "Another month like this an' the river above heah will be a mudhole. Ben, it shore was lucky when you found that spring heah."

Nevada pointed down the bank to a green spot and a little willow-shaded cove that cut somewhat into the bank. Here at the lowest stage of water ever known in the country a spring of cold running water, remarkable in volume considering the six dry years, had been discovered. Not even an Indian had ever suspected its presence, because heretofore it had been covered by the river. It belonged to Ben and was indeed a priceless possession. If both lake and river dried up he would still have that spring. Both Ben and Nevada believed the water came from the high back range to the south. They knew every foot of that country, and it was waterless. Here then must be the outlet of water stored in the mountains.

"Pard, that's why we can afford to gamble," asserted Nevada. "That gurglin' little spring hole is a gold mine."

"Nevada, guess our luck has turned," replied Ben, soberly. "I swear I forgot about this spring."

"Ahuh! Now, Ben, I'll cut out these hosses. You ride on down an' open the pasture gate. I'll leave your favorites an' a couple of mine."

Ben did as he was bidden, reconciled now and strangely glad the die had been cast. Indecision, love of horses, had always kept him from concluding profitable deals. Here was an end to his vacillation. He dared not think openly of Nevada's curt statement that the deal was the first for Ina Blaine, yet Ben could not deceive himself. The romance of it was at the back of his mind, like a muffled song, barely distinguishable. He gazed around him, with dreamy eyes of vision, at the dry waste of sage and the lonely little river, at the majestic round hills, almost yellow in the sunlight. There would always be beauty and solitude here, even in that mythical future when this wild country was settled by prosperous ranchers. Ben had a doubt that was father to his hope. It was a desert and sage country with one wandering little river to supply nourishment.

Ben assisted Nevada to drive a string of spirited horses across the gray barren, between the sage slopes, to a wide basin called Mule Deer Flat. In fertile seasons this was a beautiful and wonderful country. After six years of drought, however, it was a dusty sordid bowl with a yellow water hole in the center and gradual slopes of scant sage and grazed-off grass. A few gaunt cattle stood here and there. Bleached bones and dried carcasses were not wanting in that scene of a rancher's failure.

The three homesteads Nevada and Ben intended to purchase comprised the whole basin and part of the higher slopes. Ben had not passed by there for a year. What a deplorable change! This lake region was one of the finest bits of ranching ground in all the country. But the lake was surface water, from snow and rain, and as there had been practically no precipitation for six years it was all gone except a patch of yellow filthy water that would soon kill any stock which drank it.

Ben and Nevada drove their horses into the pole-fenced corral and went on to the little log cabin, where Modoc had stopped with the pack horses. Sims lived there. He was a fine specimen of cowboy turned rancher, a lean rangy fellow, clear-eyed and bronze-faced. He looked worn, and his person and surroundings had the appearance of hard times.

"Get down an' come in," was his cordial greeting. "Whar you goin' with all thet fine stock? Say, how on earth do you keep them hosses alive?"

"Nevada, let me do the talking," said Ben, as Nevada assumed a very important air. "Sims, we're here to buy you out. Do you and your partners want to sell?"

"Man alive! Do we?" ejaculated the rancher. "Ide, we come in hyar on a shoestring, an' if we'd had rain we'd made a success of it. But this terrible drought has ruined us. I'm tellin' you thet these three homesteads are the poorest buys in northern California. Moore's place is as bad as this, an' Nagel's is burned black."

"Will these fellows sell?"

"They'd break their necks takin' what they could get," replied Sims, abruptly.

"All right. What do you want?"

"But, Ide, you ain't really serious, are you?"

"Yes, Nevada and I are going to gamble," said Ben, frankly.

"I wish I could afford to. But I'm stone broke an' no credit. Our mistake in the first place was homesteadin' hyar without allowin' for dry seasons. We knew Mule Lake was surface water. A big reservoir would have saved us. An' there's a canyon on Moore's land where a good cement dam would have done the trick. It'd take money."

"Shore we'll build the dam," interposed Nevada, complacently.

"What's the lowest you'll take?" demanded Ben.

"Wal — would, say — eight hundred dollars be too much?" hesitatingly returned Sims.

"It's too little," replied Ben. "I'll make it a thousand. Get Moore and Nagel over here pronto. I've thirty head of fine horses out there in your corral. You can sell them tomorrow at Klamath for a hundred dollars each. And if you hang on to them a little you can get two hundred. What do you say?"

"By jiminy! I take you up," shouted Sims, "an' I'll say you are a good fellar, Ben Ide."

The deal went through, Sims's partners proving as eager as he, if not more so; and by midday Ben had the satisfaction of seeing them ready to drive off toward Klamath Falls.

It struck him that Sims acted a little queer, now jubilant, and again preoccupied. He had something on his mind. Finally Moore arrived in a spring wagon with his family.

"Wal, look at that ragged little outfit," declared Nevada, with sympathy. "Moore's woman is cryin' for very joy. Ben, you done her a good turn."

At the last, when the horses were out of the corral, headed north, Sims called Ben aside and leaned down from his saddle.

"Ide, soon as I sell my share an' fix up papers for you I'm headin' for the wheat country on the Big Bend, in Washington," he said, low-voiced. "Will you keep it under your hat?"

"Why, sure!" replied Ben, feeling a surprise, more at Sims's manner than at his disclosure.

"You're goin' strong for cattle hyar?" he went on.

"Yes, some day."

"I want to be square with you. Moore's wife is my sister. She was dyin' hyar. An' I reckon you've saved my bacon. Now if I put you wise to somethin' will you give me your word never to tell?"

Ben extended his hand and Sims wrung it. He was pale, tense, and his eyes glinted.

"I had to throw in with this cattle-thievin' outfit thet hides in the mountains back of Silver Meadow. It was thet or starve. Wal, this outfit has a big cattleman backin' it. Someone you'd never suspect. I had no use for them fellars an' I was suspicious. So I spied on them. Now my hunch to you is this. Don't throw in with anybody. Don't trust any of these big dealers or ranchers. Don't put any cattle in hyar till the thieves quit. An' do a little spyin' round on your own hook."

With that Sims spurred his horse and galloped away across the dusty flat, leaving Ben standing there dumfounded. Nevada strolled up from somewhere.

"What the devil was Sims tellin' you?" he inquired, casually, yet his keen glance scrutinized Ben.

"Nevada, I'm not at liberty to say, but it was a hell of a lot," replied Ben, drawing his breath hard.

"Ahuh! Wal, pard, Modoc an' I could tell you somethin' aboot why these homesteaders was so darned glad to sell out an' shake the dust of Tule Lake."

"It's an ill wind that blows nobody good," rejoined Ben.

"Shore. An' their loss is our gain. We've fallen into four hundred eighty acres of the best land in this country. But, Ben, my boy rancher, we'll let it lay fallow for a while. Savvy?"

"You're a cute son-of-a-gun," retorted Ben, regarding his friend with admiration, not guessing how much Nevada knew!

"Wal, if I do say it myself I reckon I'm a pretty good pard to tie to," said Nevada, complacently.

"Best in the world," returned Ben, eloquently. Then he added, quizzically: "That is, the best *man* pard."

"You darned fickle wild-goose chasin' Forlorn River hermit!" ejaculated Nevada, with infinite disgust. "No woman, not even Hettie, could ever make me say that."

"Nevada, I'll bet Hettie could make you do anything. But we're getting mushy again. Couple of fine industrious cowmen we'll be, unless —"

"Ben, the cattle business is a side bet with us. We're goin' to ketch, breed, raise an' sell hosses. Let's ride over this four eighty of ours an' see what we're up against. Then tomorrow we'll ride over to the lava beds and ice caves."

Ben gave Nevada a quick interrogating look. "Holding out on me, hey?" he flashed.

"Wal, not exactly," drawled the cowboy. "I seen your haid was full of Ina Blaine. An' I shore didn't want to see that sweet little girl forgot all in a minnit."

"Nevada, I'll biff you one right on your long jaw," declared Ben, half in earnest.

"In that case, then I'll have to elucidate. Day before yesterday Modoc spotted a big band of wild hosses. He was on the mountain yonder an' saw the hosses down in the valley, makin' straight for the ice caves."

98

"By thunder!" shouted Ben, in an instant all excitement. "What we've laid low for all these dry years!"

"You bet. Water all gone on this range. Them wild hosses are sick of drinkin' out of this mudhole. An' Forlorn River about your spring is growin' green an' bitter. There's cold clear water down in them ice caves. Modoc tells how his people used to trap hosses there. An' as you say, we've been layin' low for the chance."

"Of all the luck! You knew this when you jumped on me with both spurs — driving me to sell my horses?"

"Shore. I just wanted to see how much of a sport you was."

"Did Modoc see California Red?" asked Ben, eagerly.

"No, but I shore did," replied Nevada, quickening to the excitement of his friend. "I was ridin' north six or eight miles above heah, lookin' for tracks. I climbed pretty high, an' swingin' round a curve I run plumb into Red. He had a small bunch with him, mostly mares. They were travelin' north. Say, when he seen me! Whoopee! Talk aboot your red streak. Closest I ever was to him. I watched him out of sight. An' I'm shore he was makin' for that high black range."

"Good! Out of the way for this summer," exclaimed Ben, with gratification. "That leaves us time to work. We'll catch Red when the snow drives him down out of the hills."

"Ben, you're gettin' real human sense. I declare fallin' in love all over again . . . Hold on! Ouch! — I'll take it back."

"You'd better. Come on, now. Let's ride this four eighty, as you call it."

It required no great acumen for Ben to realize that they had secured a remarkable bargain in the homesteads. There were fully three hundred acres of level land, a gray loam very productive under normal rainfall. This did not include the area of Mule Deer Lake, which was now a ghastly yellow basin, with a small circle of muddy water left in the center. The mouth of Moore's canyon proved an ideal site for a dam. A wall thirty feet high and two hundred in length would dam up a lake of large dimensions, storing water enough for years. Irrigation in that warm protected bowl would make it a paradise. What an oversight on the part of these homesteaders! Ben and Nevada were highly elated and talked like boys and planned like ranchers with means. Yet the evidence was there to see. Ben realized he had bought a magnificent ranch for a bunch of horses. What would his father say to that? What would Ina Blaine think when some day she saw this sage-sloped valley green and verdant? Ben's heart beat with unwonted vigor. His luck had turned. He was on the track of something that would surprise those hard-fisted grasping ranchers back at Tule Lake. But he reflected he would never abandon his homestead on Forlorn River.

Toward sunset of the following day Ben and Nevada, with Modoc behind driving the pack animals, were approaching the wild region known as the lava beds. Miles of sage flat led to the forest of pine that rose in undulating steps to the bare gray cinder slope and black lava ridge and dome of the mountain. In the foreground the pine trees showed faintly yellow, gradually losing that hue for a healthy green.

At the edge of the forest Ben called a halt to make dry camp. One out of every three pine trees appeared to be dying. The pine-needle foliage was sear and yellow. Six years of drought had doomed many of these noble trees. The forest was extremely dry and almost suffocatingly odorous.

During the day the men had crossed the track of the band of wild horses; and while busy with the camp duties, and after supper round the fire, their sole topic of conversation related to the chase. Next morning they were on their way before sunrise, slowly climbing and working somewhat to the west.

When the sun rose to blaze into the open forest Ben thought he had never seen so beautiful, so dry, and so dead a place. Not a sound, not a living creature! The trees were yellow pines, large, stately, and widely separated. A thin bleached white grass stood above the strange volcanic soil. It was no less than gray granulated pumice stone, soft and springy, so light that clouds of white dust puffed up from every step of horse. The travel was therefore slow and tedious. Under the pines, where a mat of brown needles covered this treacherous ground, the travel was easier. On all sides there was a rain of dead pine needles falling from the starved trees, sifting, floating, glinting down in a weird silence.

Modoc, who took the lead, kept to the base of the gray slope, now working westward. Through openings in the forest a red cinder mountain stood up against the blue sky. It had a fringe of pines. The fine dust that puffed up from under the hoofs of the horses was hard on both man and beast. It clogged the nostrils. It choked. It had a smarting, constricting power, like that of alkali.

As the hunters progressed, getting higher all the time, the characteristics peculiar to this lava-bed country appeared to be magnified in every detail. The pine trees grew immense; the gray ridges of pumice sloped up, too steep for a horse to climb without effort; out of this strange medium the pines sprang; and the brown of trunks, the green and red of foliage, against that soft pearly gray background, was strikingly beautiful.

Toward noon Modoc worked down a little, coming to the parklike slope of a great canyon, across which loomed the steep red cinder cone. Here there began to be manifested harsher evidences of the volcanic power that had dominated the region in ages past. Outcroppings of bronze and black lava showed here and there under the pines. These increased in size and number, and presently it was noticeable that a thin layer of pumice covered a tremendous stratum of lava.

At length Ben reached a point where he could see down out of the forest to a vast belt of lava beds below. Miles and miles of ghastly ragged lava rolled away toward the gray expanse of sage. In color it was blue, black, red, like rusty iron, seamed and fissured, caked and broken, a rough file-surfaced place over which travel was almost impossible.

Modoc soon led into the region of the ice caves. Huge holes gaped abruptly; black vacant apertures stared from under ledges; windows of mysterious depths showed right out of the gray pumice. Each and every cavern was a blow-hole that had formed in the cooling lava. It was an uncanny region where riding a horse did not feel safe. Some of the holes were fifty feet deep and twice as long, black and jagged-walled, brush-filled, with the dark doors of caves somewhere at the bottom. Every one of them led into a cave. And down in these caves there was always supposed to be ice, from which cold crystal water flowed.

As to this latter fact, however, it transpired that Modoc had his doubts. He dismounted beside several holes and laboriously descended to seek water. At last he found one. But the water was not accessible for a horse, and must be drawn up with rope and bucket. Here camp was pitched. Modoc slipped away on foot to see if he could locate the wild horses. Along this canyon slope the bleached grass grew in sufficient quantity to furnish feed. Ben could not help but believe a lucky star was rising for him. Upon Modoc's return he was sure. The Indian wore a smile.

"Good — most dry time — ever see," he panted. "Find old Modoc cave — trail — water . . . We make trap — catch plenty horse."

CHAPTER
SIX

Ben and Nevada were intensely eager to see the trap Modoc spoke of with such assurance, but they were advised by the Indian to wait until a more favorable time. What little wind there was appeared to favor the horses. Toward late afternoon, however, it veered to the west and freshened a little. Whereupon Modoc took up an ax and some large nails, and bidding his comrades follow he set off on foot.

Modoc led them down out of the forest upon the lava. Like a tumultuous iron-crusted sea it waved and billowed before them, presenting a most sinister aspect. Once molten, it was now hard as steel, and broken into every conceivable manner of split, fissure, crack, cave, and cavern, colored in rusty drab lanes. Pine trees, saplings, and brush grew marvelously right out of the crevices, apparently without earth as sustenance and foundation for their roots. Many of the pines had lately died, and as many more were beginning to turn yellow at the tops, betraying starvation by thirst.

As the hunters with difficulty progressed westward, the violence of the lava stream gradually smoothed out, but the great blow-holes grew larger and more numerous. Ben peered into caves huge enough to hide a church. The whole stratum of lava appeared to be honeycombed into a labyrinthine maze of holes, passages, caves.

At length Modoc halted on the brushy tree-bordered rim of the largest depression Ben had seen. It was over an acre in extent, precipitous on three sides, and shelving very roughly on the fourth side. Deep and flat-floored, it formed a remarkable natural corral. Ben's sharp eye was quick to note where a trail had been worn, narrow and sharp and steep at the rim, and gradually growing broader and easier of descent until it resembled a road. It led into a gigantic cavern.

"Geemanee!" ejaculated Nevada. "Made to order!"

"Modoc, the water's down in that cave," asserted Ben, eagerly, pointing.

"Big hole full water. No bottom. Ice all over," replied the Indian.

"By golly! Nevada, we're rich. Let's go round to the head of that trail and have a look."

Ben had heard from the Indian how the Modocs used to lie in ambush around this cave, watch at night for the wild horses to go down to drink, then run and block the narrow place where the trail led over the rim. How absurdly simple the trap! The moment Ben laid eyes upon the head of the trail he felt almost shame to be guilty of catching wild horses so easily. There were, however, two great difficulties. One was that only in rarely occurring, extremely dry seasons were the wild horses driven to this extremity. And secondly after they were trapped in the cave, to get them out safely was a hazardous and strenuous undertaking. That did not in

105

the least daunt Ben; he had a way with horses, and as for Nevada, the cowboy was incomparable with a lasso.

Modoc shuffled away to begin chopping down saplings. When Ben had gazed his fill at that fascinating trap he drew Nevada away with him to help the Indian. They built a gate, so heavy that they had difficulty in carrying it to the objective point, where they partially hid it under brush. Two great boulders of lava, one on each side of the trail, attested to their use as anchors for trap-gates in the past.

"Doggone!" ejaculated Nevada, after heaving one of the boulders into better place. "Is this all the work we have to do? Shame to take the money!"

"The worst is to come," replied Ben, in grim satisfaction.

"You mean gettin' the hosses up out of there an' movin' them, after we do ketch them?" queried Nevada.

"I sure do. It'll be the toughest job we ever tackled."

Whereupon the cowboy subsided, and lost his enthusiasm in thoughtfulness. On the return to camp Modoc explained one of the methods adopted by the Indians for capturing the horses after they had been trapped. It was to let one or two out of the gate at a time and rope them. But Ben could not accept this plan as practical for him. The Indians wanted only a few horses, while he wanted many. It would take time to capture them.

"Well, let's wait till we see how many we trap and how good they are," decided Ben, finally.

"Reckon I figger same way," replied Nevada. "I've an idee, though, an' it's pretty darn slick."

They hurried through with their camp chores, and before daylight had failed they were snugly hidden on a high point of lava near the cave. Modoc had located the trail used by the horses coming in to drink, and had chosen the hiding place with keen regard to the direction of the wind.

Their plan was to take turns at sleeping and watching. Ben chose the early watch, and while his comrades rolled in their blankets he composed himself to a task full of infinite joy for him.

Night fell black. One by one stars appeared in the sky. A cool wind with a breath of snow came down from the lava heights. At intervals sounds of the wilderness broke the silence; and of these the honking of wild geese thrilled him most. They passed very high overhead, bound to the far north, late in their pilgrimage. From the flat country toward Mule Deer Lake the sharp staccato notes of coyotes pierced the loneliness. Then from a far ridge pealed down the wild mourn of a wolf. An owl hooted weirdly. Next Ben heard the slow, shuffling, scratching progress of a porcupine working across the lava near at hand. Then followed a swift silky rush of wild fowl flying low. The rustling of brush, the snapping of twigs, the rolling of bits of lava, the faint cracking of hoofs on hard substance acquainted Ben with the fact that deer were going down into the cave to drink. Also he caught the soft padded footsteps of a heavier animal.

These sounds of the wild were as familiar to Ben as the voices of his comrades. Yet he never tired of them. There was something about them which he could not understand. But love of them had always been in him. And this kind of a lonely vigil seemed full and all-satisfying.

Ben chose not to wake his comrades, except once to shake Nevada, who was blissfully snoring. He did not need sleep; he did not care to miss any of this night. It came to him, finally, that there was something extraordinarily more beautiful about it all — the velvet blue sky, the white stars, the silver forecast of the moon behind the black ridge, the night with its rare wild sounds, the peace of the wilderness, the glory of the solitude. And he divined that his love for Ina Blaine was responsible for this. At that hour he felt only exaltation. Unhappiness could not abide in him. The overmastering love that had grown so suddenly was something great in his heart, too splendid a privilege, too profound a gift ever to hurt him again. At such an hour, in such a place, he could feel the mystery and significance of his life.

The moon soared white and grand above the mountain and the black mantle that had obscured the billowy lava beds seemed lifted away. The soft night wind all but died away, and the wild sounds ceased. The majesty of utter solitude held full sway until Ben's rapt abstraction broke to the crack of hard hoofs on hard rock. A suffocating excitement gripped Ben. The wild horses were coming to drink! Long past midnight it was. He waited a moment to revel in his strange joy before awakening his companions.

At a touch of hand Modoc raised himself cautiously and turned his head to one side. "Ugh!" he whispered.

Nevada was harder to awaken, and noisy when he did rouse himself. "My Gawd! I dreamed I roped California Red an' gave him to Hettie an' you shot me!"

"Quiet, you big cowpuncher!" said Ben, bending low over him. "The wild horses are coming."

Instantly Nevada's lax length stiffened, and he rolled over noiselessly. "Now you're talkin', pard," he whispered. "Aha! I hear them. Steppin' along right pert."

"Wind good. No scare. We have luck. Catch lot," whispered the Modoc.

Ben had not yet been able to get the exact direction from which the horses were coming, but he kept his gaze riveted on the gray depression where the trail ran. The sound of hoofs came faintly, then distinctly, and all but ceased — to begin again. Gradually the faint clip-clops, the sharp cracks, the clear rings augmented into a steady rhythm. Then as it ceased near at hand it seemed to move away to die in the distance. Ben knew this happened when the leaders halted and the others strung out behind gradually followed suit.

"Ugh! See 'em," whispered Modoc.

Dark shadows began to form in the gray obscurity. Ben felt thrilling expectation and satisfaction. Who would not be a wild-horse hunter? He preferred his state to that of kings. Yet on the instant a pang pierced his joy. No chance of California Red being leader of this band! The great stallion was not to be caught in caves.

Nevada laid a clutching hand on Ben. "Look! Way over heah!" he whispered.

Ben withdrew his gaze from the gray depression out of which the dark forms were coming, and looked down upon the moon-blanched lava. A noble black stallion stood shining in the moonlight. He had come around a huge abutment ahead of the string of horses Ben had been watching. Obviously he was the leader. He looked rough and wild. But evidently his halt was only the caution of leadership. He stood motionless until a string of horses filed from behind the lava bank and another column filed up out of the gray depression, then proceeded toward the cave and disappeared over the rim. Long lines of horses followed him, blacks and grays, spotted and light, to mass in a dark group at the head of the trail. Ben heard the rattling and cracking of pieces of lava, the uneasy tramp of many hoofs. He crouched there transfixed with the excitement of the moment. Nevada was whispering to himself. The Indian rose noiselessly to his feet.

"Get ready to run!" whispered Ben, also rising.

"Give them time," said Nevada. "Nothin' on their minds but a nice cold drink."

It seemed long to Ben before the last of that black mass of horses melted over the rim. He waited in a tingling suspense until the crackling, rolling, rattling sounds became fused by distance, then gave the word to run. Ben was a swift runner and Nevada had long

110

legs, but the Indian beat both of them to the rim and was dragging at the heavy gate when they arrived.

"All together," whispered Ben, hoarsely, laying hold of the gate. "Now, heave."

They staggered with the heavy burden to the wide crack in the rim. In a few more seconds the opening was covered, the huge rocks in place to hold the gate.

Then Ben stood up, wet with sweat, and stared speechlessly at the cool cowboy.

"Wal, Ben, how aboot my hunch now?" he drawled.

"Hunch?" echoed Ben.

"Shore. Aboot the change in our luck. Reckon you was so crazy you couldn't see. But I figgered there was over a hundred haid of horses in that bunch. They're trapped. They're ours. Nothin' to it but a little work. An' what do we care for work?"

"Nevada — your hunch — must be straight," panted Ben, sitting down and wiping his wet face. "My heavens! How easy! It's too good to be true."

"Nope. It's good enough to be true. When we ketch California Red — then you can rave. This is all just in the day's work for us."

"Let's get back — from the rim," said Ben, rising to peer into the huge shadowy abyss. One side was black in gloom, the other silver in the moonlight. The wild horses did not yet know that they had been trapped. Hollow ring of hoofs came from the cavern. It seemed tremendously deep and large, magnified by the night.

"Wal, heah's my idee," began Nevada, very businesslike, when they had moved back from the rim. "It's a big haul of wild hosses. They'll be some fine ones, an' a lot of good stock. It'll cost money to save them, but nothin' compared to what they're worth. Send Modoc to Hammell for hay an' grain, wire an' rope an' nails. We'll need a couple wagon loads of stuff. We can pack in heah from the road. While Modoc is gone we'll cut fence posts. We'll build a big corral. We'll feed them hosses, an' when we're ready we'll let some up into the corral where we can ketch them. A few at a time, while the main bunch down there is gettin' used to us. Huh?"

"It's a grand idea, Nevada," averred Ben. "If there are as many as you think we'll be a month and more on the job."

"Ben, you know a bunch of hosses at night is always deceivin'," said Nevada, seriously. "Even a small bunch will have a lot of hosses. An' that was an awful big bunch crowdin' to go down the trail."

"Nevada, you're a comforting cuss," returned Ben, happily. He breathed a long deep sigh. "By golly! Some day —"

"Ahuh!" drawled Nevada, interrupting. "Don't you try to steal my hunch. Suppose we take another little snooze."

"Not me!" exclaimed Ben, shortly. "Dawn is not far away. I'll sit up."

"Wal, it's shore nice to be in love, but I got to sleep, an' eat regular, too."

Modoc, who had been standing to one side, suddenly uttered a low exclamation. Then he said: "More wild horse come."

Instantly Ben and Nevada became silent statues.

112

"Shore as you're born," whispered the cowboy, in elation.

Ben was the last to hear the unmistakable dull thud and slow clip-clop of hoofs.

"Catch lot more," announced the Indian.

"By golly! Ben, we shore can," returned Nevada, now excited. "Listen. You see the bunch we've trapped are far down in the cave drinkin', an' waitin' for their turn. They don't know they're ketched. Wal, we can raise the gate, stand it to one side, an' hide close by. Some of the new hosses will go down shore."

Ben felt the leap of temptation, but he found strength to deliberate, and attractive as the idea was he decided against it.

"We'll let well enough alone," he said. "A bird in the hand, you know. We might catch more. But we stand a chance to lose what we've got. Suppose the horses down there would start a stampede up that trail. We could never close the gate on them. It's too risky."

"Wal, second thought is best. I reckon you're right," returned Nevada, reluctantly. "An' even if our luck held we might ketch too many to handle."

It seemed to Ben that the moon would never go down and dawn never come. To and fro he strolled over the lava, under the pines, revolving thoughts new to him. Several times a trampling, snorting uproar came from the cave. The trap was an efficient affair, because in the upper part of the trail there was room for only one horse at a time. With the gate closed over the outlet the

113

horses could not get started. Ben had an idea they would give up rather quickly for wild horses.

At length the moon went down and gradually the gray obscurity turned to black shadow. The darkest hour came and passed. Then a faint brightening in the east told of the approach of day. Soon the sky lightened and turned rose; the shadows paled and vanished; quickly then, it seemed, day was at hand.

Ben and his two companions crawled into a covert of brush and peeped over the rim of the cave. Nevada evidently got the first glimpse of the wild horses, for he gave Ben a tremendous punch that all but knocked both breath and sight out of him. It certainly was not because Ben discovered anything that he returned the punch with good measure. In another instant, however, he saw clearly. The white ash floor of the great hole was covered with wild horses, and toward the ascent where the trail started up horses were packed closely. A line of them narrowed up the trail clear to the top. They stood motionless, dejected, as if they knew their case was hopeless.

Ben drew back to relax and collect his wits. Nevada kept looking for a long time. When at length he did move back to confront Ben his face was alight with amaze and joy, and his disheveled black hair appeared to stand on end.

"By — golly!" he whispered, hoarsely. "Did you see that bunch of hosses?"

"I — sure did — but not very clear," replied Ben, breathlessly.

"Pard, we're rich!"

"Oh, now, Nevada, don't *you* go off your head," whispered Ben, hurriedly.

Modoc drew back to join his two comrades. His bronze face was wreathed in a smile seldom seen there.

"Lot horses all good," he said.

"Ben, I'm knocked into a cocked hat," whispered the cowboy. "There's at least a hundred an' fifty haid in that bunch. Reckon I never seen a finer lot of wild hosses."

"Let's peep again, then chase back to camp and get things started," said Ben.

This time Ben took his fill gazing, and his sober conclusion was that Nevada had not exaggerated in the least. What a splendid catch! Ben could not locate the magnificent black stallion that had been the leader but he saw enough individually fine horses to fulfil the most exacting hopes of a wild-horse hunter.

"Reckon they might just as well have a look at us," said Nevada, and rising he exposed himself on the rim. Ben got up in time to see the horses break into a trampling, whistling, plunging uproar. They surged from one side to the other, plunged at the ascent, only to press closer into a dense mass. Many on the outside ran back into the dark cavern; some pounded at the steep iron walls; those on the trail were crowded off to admit of others. A cloud of white and red dust rose to hide them. Nevada called down to the captured horses, but in the din Ben could not distinguish what he said. Drawing the cowboy back, Ben led him in the steps of Modoc, who was hurrying toward camp.

They partook merrily of a hearty breakfast. Then after Modoc had been dispatched posthaste on the important mission, Ben and Nevada set to work in grim earnest on the long strenuous task.

During the day they often left off cutting poles and posts to walk around the rim of the cave, purposely showing themselves to the trapped horses. On each occasion a terrific mêlée ensued. The second day was like the first, and on the third the wild horses began to get used to their captors.

Modoc arrived eventually with all Ben's pack horses heavily laden, and he announced the wagons would reach the end of the road late that day.

It took two whole days to pack the supply of hay, grain, rope, hardware, and other supplies up to the camp. By this time the wild horses had grown thin and gaunt, but not to the extent that Ben was concerned about them.

While Ben and his comrades were in sight on the rim the wild horses would not eat the hay thrown down to them, but when morning of the next day came it had all been consumed.

With these important initial steps of the plan wholly successful, Ben and his men were jubilant, and confident of the outcome. They built a large corral around the level space on the trail side of the cave, with high fences running to the gate. Then began the strenuous job of letting out a few of the horses at a time, roping them, and breaking them sufficiently to lead them across the miles of forest and sage to Ben's pasture on Forlorn River.

Early and late they toiled, dexterous, patient, indefatigable. Horses were skinned, bruised, lamed during the laborsome process, but not one was seriously crippled. The hardest job of all was to drive the half-broken horses across to Ben's pasture. Nevada managed four, while Ben and Modoc had about all they wanted with three each.

Once out of the corral, these horses plunged into a run, stretching the lassoes and dragging their captors at a breakneck pace. They ran until they gave out. Then the task was to pull them the remaining distance to the pasture. This drive took half a day. Then, after a rest, the men, mounting fresh horses, rode back to their camp.

Ben lost track of days. But he knew indeed that summer had come, for the days grew hot and hotter, and the drought correspondingly worse. The situation as regarded cattle and horses on the ranges became aggravated. If the fall rains failed this year all livestock in that section was doomed.

CHAPTER
SEVEN

For Ina Blaine the early summer weeks were full and sweet, despite the slow tangling of threads that bade fair to grow into an inextricable knot.

It became a certainty that she was helping her mother. Her merry presence, her patience and tact, her affection were making life easier for that perplexed woman. And Ina saw how greatly she was influencing Dall and Marvie in a situation their youthful minds could not have encompassed. Then she had become an intimate friend of Hettie Ide, to their mutual benefit. The more she saw of Hettie the more she found her to be good and lovable, the comfort and stay of a broken-hearted mother.

Over against these happy facts were arrayed others fraught with bitterness. Ina's father, finding that he could not dominate her, had become harsh and hard, unyielding to the genuine love he bore her. The older brothers did not understand her. Kate from being covertly jealous had grown openly hostile which situation, however, had been relieved by her marriage and consequent absence from home. Sewell McAdam had in no wise been discouraged by her indifference. Every Sunday he went regularly to church with the family, and spent the rest of the day with them, complacently vain in the position gossip gave him as Ina's suitor. On these occasions he was her shadow, until Ina could scarcely conceal her disgust and chagrin. Her resentment had grown to the proportions of a revolt. The last time her father had broached the subject of marriage with McAdam he had intimated an obligation to the McAdams that was beginning to be serious. Ina had refused, appealed, protested, argued, all to no avail. She began to be afraid he might marry her to McAdam against her will, though she did not see how that could be possible.

Lastly, and most disturbing, her father had become deeply involved with Less Setter in horse dealing on a large scale, in land and cattle deals, in the foreclosing of mortgages on small ranchers forced to the wall by the unprecedented drought. Ina's keen ears had heard a good deal not intended for her. Less Setter was the big factor in these deals, but her father furnished the money. Several worthy ranchers had been ruined by Setter's drastic measures. To be sure, the law was on Blaine's side, but the consensus of opinion around Hammell appeared to be that Blaine had not gained any liking or respect through his partner's high-handed methods. Added to all this there was a personal implication for Ina, inasmuch as Setter had been making preposterous and offensive advances to her. Ina had not told her father, because she had sensed veiled threat and power in this man's talk. She exercised all her wits to keep out of his way, but sometimes it was impossible.

119

One day, early in June, Blaine announced to his family that he would close the house at Tule Lake Ranch for the summer.

"I've got hold of a place on Wild Goose Lake," he said. "It's all run down an' cabins ain't fit for women folks. But we'll put up some tents for you an' the kids."

Marvie and Dall, who happened at the time to be in the good graces of their father, let out yelps of joy. Ina was taken aback, but she managed otherwise to hide her own amaze and delight. Mrs. Blaine did not evince any regrets at the idea of closing the big house for the summer.

"Sort of summer outin', as they call it in town," went on Blaine, blandly. "Lots of families with means do this nowadays. The McAdams go to Upper Klamath Lake . . . Now as I expect to have large interests around Wild Goose Lake an' up Forlorn River, we may just as well start developin' a summer place up there. Reckon it's about forty miles, considerable higher an' cooler. There's a fine grove of trees a little ways from the cabins, an' I aim to put up the tents in it. The problem is water. But that's a terrible problem everywhere this year. I've sent well-diggers. If they fail to reach water Setter has a plan he thinks will work. So I reckon you can all pack up an' get ready to move."

Whereupon there followed considerable excitement and bustle in the Blaine household. Marvie's first statement to Ina, when they were alone, proved the predominance of his ruling passion.

120

"Sis, the fishin' in Forlorn River is grand. Only ten miles across the lake," he whispered, with wide bright eyes.

"But, Marvie, the lake and river are drying up, I hear," replied Ina, who was conscious of disturbing and not unpleasant emotions on her own behalf.

"There're spring holes in Forlorn River an' the trout will collect there," asserted the boy. "Ben Ide will show us."

Ina found herself blushing, and consciousness of the fact brought an added wave of scarlet.

"Say, Sis, you're as red as a beet," declared Marvie, wonderingly.

"Am I? . . . Oh, it's nothing," replied Ina, feeling her hot cheeks. But she knew it was a great deal.

Marvie leaned close to her and his loyal eyes pierced her. "Ben lives across the lake, at the mouth of the river. We can see his home from where we'll be campin'."

"Well, what of that?" queried Ina, smiling at him.

"Why, nothin' much, except you can bet I'll slip over there to see Ben, an' take you along if you want to go."

"Marvie, you think I'll want to?" went on Ina, composedly. Marvie was showing depths hitherto unsuspected.

"I've a hunch you will," declared the boy, bluntly. "Outside of ridin' an' fishin'! . . . Now listen, Sis. I knew about this plan of Dad's before he sprung it on us. I heard him an' Less Setter talkin' out by the barn. They were talkin' about gettin' hold of Ben Ide's water an' land. Dad wanted to buy from Ben, but Setter

121

swore he was goin' to run Ben out of the country. An', Ina, after that I heard one of our cowboys say Setter had dad buffaloed."

"Well!" ejaculated Ina, with difficulty controlling the flash of resentment that swept over her. "Marvie, I don't like that," she added, deliberating.

"Neither do I," rejoined the lad, stoutly. "An' worse than that I hate the way Setter looks at you, Ina. Goodness knows I thought that McAdam fellar was hard enough to stand. But Setter's different . . . I wish I was older an' bigger."

"Marvie, you're fine, just as you are," said Ina, sweetly. "We've a secret between us. I — almost hate Mr. Setter myself. I'm afraid he is not what Dad thinks. And between them they are going to injure Ben Ide . . . Marvie, Ben was — is a dear old friend. I don't believe what they say about him."

"Ina, I'm for Ben any day, an' you can bet on that," replied Marvie.

"That's fine, Marvie. I don't believe you will be sorry. Let's keep our eyes and ears open. It's not dishonest, considering what we believe is injustice to Ben Ide. Let's play a game, Marvie."

Ina did not explain just what kind of a game she meant; nevertheless Marvie fell into it with an air of intense eagerness and importance.

"Don't tell Dall nothin'," he said, finally. "She's only a girl an' can't be trusted. An' she's afraid of Dad."

At the end of this little conversation Ina found that, no matter what had heretofore been the state of her mind regarding Mr. Setter, she was now convinced of his crookedness. This related to his business relations with her father; she had long been satisfied that both she and Hettie Ide were objects of Less Setter's dishonest intentions.

Ina spent the day packing, with frequent periods of abstraction, part of which were so dreamy and pleasant that she felt guilty of being very happy over this summer-camp plan.

Next morning before sunrise she and Marvie were off on horseback at the head of a string of pack horses and wagons. Marvie was not only good company, but also served somewhat to embarrass the several ambitious cowboys who approached Ina on every possible occasion. Ina liked them, and liked their company, except when they got what Marvie called "sweet on her".

Riding in the early morning was delightful, and the long winding dusty road toward the sage hills was not formidable. But when the flat country lay behind and the ascent of the great basin slope began and the sun grew hot, then it was different. It became work, yet not without satisfying sense of achievement. At noon the cavalcade had crossed the divide between two of the huge sage hills and found easier travel downward. Presently Blaine ordered a halt at the last ranch on the north side of Wild Goose Lake. The owner's name was Blake, and like all poor ranchers in that country he was, as a cowboy tersely put it, "holdin' on heah by the skin of his teeth". They rested and had lunch in the shade. Ina was pleased with Marvie's keenness when the boy whispered to her: "Did you see we wasn't very welcome? This fellar Blake is scared of Dad." For her own observation tallied exactly with Marvie's.

For two hours following that noonday rest the ride was most uncomfortable, hot, dusty, slow, over a rough road, from which nothing but bleached and sear grass slopes could be seen. But at last, when they emerged on the outlook above Wild Goose Lake, Ina suddenly felt rejuvenated.

A breeze which was hot, but still a breeze, swept up from the vast gray-and-black basin. The slope was long, rolling, somehow beautiful despite the aridity. At a distance the sage appeared softly gray, merging into purple. Wild Goose Lake was an immense round body of muddy water, surrounded by mile-wide shore lines, denuded, stark in the sunlight. The sage hills now appeared to rise to the dignity of mountains, long-sloping, domelike. A cowboy called Marvie's attention to black and white dots on the far high slope. Wild horses! How Ina thrilled to the words and the sight! Yet this feeling was slight to that which gripped her when Marvie pointed across the great open space of land and water to a winding pale ribbon — Forlorn River. Could a more felicitous name have been given it? Dim and almost indistinct was the mouth of the river. It looked as if it sank into the sands. And scarcely clearer was the point of land, with its dark blur of trees, that marked the wild and lonely homestead of Ben Ide.

Ina's heart swelled into her throat. No wonder he loved that place. She loved it herself, at first sight; and a vague sweet emotion attended the assurance. Far across and above the gray monotony where Forlorn

River wound its way climbed the black ranges into the sky. These, a cowboy said, were the mountains of Nevada.

The hours of riding that followed did not wear on Ina's spirit, though at the last she suffered in flesh and bone. She had an ever-changing, ever-wonderful prospect to gaze upon, and always a feeling of some intimate connection with it. She did not trouble to explain this latter complex assumption. But she thought once — what extraordinary good luck for her that Hart Blaine and Less Setter should have chosen Wild Goose Lake and Forlorn River for their field of operations this summer! Almost she laughed aloud in a strange exultation, totally foreign to her. But deep in her there had been born a rankling strife. Here, approaching an environment she had cherished in her thoughts, she was conscious of roused and accepted conflict. And like a lightning flash came the query — why? Ina dared not answer it with her mind. Involuntarily her pulse, her blood, the leap of flesh answered it physically.

It was four o'clock in the afternoon when the Blaine party arrived at the deserted ranch. Ina had never seen such a squalid place. Dilapidated sheds, fences rotting on the ground, mummified remains of dead cattle, two old flat black log cabins, patched with yellow boards and sheets of tin, dust and dirt and rocks everywhere, with not a blade of grass or living shrub of green — these were the dominant characteristics of the latest acquisition of Hart Blaine.

To Ina's great relief one of the wagons and some of the pack mules were driven on past the ranch to a grove of scattered junipers on a high bench facing a deep brushy canyon that opened out into the lake basin. This location afforded a wonderful view of the sage mountains that towered above, and the great round bowl below. The ground was carpeted with bleached grass and brown mats from the junipers. In the shade of these bushy trees there was retreat from the hot sun. What a dry, fragrant spot! It was somewhat removed from the bare open ranch, and far enough from the lake basin for distance to lend enchantment. Ina calculated that as a crow flies it was ten miles across to Ben Ide's homestead. She could see the little gray cabin facing the west.

Half a dozen lusty cowboys made short work of unpacking the horses and wagon and pitching a few tents for temporary use. Marvie and Dall were in a seventh heaven of youthful experience. The forty-mile ride had only served to liberate their exuberance. Ina, however, had made the whole distance in the saddle, and she was tired. Her mother showed a surprising alacrity and pleasure. Ina reflected that her mother, as a young woman, had spent a good deal of her time on the open cattle ranges.

That night Ina went to bed with Dall under a juniper tree with no covering except blanket and tarpaulin. It was really her first experience of the kind and she shared Dall's excitement. The night was dark, with only flickering lights from a camp fire. The wind swept over their bed, tugged at their hair, and rustled through the junipers. Coyotes barked from the black mountain slope. Where was the heat that had made the nights uncomfortable at Tule Lake? Ina saw white stars crowning the black dome of the looming mountain. Dall nestled close to her, whispering her wonder and delight and, as well, a fear of crawling things and prowling animals. Presently it seemed to Ina as if a ponderous sticky weight had closed her eyelids. How restful, languid, sweet the sensation! And that was her last conscious thought.

She awakened at sunrise, to become aware that Marvie was poking at her with a fishing pole.

"Sleepyhead!" he called, derisively. "What kinda ranchman's wife are you goin' to make, anyhow? . . . Somethin' to tell you, Sis." And he winked mysteriously at her.

Ina felt stiff and sore from the long ride, and found it hard to arise and begin the day. A little exercise, however, rendered her more fit for the multiplicity of tasks. Marvie vanished like a will-o'-the-wisp, and that added to Ina's curiosity. She went with her mother and Dall to get breakfast at the chuck wagon, which had been stationed halfway between the two cabins on the ranch. Ina did not linger long at that meal, and she shared her mother's express wish to have a cook tent of their own over at their camp. This her father promised would be put up that very day. Indeed, he was unusually jovial, energetic, and forceful. Ina felt a strengthening of her conviction that he had considerable on his mind regarding this Wild Goose Lake country. He had started his army of cowboys to work

127

cleaning up the squalid ranch. The stench of burning carcasses, rotten wood, rubbish, and what not assailed Ina's nostrils. She saw cowboys tearing out the insides of the cabins, demolishing the old sheds and fences, digging and raking and hauling. Manifestly her father meant to make this ranch livable. Water had been brought in barrels from Tule Lake. She heard her father complain because the well-diggers had not arrived.

Upon returning to the grove, Ina found several of the cowboys there with tents, lumber, tools, all eager to set to work, and incidentally to make sheep's-eyes at her. Presently her father and mother arrived and the task of making a comfortable summer camp began.

"Daughter, show us where you want your tent," he said, "an' I'll set these lazy boys to work."

Ina chose a spot beside the large juniper under which she had slept. By the magic of swift cowboy hands a floor of boards was quickly erected high off the ground, with a skeleton framework over which the tent was stretched. And over this they put up a wide canvas fly that projected out in front, serving as a roof for a porch.

For the present Ina and Dall decided to sleep out in the open, under the spreading juniper, and use their tent for all other purposes. To which end they carried their numerous bags and boxes into the tent, where they proceeded to unpack them. While they were thus engaged two cowboys appeared at the tent door, one with hammer and nails, and the other with a huge pine box into which shelves had been built.

"Wal now, Miss Ina, I reckon you'll need somethin' to hang things on," said one, proceeding to hammer nails into the wooden crossbeam of the framework.

"Heah's a box I fixed for a washstand," offered the other cowboy. "It ain't very good, but I couldn't find no better. An' I spotted a big new water pail down by the chuck wagon. I'll fetch it up full of water, if I don't happen to run into your dad."

"Why, what difference would that make?" laughed Ina, looking up.

The cowboy, a fine-faced, square-jawed young fellow, stood bareheaded and respectful, but he was all eyes.

"Wal, he says go slow on the water we fetched from Tule, an' if we *have* to wash, to use the lake water heah."

"But, my gracious! we *have* to wash — and that muddy water is impossible!" protested Ina.

"Shore. We told him so. But you know your dad. He didn't say just us cowboys, so he might have meant everybody."

Ina knew full well that her father was quite capable of including his women folk in an order forbidding the use of water.

"Why in the world did Dad buy this place?" she queried, blankly.

"He got it for nothin', Miss Ina. An' he has his eye on Forlorn River. We shore tried to persuade him not to come heah, this awful dry time, anyhow. There ain't any water. It's all dried up. Diggin' wells won't do no good. An' we'd have talked him into waitin' till the rains come if it hadn't been for Mr. Setter. He shore was set on comin'."

"Well . . . thank you, boys," replied Ina, thoughtfully. "Fetch a bucket of water, anyway. I'll take the responsibility."

Ina almost yielded to the temptation to ask a pertinent question about Mr. Setter. Upon reflection, however, she felt that the frank cowboy's tone had intimated a dislike for her father's partner. At former times she had received impressions as to the regard in which some of the cowboys held Less Setter. The sum of these impressions added weight to her own, and she had an inkling that the next few weeks would be prolific of most interesting developments.

The day passed so quickly that Ina could not realize what had become of the hours. There had been no noon meal to mark the flight of time. Her father had placed the summer camp under the same rule that prevailed among his cowboys' outfits when on the open range — two meals a day.

Ina's appetite this evening was not a thing to be denied, and she had the pleasure of helping her mother in the little cook tent of their own. Supper time brought Marvie, muddy and disheveled, wearing a long weary face.

"Aw, there ain't any fish," he burst out in reply to Ina's solicitude. "I rode an' walked about nine hundred miles. Nothin' but mud. Nothin' but tadpoles in that darned lake."

"Did you get as — as far as Forlorn River?" asked Ina, experiencing a strange little thrill at the spoken words.

130

"Yep, but not very far up. I went to Ben Ide's place. Doggone it, he wasn't home! Looks like he's been gone a long time. An' I was just bankin' on Ben."

"Surely he will return soon," said Ina, encouragingly, while she wondered on her own behalf. No doubt Ben was away on one of his wild-horse jaunts.

Marvie was not to be consoled, and his misfortunes of the day were brought to a climax when his father saw him.

"Where you been?" was the demand.

"Fishin'," replied Marvie.

"Do you have to get dirty like that when you fish?"

"'Course. I'm no city fisherman."

"Marvin, I've a hunch you are a lazy good-for-nothin' boy who hates work," declared Mr. Blaine, severely.

"It ain't so," retorted Marvie, hotly. "You said I could fish all I wanted. This here is vacation time. I passed high in all my studies."

"Yes, I know. An' I'm not goin' back on what I said. I was just thinkin' how maybe this fishin' an' huntin' might make you turn out like young Ben Ide."

Marvie flushed red over all his dirty face, and manifestly there was an angry retort on his lips, but he caught Ina's quick glance and held his tongue. He appeared at supper with clean blouse, shining face and hair, tactful improvement not lost upon the head of the family. Later Marvie came to Ina as she lay in her hammock watching the sunset, and he said with a thoughtfulness beyond his years:

131

"Sis, Dad's got Ben Ide on the brain. It's funny, an' I'd like to know why. Now what's Dad goin' to say when it comes out that Ben isn't what they make him?"

"Marvie, I wonder about that, too," murmured Ina, with dimming eyes. She wanted to kiss Marvie for his boyish simplicity and faith.

Several days sped by, at once busy and restful for Ina, and altogether happy. The best development of this summer-camp plan was the improved mental condition of her mother. Mrs. Blaine had fallen upon old tasks, the habits of a lifetime that sudden wealth had denied her, and she became another woman. Ina noted with eager curiosity how her father was struck by the change, and thereby rendered thoughtful. At heart he was good and loving; and if an idea only pierced his dense brain it lodged there to become productive.

Saturday found the old worn-out ranch vastly renewed. All the débris had been burned; new fences, sheds, corrals, newly shingled roofs, shone in the sun; a large barn was under course of construction; and other improvements attested to Hart Blaine's energy and management.

The end of this eventful week brought two other circumstances, both disturbing to Ina. The first was the arrival of Less Setter, subtly more forceful and bold than ever, showing in his sleek blond features and suave tones something of hidden power and confidence that heretofore had been veiled. He presented himself before Ina with all the assurance of Sewell McAdam, as an equal, as one who always got what he wanted. Ina saw that her father was as blind as a bat where this man was concerned. And for the few moments before she could escape, when she had to be courteous, she raged in impotent fury.

The other circumstance affected Ina quite as powerfully but in an immeasurably different way. Marvie was her informant and his jubilance permeated her like a breath of fresh air. "Gee, Ina — whatju think?" he panted, evidently having run to her with the news. "Ben Ide come home — to-day. Bill Sneed rode in — just now — an' I heard him tell Dad. Bill said Ben an' his Modoc Indian — drove a bunch of wild horses — into Ben's river pasture. An' Bill was sure spoutin'. 'Dingest purtiest lot of hosses I ever seen in my life. One was a black stallion an' he shore hit me as hard as California Red.' . . . There, Ina, that's what Bill Sneed said."

Ina was glad the dusk hid her face from this keen little brother. She felt concerned about it and the strange rioting thrill that coursed through her.

"An', Ina," went on the lad, "Less Setter heard Bill tell Dad. I was keepin' my eyes an' ears peeled, you can bet. An' I wish you could have seen Setter look at Dad. But all he said was, 'Blaine, I'll take some boys an' ride over there tomorrow.' Dad pulled him in the cabin an' shut the door. I listened by the window, but couldn't hear nothin'. Now I'm goin' back an' hang around."

"Marvie, be very careful," whispered Ina, trembling for she knew not what.

"I'll be like an Indian," asserted Marvie, loftily. "Less Setter doesn't dream I'm anythin' but a stupid kid. Neither does Dad."

Then he darted off, leaving Ina a prey to conflicting thoughts. She went to sleep, however, before Marvie returned from the ranch; and next morning he was gone with the cowboys before she awoke.

Ina was destined to miss Marvie for quite another reason, which presented itself in the shape of Sewell McAdam on his regular Sunday visit. Now Marvie had always been her ally in extricating her from embarrassing situations, and he had deserted her to go fishing. Ina had depended upon being free from McAdam's attentions during the summer months. It was too exasperating. She had reached the end of her patience. An instant decision to tell him flatly that she would not waste any more precious time listening to his inane conceited talk acquainted Ina with the development of her revolt.

McAdam arrived early, in a light buggy, drawn by a team of spirited horses. Their heaving dust-lathered flanks attested to the manner in which they had been driven. One of the cowboys unhitched the horses, while the stylishly groomed young man strolled, whip in hand, toward the cabin, where her father was breaking his Sunday rule by working. Ina saw distinctly from her hammock, and precisely what she expected happened. McAdam at once came out of the cabin and headed toward the grove. Ina watched him coming with mingled contempt and disgust. Even Less Setter struck her as being more of a man. At least she could feel fear of him.

When McAdam had approached within a few rods Ina pretended to be asleep, in the hope that he might

134

show something of the instinct of a gentleman. But as he drew near he began to tiptoe, and he came so softly that Ina could scarcely hear him. She regretted her pretense, but she meant to stick it out as long as possible. Suddenly she felt him close — caught the odor of liquor. And she opened her eyes and violently swerved in the hammock just in time to avoid being kissed. Then she sat up. Anger would have consumed her, but for the flashing thought that at last he had given her real offense. She was almost glad to see him.

"How do, Ina! Thought you were asleep," he greeted her, in no wise discomfited.

"I'm quite well, thank you, Mr. McAdam," replied Ina, pertly. "But I wasn't asleep."

"What'd you lay that way for?" he demanded, his eyes losing their smile. His face was slightly heated, but he did not appear under the influence of drink.

"I wanted to see what you'd do if I had been asleep. I found out."

"Well, I was only going to kiss you. What of that?"

"You insulting cad!" retorted Ina, rising to her feet. Even on the moment she was struck by something in McAdam very similar to what she had noted in Setter. These men had returned to the Blaine environment with singular suppositions.

"It's no insult for a fellow to try to kiss his girl, is it?" he asked, with the most amazing effrontery.

"I'm not your girl," returned Ina, icily.

"Well, if you're honest about it, and you're *not*, then my dad and me are getting a rotten deal," he said,

135

bluntly. But he doubted her honesty. The half smile on his smug face attested to his half-won conquest.

"Mr. McAdam, you amaze me. If you and your father are getting a rotten deal, or any kind of a deal, it is absolutely without my knowledge. I've been perfectly honest with you. I never liked you. I despise you now. You never struck me as particularly bright. Besides, your enormous conceit makes you blind to the truth. But do you understand me now? If not —"

"Yes, that's enough, Ina Blaine," he returned, hoarsely, his face growing darkly red, and he shook a gloved fist in her face. "Your father let us think you were as good as engaged to me. On the strength of that my dad went thousands of dollars into cattle and ranch deals. And more — he got all balled up with that damned slick Less Setter. You —"

Ina silenced him with a raised hand. She felt her face growing white.

"I won't hear any more," she said, ringingly. "I know nothing of the deals you mention. If my father really did what you claim — it — it was doing me a terrible wrong. Now all that remains for me to say is this. I wouldn't marry you to save my father from ruin — or even my own life."

"You've changed some since I last saw you, Ina Blaine," declared McAdam, with the studious bitter acumen of jealousy. "I haven't forgotten the way you greeted Ben Ide that day in Hammell. If I have to lay this throw-down to that lousy wild-horse hunter it'll be bad for him."

136

Ina checked on the tips of her opening lips a flippant retort that he was precisely right in his suspicions.

"You wouldn't dare say that to Ben Ide's face," she blazed, instead.

"*Now* I've got you straight," he hissed. "I see it in your face. You pretty lying cat! Coming home with all your education and style to take up with that horse thief!"

There were, it seemed, limits to Ina's endurance. She gave McAdam a stinging slap across his sneering mouth. The blow brought the blood.

"I'll tell Ben Ide what you've said," she cried, passionately. "And I hope I'm around when he meets you. That, Mr. McAdam, is the last word I'll ever speak to you."

Whereupon Ina went into her tent, shut and hooked the screen door, and pulled down the blind. She heard McAdam stride away, cursing, striking the junipers with his whip. Then she sank into a chair, suddenly limp and weak.

"Whew! All in a minute! Something's got into me, surely . . . But he was insufferably rude. I'm glad it happened just that way . . . Now for Dad! He'll come like a mad bull . . . Well, I'll just settle him, too."

Ina did not have long to wait, certainly not long enough to cool off or lose her nerve. She heard the stamp of his heavy boots.

"Ina!" he called, stridently.

She waited until he called again, louder this time. Then she answered:

"Dad, I'm in my tent."

"Wal, come out."

"But I'm not coming out just yet."

"Wha-at?" he roared, stamping to the front of her tent.

"I'm expecting to feel very bad — pretty soon — so I don't want to come out." How cool and audacious she felt! Almost she could have laughed. But at the depths of her feeling there was a new and cold emotion, sterner than any she had ever felt.

"You come hyar an' apologize to young McAdam," shouted her father.

"I won't do anything of the kind," flashed Ina, in a voice her father had certainly never heard. Nor had she ever heard it! Still, she was frightened.

"What's wrong? What happened?"

"Mr. McAdam insulted me."

"He did, now! — an' how?"

"He tried to kiss me. Then after a few pretty plain words from me he insulted me again. So I slapped his face. And I ended by saying I'd never speak to him again."

"But, Ina, you will? This is serious business for me," implored her father, hoarsely.

"I'm sorry, Dad. You were wrong to encourage him," replied Ina, softening for an instant. "For I absolutely will never look at him again."

"Girl, who are you to cross me this way? I'll have obedience," he went on, in low-voiced fury. "Come out hyar, before I break down that door."

He laid a heavy hand on the knob and shook it violently. Ina stood up to face him, and she paused

138

before answering. This was the crucial moment. Alas! She felt sick at heart. But it was her life, her happiness at stake, and she knew he was hard, ignorant, intolerant, if not worse. Then she heard herself speaking coldly, clearly:

"Father, if you break in here and drag me out in front of that cur, I'll go to Hammell if I have to walk — and I'll get a job if I have to be waitress in the hotel."

She heard his choking, husky ejaculation. Then silence ensued for a long moment. The handle of the door turned, but it was only with release. Her father's step sounded heavily, backing away. Then her mother's voice broke the silence: "Hart, I couldn't help but hear. Don't be mad at Ina."

"Mad? Haw, haw, haw!" he rejoined, harshly. "Reckon I was mad, but she licked me — that college daughter of yours — by Gawd! she's licked me."

CHAPTER
EIGHT

Shortly after the altercation with her father Ina had a visit from her mother.

"He's gone, daughter, an' I reckon I never saw him so stumped in all our years together," she said, with unconscious satisfaction.

"I feel pretty shaky now," replied Ina, with a queer little laugh. "But, Mother, I couldn't stand it any longer."

They sat on the steps of Ina's tent porch, from which the ranch cabins could be plainly seen. Her father and McAdam were standing in plain sight. Ina could translate that interview from the deprecatory gestures of her father and the wild ones of her rejected suitor. The most amazing thing then was to see her father abruptly turn his back upon McAdam and go into the cabin.

"Hart can be awful bullheaded when he's mad," muttered Mrs. Blaine, as if speaking to herself.

"Mother, it's a wonder to me that young nincompoop didn't make Dad mad long ago," rejoined Ina, with a giggle.

"Your father has a mighty lot of patience where money is concerned."

"I'm afraid he has become deeply involved with the McAdams."

"Hart Blaine has got involved with everybody, particularly this man Setter," said Mrs. Blaine, in bitter impatience. "He's changed. He won't listen to me. We were poor so long that money when it came set him crazy."

"Then it'd be a good thing for him to lose some of it," declared Ina.

"That's what I told him. Land's sake! I thought he'd knock me over . . . Well, well, maybe things will come out. You needn't tell it, daughter, but I'm glad you wouldn't marry young McAdam. He didn't suit me at all. I try to keep my ideas to myself, as I don't seem to fit well in this new world of ours. Just now I happened to be at the door of my tent when young McAdam came up to you. I thought you was asleep in the hammock. An' when you jumped away from him I sure wanted one of the cowboys to happen along. Then when you slapped him — that tickled me. Well, I hope we've seen the last of McAdam an' can have a little comfort by ourselves on Sundays."

"Mother, bless your heart, you do understand. I feel suddenly freed . . . But, oh, I forgot Mr. Setter," exclaimed Ina, impulsively.

"What do you mean, daughter?"

"I didn't mean to let that slip. But maybe it's just as well. Mother, of late Setter has been — well, offensive, where McAdam was only silly. McAdam only annoyed me, but Setter has worried me, even frightened me."

141

"For the land's sake! What's he done?" exclaimed her mother, bewildered.

"It's enough to say, Mother, that he has neither scruples nor decency," declared Ina, with heat. "The last few weeks before we moved over here he waylaid me in the parlor, out under the pines, on the road when I went to meet Dall, in fact, everywhere I was alone."

"Waylaid you! What's that word? . . . You don't mean courtin' you? Why, he's old enough to be your father!"

"Courting is a mild way to put it, Mother," continued Ina, gravely. "Courting implies marriage. And Mr. Less Setter has not done me the honor to hint of marriage. But he makes brazen love to me. I have to fight, even *run* to get away from him. There, it's out!"

Mrs. Blaine passed from astonishment to anger. A slow dull red colored her lined face and her usually mild eyes snapped.

"You never told your father," she asserted.

"No. Once or twice I've said sharp things to Mr. Setter and got a terrible scolding from Dad. Then of late Dad has got so thick with him that I was actually afraid. He'd get terribly angry now and he wouldn't believe me. Then I've had suspicions that Setter would cheat Dad sooner or later. So I just relied on my wits to avoid this gay Lothario of a cattleman."

"Ina, I'm glad you told me," said her mother. "I hope Hart Blaine learns a lesson. If he can't protect his own daughter an' lets her brothers go gallivantin' to the city — well, it's a great pity. If I was in your place I'd make up to some strappin' big cowboy who would protect me from a man like Less Setter."

142

"Mother!" cried Ina, incredulously.

"That's plain talk, Ina, an' maybe common, as young McAdam's mother said I was. But I don't care what it is. Wealth isn't everythin'. I know good from bad. An' pretty soon I'll give your father a piece of my mind."

Dall came noisily into sight then, dragging a puppy and a rabbit. Whereupon Mrs. Blaine left Ina and went to her tent.

"Ina, you look like the dickens," said Dall. "Come play with us."

"Surely, if you and your menagerie will stick close to my lookout station here," replied Ina.

"Lookout station! You mean a forest-fire lookout?"

"Forest fire, thunder and lightning, earthquake, any kind of catastrophe," said Ina, pointing to the juniper tree, the white tarpaulin spread over their bed, the comfortable wide hammock with its cushions, and the box table littered with books.

"I savvy," returned Dall, seriously. "You want to see when to run from Dad and Mr. Klamath Falls and Mr. Blondy Pop-eyes."

"Dall, despite what Marvie says, your brain seems to be growing along with your legs. You hit it right on the head. Come on; I'll play with you. And we must not forget to read over your Sunday-school lesson."

The rest of the morning hours passed swiftly and pleasantly. Perhaps the most pleasant incident for Ina was to see Sewell McAdam drive away with his high-stepping horses and shiny black buggy. Marvie did not return. Mrs. Blaine served dinner outside in the shade of a juniper, but her husband failed to appear.

Mother and daughters had dinner to themselves, and Ina reflected that it was the first Sunday meal for weeks at which she had felt at ease. Afterward she and Dall helped their mother wash and dry the dishes. "Your father forgot this was Sunday," said Mrs. Blaine, complacently. "We always have Sunday dinner at noon. He'll miss his an' have to eat with the cowboys."

Ina spent most of the afternoon in her hammock, reading, dreaming, both wide-eyed and asleep. In truth, her sleeping dreams were disturbed by a very abashed and respectful cowboy who brought a message from her father, requiring her presence at his office at once. Ina, somewhat upset in mind, walked over to the ranch with the cowboy, and took advantage of the few moments to make casual inquiries.

One of the cabins had been fitted up to serve as a living room and office for Mr. Blaine. It did not look very tidy, but it was a pleasant light room, an improvement on the one used for the same purpose at Tule Lake Ranch.

Ina's father was not in. She glanced at the large table, covered with letters and papers, deeds and contracts, all jumbled together in hopeless confusion. She had often asked her father to let her keep his books, and file his papers for convenience, but he had scouted the idea. He did not need any bookkeeper. Ina studying that table load of documents, wondered just why her father did not care to have her in his office. Then she heard trotting horses outside. Through the window she espied Setter and three cowboys riding in.

144

Also her father appeared crossing the space between the cabins. Setter intercepted him, and waving the cowboys away, he dismounted and walked beside him toward the office. The window was open, and Ina stood a little back from it. As her father and his partner approached she remained motionless, without compunction attending to their conversation.

". . . twenty head of wild horses, half broke," Setter was saying with enthusiasm. "Ide must have left last night. Anyway, he wasn't home. His cabin door was nailed shut. But I pried it open. Nice place he's got, clean as if he had a woman there. Nothin' there but grub, which we helped ourselves to."

"Wal, if Ben Ide wasn't home, of course you couldn't talk business," said Blaine, thoughtfully.

"No, but I'll go again an' stay till he comes," rejoined Setter.

"Suit yourself, but I'm advisin' ag'in' it."

"I know you are," replied the other, patiently. "But why? You don't give me any good reasons."

"Wal, I reckon I haven't any 'cept I know his father, Amos Ide."

"Hart, I don't care a damn for Amos Ide, or his son, either," retorted Setter, coolly. "Ben Ide has the key to this valley. Why, his place will be priceless some day! With that an' the three ranches round Mule Deer Lake we can control all the good range clear to your holdings at Silver Meadow. Thirty miles of Forlorn River! That's the cream of this country. How did you cattlemen fail to see it?"

"Wal, we've all been workin' too hard, till lately," responded Blaine, dryly. "But I agree with you. There's a fortune to be made on Forlorn River."

"Fortune? Well, I should snigger," said Setter, scornfully. "Ide's got one spring over there that's worth a million. Your cowboys said it had always been under water — under the river. If Ide knew it he sure kept his mouth shut."

"Reckon he did know. He always was a smart boy. Perhaps he's seen the future of this valley. Mebbe that's why he bucked his father so hard. If so we'll never buy him out."

"See here, Hart, it's only you talkin' about buyin' out this boy's holdings," returned Setter, testily. "We won't buy him out. We'll drive him out. Remember I told you Ben Ide is tied up with a Nevada outlaw. I know him. Their ranchin' an' wild-horse huntin' are only bluffs. Blinds to hide their cattle rustlin'. It's an old gag. I've seen it work in Montana, Arizona, Nevada. But it's new here in California."

"Strong talk again, Setter," said Blaine, tersely.

"Yes, an' it comes natural to me," replied Setter, meaningly. "I'll make these plans an' carry them out. All you do is furnish what ready cash we need, an' I'll bet we can buy out Sims an' his neighbor homesteaders for next to nothin'."

"Poor devils! I shouldn't wonder. I'm givin' you a hunch that I ain't as keen about this ranch buyin' as I was. Some of my old friends have turned ag'in' me for it. My wife, too, is worryin' me."

146

"I've seen all that, Blaine, an' am allowin' for it," rejoined Setter, suavely. "But business is business. These poor devils would be all the worse off if we didn't buy. Let's put this big Forlorn River deal through an' then we'll have about all we can handle."

"Huh! Reckon I've got that now," said Blaine, gruffly. "There was hell to pay today."

"What?" queried Setter, sharply.

Ina, watching keenly, saw in this man's swift responsiveness, in the alert intent flash of his prominent eyes, a preparedness, a reserve force not to be accounted for by what lay behind her father's statement. This man wore a mask. He was two men at the same time.

"Young McAdam showed up here today," explained Blaine. "He got to monkeyin' round Ina an' she slapped his face. Then she turned him down cold. Wal, he came to me, ugly an' mean. Reckon I didn't savvy him. An' I got ugly, too, an' called him a few names on my own hook. He left swearin' he'd have me in court. Now I'll have to go to Klamath tomorrow an' raise that thirty thousand old McAdam put in one of our deals. You see, I didn't tell you he was set on his son Sewell marryin' Ina. An' I, like a damn fool, encouraged them. Without thinkin' much about my girl, I'm bound to say. But I got the thirty thousand on the strength of a marriage between Sewell an' Ina."

"I'd call you somethin' stronger'n that," declared Setter, with sarcasm. "Why didn't you tell me the terms of that deal? I'd have blocked it. Sewell McAdam! That pasty-faced potato-head on a whip handle! . . . Blaine, even if you could have arranged this marriage I'd have blocked it."

"You would?" blurted out Blaine.

"Yes, I would."

"The hell you say!" Here the old independence of a hard pioneer of the West spoke, dry, crisp, somehow menacing, with just a hint of curiosity. It thrilled Ina more deeply than any word or deed she remembered of her father's.

"No need to argue about that now," added Setter, smooth and conciliatory again. "The McAdam deal is off. Probably we're well rid of that shrewd old *hombre*."

"Reckon so, 'specially as he's thick with Amos Ide's banker. I had a devil of a time persuadin' Amos to throw in with us."

"Don't worry, Hart. That's done. Ide is in with us, up to his neck, deeper than he knows . . . Hello! there are the cowboys ridin' in from Mule Deer Lake. I sent them over. Hey, boys!"

A lean rider detached himself from his companions riding up the road and trotted over to Setter and Blaine.

"Nobody at home at Mule Deer Lake," he announced. "Reckon the drought drove them out. No water. Place all burned brown. Few cattle an' deer dead from drinkin' mud."

"That's strange," muttered Setter. "Moved out . . . But of course those homesteaders couldn't live there without water. Blaine, I'll bet you can find Sims at Hammell tomorrow."

148

"Wal, I'll ask for him," replied Blaine, turning on his heel.

When he entered the office Ina was sitting at the other end of the room, apparently reading. He was surprised to find her there.

"Dad, you sent for me," she said.

"Wal, so I did. I forgot."

He looked harassed and worn; he ran a horny hand through his grizzled hair as if to revive vague thoughts.

"Ina, I'm out of favor with you an' Ma," he began, not appealingly, but merely making a statement. "In your case I want to make clear that I thought you'd sure care for Sewell McAdam. Kate's case with her city beau might be some to blame. I couldn't bide what I took for your disobeyin' me, an' I got mad. Now I want to know if you really meant you'd run off from me an' be a waitress in a hotel."

"Dad, I certainly meant it. But I could surely get a better job than that."

"Wal, you needn't think about it again. I'm sort of ashamed, an' I don't take kind to your mother's late opinion of me. After all, I'm workin' an' storin' up for my family, not for myself."

"Yes, I know, Dad. But Mother and I and Dall — Marvie too, would like kindness and love *now*, rather than any material proof of them in the future."

"Ahuh. Reckon I've had a heap on my mind lately," he replied, not quite comprehending. He had received a shock, but it would take a great deal more to clarify his obtuse mind, if that were ever possible. "An' from the hunches I'm gettin' it looks like I'd have more. But

149

your old dad ain't done for yet, even if his favorite daughter did lick him."

Ina kissed his brown cheek and laid a hand on his broad shoulder.

"You will be glad some day that I had the independence to stand by my rights . . . Dad, I think sudden wealth has placed you in a position where you make new decisions. They're strange to you. And some of them are beginning to get you into trouble."

"Lordy! you hit it. Half the time lately these deals stump me. Reckon I don't mean cattle an' land. I know them. But the papers, figgers, mortgages an' interest — they get me buffaloed. If it wasn't for Setter I'd be worse than stumped."

"Dad, have you talked over all your deals with a good lawyer?" asked Ina, earnestly.

"Not one of them. What do I want to pay lawyer's fees for? Setter is lawyer enough."

"But, Dad — how do you know he is honest?"

Her father straightened up with a jerk. "What? Honest? I never thought anythin' else. Setter's a mighty big man. He could buy an' sell me ten times over . . . Child, where did you get a queer idee that he might be — ?"

A crunching of the gravel outside and a jingling of spurs interrupted Blaine's question. Setter stepped into the doorway. When he saw Ina his wine-dark eyes leaped and his mobile face lighted with a smile that made him rather handsome. His gladness at sight of her was unmistakably sincere.

150

"Evenin', Ina, was wonderin' when I'd see you," he said, approaching her. "Your dad told me how you chased that false-face with its little mustache back to Klamath. I'm tellin' you I'd have chased him myself pretty soon."

"Oh, I guess Dad did the chasing," replied Ina, nervously.

"Now some older chaps, like me, can have a chance," he said, and taking hold of her arms above her elbows he gave her a gentle pull. He appeared smiling, suave, yet there was unveiled boldness in eyes and manner.

Ina did not move, nor look up at Setter. She watched her father while she stood there in Setter's grasp. What she saw confirmed a suspicion born of that very moment. Setter had a hold on her father, who was realizing this and that it involved his daughter.

Then Ina slipped not gently out of Setter's grasp and left the room. Soberly she bent her steps toward camp. What had only seemed vexatious and offensive had developed into a plot. In the first flush of this possibility she felt trapped, helpless. Her father was no match for Less Setter. How deeply he must have become involved! Setter's air was that of a master of a situation, a conquest over which he exulted. Then Ina's temper fired away her dread and into her mind flashed her mother's advice.

"A strapping big cowboy who would fight for me!" murmured Ina, half aloud. "Oh, it sounds beautiful! I'd find one. But how can I — when — when I love Ben Ide."

Here Ina halted in her tracks, aghast. Suddenly she began to tremble. Her heart had ambushed her and in a moment of poignant uncertainty had betrayed her with the truth. A simple natural confession, spoken aloud, suddenly grew to astounding proportions. Ben Ide! Love! — Ever since her childhood! The truth burst imperiously upon Ina, overwhelming her. Friendship, loyalty had been guises to deceive herself. She hurried on, suddenly afraid of being seen, of the sunlight, of herself. She ran, at first fleetly, to the grove, under the juniper trees, and then almost blindly into her tent, where she locked herself in, and leaned back against the door, hands clutched to her surging breast. Her terrible predicament dawned upon her. It was agony — that piercing staggering surrender to love. "Ben! Ben!" she whispered, wildly. "My God — it's my life!"

Not for many hours, indeed not until late the next day, did Ina recover from the storm of emotion that had overwhelmed her, and then it seemed she was herself again intensified and magnified beyond understanding. Out of the spiritual chaos emerged a woman infinitely surer of herself, one who scorned weakening before the problems of yesterday.

From that crucial time every hour seemed full, dreamy, prophetic, yet they passed swiftly. She kept busy and active as much as the limited opportunities permitted. She helped her mother, sewed, read, studied, played with Dall, rode horseback with Marvie, but there were often intervals in which she idled, dreamed, waited for something that she knew was going to happen. Dread had departed. She had no more fear of Setter and made no effort to avoid him, a circumstance he manifestly grasped. It puzzled him. Whatever his mental attributes, he was not thickheaded and egotistical like McAdam. Ina's changed attitude, however, did not affect him, as it was plain he was indifferent to the state of her mind and heart. Ina saw that he had no conception of the spirit of a woman. He was merely base, bold, brutal. He did not want love or respect. She was no more than a horse to be possessed and beaten.

In a clever and unobtrusive way Ina managed to dip into her father's affairs. After all, he could be approached. It was Setter who resented Ina's interest and suggestion. But with regard to this situation he was between the devil and the deep sea, because he reveled in Ina's visits to the ranch and office.

Late in the afternoon of the day Setter had again ridden to Forlorn River, Ina was startled by clattering hoofs outside her tent, and then Marvie's yell. Hurriedly she ran out.

Marvie was slipping off a wet and heaving pony. The lad's face, hot, red, radiant, electrified Ina, and before she could utter a word he burst out.

"Oh, gee! — I'm out of breath," he panted. "Rode fast — to get here first . . . Dad yelled like mad — as I come by. He'll kill me. I run off — you know . . .Was at Ben Ide's — when Setter got there . . . Ina, what happened will tickle you — half to death. But don't make me — tell now. You want to be over at the ranch — when Setter rides in. Hop my pony — an' ride over."

Ina was not dressed for riding, but she did not let that interfere. As she mounted, Marvie added: "I'm hopin' Dad'll be so upset he'll forget about me. If he isn't — you —"

Ina, galloping away, did not catch the conclusion of Marvie's speech, but she guessed at it. She was tremendously excited and curious and thrilled. Marvie had said she would be tickled half to death. What had happened to Setter? To Ben Ide? Ina did not like to urge the tired pony, and when, looking down the road beyond the ranch, she espied Setter and three cowboys coming, she restrained her hurry. She found her father and some of his men out in front of the cabin, evidently much interested in Setter's return.

"Where's that young rascal Marvin?" he demanded, irately.

"I think he fled to Mother for protection," replied Ina, demurely.

"Ahuh! Wal, that won't save him. I'll lick him good."

"What for, Dad?" asked Ina, sharing the smiles of the men.

"He rode by hyar yellin' like an Injun, an' wouldn't stop for me," replied her father.

"What was he yelling?" inquired Ina.

"Reckon somethin' about Setter. I didn't ketch it. Never seen the lad like that before. He's growin' up an' gettin' wild. I'll have to use a halter on him."

"Dad, wait till you see what has happened. Marvie was terribly excited. I think there has been a fight at Forlorn River."

"Fight? . . . Wal, wal!" he ejaculated, and his rugged face changed. "I *told* Setter to be careful."

One of the men pointed down the road toward the group entering the ranch gate.

"Boss, looks like Bill Sneed was holdin' Setter on his hoss."

Blaine, muttering under his breath, started to stride across the open to intercept the horsemen, who were heading toward the second cabin. Ina's keen eye caught Setter's impatient gesture, clearly significant of the fact that he preferred not to be met just then. But Blaine strode on, with his men close behind. Ina did not intend to miss anything and she followed. The result was that Setter and the three cowboys with him were intercepted in front of the cabin.

"What'n hell happened to you?" shouted Blaine, astounded, as he strode forward.

Setter wore no coat. His white shirt was torn half off, soaking wet with sweat, discolored by blood and dust. Ina would not have recognized him. His face was a spectacle to behold. A great black puffy lump hid one of his eyes. The other glared with sullen fury. His mouth was swollen and bleeding.

Raising a dirty shaking hand, Setter began to speak huskily: "Ide an' his cronies beat me."

"Wha-at?" demanded Blaine, hotly, and his grizzled mane bristled.

"They took my gun an' set on me," said Setter as he painfully dismounted. Evidently he was pretty severely crippled.

"Them damn hoss-wranglers! Wal, by heavens! we can't overlook this!" ejaculated Blaine, divided between rage and amaze. "Looks like a job for Strobel . . . But, say, did my cowboys stand around to see you beat by three men?"

One of the cowboys started up as if he had been struck. Ina recognized the clean-cut, red-faced Bill Sneed, who was Marvie's particular chum. This young man flung out a gauntleted hand in fiery gesture of repudiation. His blue eyes flashed fire. The look of him sent Ina's blood racing.

"Aw, Setter, tell it straight," he said, stingingly.

"You shut up or I'll fire you," shouted Setter.

"Fire, hell!" retorted Sneed, with passionate disgust. "You couldn't fire me. I quit. An' I'm goin' to tell this straight."

"So you're in with Ben Ide, hey? Well, I'll tend to all of you later," rasped Setter, shaking from weakness and fury. His bloody face expressed a hideous malignancy. Then he surged away to enter his cabin and bang the door.

"Bill, he's my pardner, but he's not firin' my hands," spoke up Blaine, gazing up at the angry cowboy.

"All the same, I quit, Mr. Blaine. I wouldn't be caught dead workin' for anyone who can stand for Setter."

"All right, Bill. Reckon I was independent once myself. I'm waitin' to hear what you said was the straight of this mess."

"Setter offered us boys a hundred dollars apiece to let him make you-all think Ben an' his pards had pounded him up three to one. But it didn't happen that way. Ben did it alone. He slugged Setter, an' it shore was good to see."

"Wal, what about?"

Sneed settled back in his saddle, with less belligerent air. Evidently it relieved him to see he was going to be heard.

"We got to Forlorn River along about noon," began Sneed. "Ben Ide was home with his Indian, an' he asked us to eat hospitable as anybody could be. Told us his pard was over at the lava beds, where they'd ketched a bunch of wild hosses. He an' Modoc had been drivin' some of them to Forlorn River every day. After havin' grub we went out to look over the hosses. They shore was a purty lot. Ben must be a wonder with wild hosses. Setter had a fit over them. He got excited. An' presently he up an' said: 'My pardner Blaine aims to buy you out, along with Sims an' his neighbors, an' you can throw them hosses in the bargain.' Ben looked sort of queer an' spoke up quietlike that he wouldn't sell. An' as for Sims an' his neighbors — they couldn't sell because Ben had bought them out long ago."

Sneed halted here long enough to laugh outright.

"Why, Mr. Blaine, it was funny the way Setter went up in the air. He just hopped, he was so mad. An' when Ben had refused again cold an' curt, Setter yelled: 'You'll sell out or be drove off!' Ben wanted to know who'd undertake to do that little job. Setter swore by God he could an' would. Then Ben said as it was a free country, an' he'd proved up on his own ranch an' paid for the others, he didn't see how he could be drove off.

157

Then Setter said, 'You know damn right well this hoss-wranglin' of yours is only a bluff — a blind.'"

Here Sneed paused again, his frank steely-blue eyes fixed upon Blaine's intent face, and as if to augment the suspense he shifted a leg over the pommel of his saddle. Ina thrilled at the power she felt he held in the *dénouement* of his story. He was enjoying the telling.

"Spit it out," growled Blaine, clenching his big fist. No doubt he knew before being told.

"Ben got kinda white," resumed Sneed, "an' he stepped close to Setter, an' he asked, very cuttin', 'What do you mean by bluff an' blind?' . . . Then Setter said, 'Ide, you better take Blaine's offer an' clear out.' . . . Ben roared, 'No, I tell you. An' I'm callin' *your* bluff.' . . . Setter got black in the face an' yelled: 'We're on to your shady deals!'

"Ben hit him square in the eye. Oh, what a soak! Setter'd have fallen a mile but for the fence. He throwed his gun. But Ben grabbed it — shoved it up as it went off. If he hadn't been quick as lightnin' he'd have been bored. They fought an' Ben got the gun. I thought he'd kill Setter, but he throwed the gun away. An' then he gave Setter the damnedest beatin' I ever seen any man git. It took us an hour to fetch him to an' we've been all afternoon packin' him back here . . . That's all, sir, an' the boys will tell you I gave it straight."

Old Blaine did not glance at Sneed's comrades for corroboration of the story.

"Ahuh! . . . Wal, Bill, I'll take it as a favor if you'll change your mind about quittin' me," he said.

"Thank you, sir. I'll sleep on it," replied Sneed, soberly.

Ina dismounted and followed her father into his office. He did not appear upset.

"Wal, daughter, reckon supper's not ready, an' I'll just have time to lick Marvie."

"Oh, Dad, don't whip the boy. Consider how wildly excited he was. He saw that fight."

"Humph! You look pretty wild yourself," returned her father, shrewdly. "Reckon I shouldn't have let you stay to hear that yarn. Marvie wanted you to hear it, didn't he?"

"Yes, he did," confessed Ina.

"Wal, I'll lick him for that, too. I'll lock up now . . . Come on, daughter. What's on your mind, that you stand there sort of queer?"

"There's a good deal, Dad, and I must confess it isn't worry over Marvie," said Ina. "Haven't *you* been made thoughtful?"

"What about?" he drawled as he locked the door.

Ina led Marvie's pony and walked beside her father toward the camp. On her own account Ina wanted much to be alone to dwell on Sneed's story, to thrill and gloat over Ben Ide's repudiation of a slur upon his honesty. But likewise she was intensely curious to find out what her father thought.

"About the way Setter approached Ben Ide," she replied.

"Wal, I don't see nothin' there to make me thoughtful."

"Then about the way Ben whipped him?"

"Nope. All I think about that is Setter deserved it good an' plenty," he returned, somewhat grimly.

"Oh, Dad!" Ina had to bite her lips to restrain impulsive and perhaps self-betraying utterance. "Then — doesn't it make you thoughtful — the way Setter *lied*?"

"Lass, I'm afraid to think," said Blaine, bluntly. "I'm up to my neck in deals with Setter. He has my paper for thousands. I can't back out. I must go on . . . Now about the fight I'll say this. I knowed there'd be one. I advised Setter. What surprises me an' does make me thoughtful is that Ben Ide didn't kill him."

"Dad, I think I know why," murmured Ina, and then she fled to hide her face.

From the safe sanctity of her tent she heard Marvie's shrill voice in protest:

"Dad, what're you lickin' me for?"

"Reckon for runnin' off when I told you to stay home," was the stern rejoinder.

Then followed sundry slaps and cracks, and shuffling sounds, pierced by Marvie's wail: "I'll never — do it — no more!"

CHAPTER
NINE

Ina's father left for Klamath Falls and was absent four days, during which period Mr. Setter did not show himself, at least away from the ranch.

Marvie took his whipping more as a disgrace than a punishment, and appeared more rebellious than ever. He coaxed Ina to ride with him over to Forlorn River, and never guessed that her calm refusal hid a tremendous tumult of temptation. Ina yearned to see Ben Ide, but she could not yet bring herself to go to him, though she knew he was not likely to approach her without invitation.

Mr. Blaine returned from his trip accompanied by Sheriff Strobel of Hammell. Ina was filled with consternation and alarm. Her father proved evasive and stern; perhaps something untoward had happened in Klamath or Hammell. Ina determined to find out. Sheriff Strobel was a tall rangy man with a big sandy mustache and keen gray eyes. He wore a huge black sombrero and did not appear to own a coat. Ina took his measure in one intuitive survey, and watching her chance, she contrived to meet him alone, in her father's office.

"Mr. Strobel, will you talk to me a little?" she asked, earnestly, with her most appealing smile.

"Now, Miss Ina, I'd be de-lighted," he replied, in kindly interest and humor. "I'd like to make these young buck cowboys jealous."

"I'm terribly serious. Your coming here — frightens me," she said, gravely looking up into his clear gray eyes. "Did my father fetch you here?"

"No. Reckon I come on my own invitation," he returned.

"Father told you of that — that terrible fight?" she went on, hurriedly.

"Yes, but not till we were on the way out."

"Oh — that relieves me . . . Please tell me why you came."

"Wal, Miss Ina, the ranchers round Hammell, your dad an' Amos Ide in particular, want this cattle-stealin' band broke up. I sent deputies roundabout through the hills, an' I'm goin' on to Silver Meadow. There's one gang of rustlers operatin' up that way."

"Silver Meadow. Is that near the lava beds?"

"No. Silver Meadow is straight up Forlorn River forty miles, I reckon. The lava beds are west of Tule Lake."

His searching eyes inspired Ina with trust. He seemed curious, respectful, sympathetic.

"Mr. Strobel," she began, eloquently, "Ben Ide and I were once schoolmate friends. I have come home after four years' absence to find him an outcast. Lying tongues have made him out a — a thief. It's criminal. Ben loves wild life — the chasing of horses, particularly.

162

But he's honest. I *know*, Mr. Strobel. This is no silly girl sentiment . . . I've talked with Ben and I'm going to stand by him."

"Wal, wal, Miss Ina, 'pears like Ben ain't so bad off for friends," replied Strobel, his penetrating gaze on her. He spoke constrainedly, but there seemed to be something behind his speech.

Swiftly then Ina told the story of Setter's visit to Ben and the fight exactly as she had heard it related by Bill Sneed. Roused as she was, with faculties intensely keen, she was quick to see a subtle effect of the narrative upon the sheriff.

"Your dad didn't tell it that way," he said, quietly.

"No, I dare say he wouldn't. But I've told you word for word," replied Ina, forcibly. "Get hold of Bill Sneed. Hear it from him. Setter will swear Bill is in with Ben. But Bill never saw Ben Ide until the other day. He's straight. Setter couldn't corrupt him."

"Wal, now, Miss Ina, I reckon I'm to understand you're a secret deputy of mine?" he queried, with a droll shrewd smile.

Ina's heart bounded at the significance of his words. "I am — if you'll have me," she replied, in breathless surprise.

"Wal, we'll shake on that . . . Reckon I'm proud to have you. An' I'm not underratin' your value. A smart woman beats a man all hollow for figgerin' things you can't see. Now give me your angle on this Less Setter. Remember any confidences will never pass me."

"Very well, then. First I'll give you my personal angle, as you call it," returned Ina, warmly. "Less Setter is a bad man, morally I mean. I felt that before I knew it. He insulted Hettie Ide once — frightened her terribly another time. Where women are concerned he is brazen, unscrupulous, treacherous. His advances toward me were at first smooth, flattering. Then when he found he made no headway with me, so to speak, he changed his tactics. Briefly he made violent love to me — waylaid me on all possible occasions. It wasn't safe for me to go anywhere alone."

"Miss Ina!" exclaimed the sheriff, incredulously. "You mean — he would have laid hold of you?"

"My dear Mr. Strobel," replied Ina, almost impatiently, "I'm telling you as plainly as I know how. He *did* lay hold of me, more than once. But I'm strong — and, well, I got away from him."

She thought no less of this man that his bronze face grew like iron and he cursed under his breath.

"Lately Setter's attitude toward me has changed somewhat," went on Ina. "There's a hint of possession in it. I think he means marriage now. At first that never entered his mind."

Strobel's mute acceptance of these statements left no doubt in Ina's mind that she had been wise to confide in him. Intuitively she felt more of his stand than he realized on the moment.

"Now as to what I *think*," she hurried on, "you must take for what it's worth. Dad's sudden rise from hard times if not actual poverty — his opportunities to make money have gone to his head. Dad knows farming and that's all. He's simple, trusting, enthusiastic as a boy. Setter has gotten around him. They're in all kinds of

164

deals. Dad has furnished money, paper, collateral, and Setter has furnished the brains. No doubt to his own profit! It wouldn't surprise me in the least if Setter has Dad involved in really crooked deals. Certainly he's got Dad tied up. Pretty soon he's going to try to make Dad force me to marry him."

"An' that will be funny, won't it?" blurted out Strobel, suddenly revealing his depth of warmth.

"It certainly will," laughed Ina, spiritedly.

"Wal, I'm sure thankin' you, Miss Ina," he said. "You've given me a different angle to work on. You're a smart girl. Reckon I'd rather be in Ben's boots right now than in your dad's."

His smile, his tone, seemed an unmasking of an aloof and unresponsive character. Ina began to quiver with a fear that she was hoping too much.

"You don't mean — on account — of me?" she queried, falteringly.

"No, just on the face of things, as they look now," he replied, thoughtfully. "Still, you can never tell. I represent the law hereabouts, but if I don't round up these rustlers this summer I'll lose my job. Amos Ide, your dad, Setter, an' other ranchers on the board have given me that hunch. An' if they fetch officers from Redlands, or Klamath, it might result in trouble for Ben. They're after him. Even Ben's own father says he ought to be run out of the country . . . But as for me — wal, even before I had this talk with you I'd have had to *ketch* Ben Ide stealin' cattle before I'd arrest him."

Toward the close Strobel had spoken ringingly, the force and content of which words quite overcame Ina.

She could only stare up at this tall sheriff in speechless gratitude.

"An' here's why, Miss Ina," he concluded, smiling down on her. "I've known Ben Ide since he was a kid. I taught him to fish. He's no more a cattle an' hoss thief than I am."

That was too much for Ina's dignity and reserve, already sadly decimated by her success in propitiating this sheriff. She answered only to joyous impulse. She wanted to give him all she owned; she could have bestowed a fortune upon him, had she possessed one. But she had nothing to give a man — except gratitude, admiration, affection. His smile was understanding though wistful. Suddenly Ina reached up and warmly kissed his brown cheek. Then she sank down, abashed and scarlet of face, yet laughing at the spectacle of this matured man standing as if petrified.

"There, Mr. Strobel, that's not from your deputy — but from your friend — forever," she said, with a gaiety full of depth, and then she fled out of the office.

Next day Sheriff Strobel rode away down the lake trail toward Forlorn River. No doubt he intended to visit Ben Ide on his way south. At first the idea pleased Ina, then on second thought it frightened her. Surely Strobel would mention her tremendous interest in Ben and his fortunes. That might be all right and then again it might not. It depended upon how Strobel had interpreted her interest and upon what he told. Big-hearted, simple man, he might take for granted that Ben knew she loved him! Most assuredly she had betrayed that love to Strobel. She didn't mind his knowing. But Ben! Ina suffered an incomprehensible attack of fright, dread, wonder and horror, shame and glory, all inextricably mixed together. She had a bad hour, and when she came out of it she was downcast and thoughtful all the rest of the day. At supper time Marvie brought news that ordinarily would have been sufficient to make her happy.

"Setter drove off fer Klamath," announced Marvie, with fine satisfaction. "Heard him say he'd be gone a week on business. But Bill Sneed said Setter was goin' to a dentist to have the teeth put back that Ben Ide knocked out."

Marvie had other news which he reserved for Ina's private ear when after supper she lay in her hammock watching the sunset. Some of the cowboys had been at Forlorn River that day. Ben Ide had come home again. He had a pasture full of the finest wild horses ever captured in that country. In another few days Ben's partner and the Indian would get back with the last of the horses caught at the lava beds, and then they would make a prolonged stay at the ranch.

"An' you bet I'm ridin' over to see Ben soon as Dad's gone," averred Marvie. "You knew, Sis, didn't you, about Dad's goin'?"

"No, I didn't," replied Ina, sitting up with interest. "When? Where?"

"Tomorrow, the boys said. I'm sure gettin' up early so I'll be away when Dad leaves. Then he can't tell me not to do nothin'. He's goin' with the chuck wagon an' outfit of cowboys to one of his ranches near Silver

Meadow. Lots of talk among the men about this Silver Meadow. I'm darned curious, fer they always shut up when they see me."

"Why don't you keep out of sight, then?" asked Ina.

"I forget sometimes. Say, Ina, this'll be a good chance for you to ride over to Forlorn River with me," returned Marvie, lowering his voice.

"Oh, Marvie!" murmured Ina. "I — I couldn't think of it now."

"Why, sure, you could," whispered the tempter. "Are you afraid of Dad an' old Pop-eyes?"

"It's not on their account," said Ina. "No — Marvie, I can't."

"Aw, you said you would. What ails you now? Ben will be tickled stiff. He'll show us that spring hole under the bank which the boys say is chuck-full of trout. We won't let anybody see us an' Dad'll never know . . . Ina, I'd go anywheres with you."

She was weak, she was helpless, she was won. Marvie did not need to discourse so eloquently, had he but known.

"All right, I'll go — some day," she replied, trying to pretend it was his persuasion and not her longing that prompted the reconsideration. What a relief when Marvie went whooping and bounding away! She could sink back in the hammock, unseen, and relax, and be herself, communing with her traitor heart.

Nevertheless the hammock did not hold her long. A restless mood came upon her. To and fro under the junipers she walked, until action and reason had restored a semblance to calm thought. Meanwhile the sun had sunk behind the gray sage mountains. The light, however, still shone on the far slopes of the basin, and the uplands beyond leading to the black ranges and the crowning clouds of gold and rose.

Ina found her favorite seat on a rock at the extreme point of the elevated bench, out of sight from the tents and affording unrestricted view in all other directions.

"I can't go to Forlorn River," she soliloquized. "I *want* to see Ben — oh, how I want to! . . . I love him. And perhaps — probably — surely he doesn't love me . . . I didn't seem to feel he did. My heart would have told me . . . I mustn't go to him. Still I'll fight for him — just the same."

The golden sunlight receded from the wooded cape and little cabin across the lake where Ben Ide lived; and to Ina there seemed to be a similarity between that passing and her mood of the moment. She changed every day, every hour. She was growing toward something — perhaps a great sadness.

The spectacle before her was sad as well as grand. Twilight was stealing out from under the sage mountains behind her, down across the basin, dark and melancholy in its barrenness, while there was still a mantle of gold and rose, turning purple, on the vast reaches of open country leading up to the heavy cloud banks in the sky. The day had been hot and that country, rendered a desert by the years of drought, showed the ghastly lifelessness of sun-baked earth and seared sage. Forlorn River wound away between the hills, a thread of fire growing pale, dying out in the dim purple. Soon it would be lost in the sands. Narrow strips of black lined some of the deep valleys. A stillness, an austerity, pervaded the scene, filling Ina with a sense of the magnitude of the earth and the inscrutableness of nature. She was only a living, palpitating atom in all that immensity.

She realized fully now how this wild country had taken hold of her imagination and heart. She wanted to stay there most of the time, if it was livable. She felt that she preferred strife with the elements, with a hard lonely wilderness, to misunderstanding and dependence, to the dislikes and hatreds of people, to life such as she imagined her sister Kate had embraced.

"I have pioneer blood, so Uncle Charlie always said," she mused. "All I need is the pioneer!"

She laughed at this, but not mirthfully. All that was necessary to round out her life, make it full and happy and productive, was for Ben Ide to come over here and take her back as his wife to that little gray cabin facing the west. As she looked, the last glow of light receded from it. Was Ben there gazing across the lake? Surely he knew she was at this newest of the Blaine ranches.

"Oh, I must not dream this way," she whispered, rousing herself. "It's madness. He'll never know — and if he did he'd never come."

Next day she had the same struggle all over again, and so it went on for days, augmented by the loyal and loving Marvie, who nagged at her to come with him to see Ben. She was driven to impatience with him.

"Aw, say, I'd a crazy notion you *liked* Ben," he retorted, in a huff. "Stay home. Play with Dall. You're no pardner for a man. You don't know your mind one darned little minnit. I'll go alone, an' what I'll tell Ben will be aplenty."

That fired Ina with panic-stricken wrath.

"Don't you dare," she flashed.

"Geewhiz! Ina, you're gettin' to be a myst'ry," complained Marvie. "I've a hunch you'll tell Dad I run off again."

"You bet I will, unless you promise," added Ina, grasping her opportunity.

"All right, I promise to say only what you tell me to," capitulated Marvie, rather lamely. "I can't go to see Ben an' tell him nothin'."

"Why can't you?"

"'Cause I'll *have* to tell Ben somethin' you said. We're on his side of the fence. He knows that. Wasn't you nice to him over at Hettie Ide's? Say, it looked so to me. Have you quit all of a sudden? Do you want to be yellow an' hurt his feelings? There's that fight he had with Setter. We was tickled to death. Don't you want him to know it?"

"Wait, Marvie!" implored Ina, succumbing before this bombardment of logic, scorn, and loyalty. The boy was perfectly right. Ben would misunderstand silence. She must send a message — something as kind, as trusting as had been her words to him that night at the Ide ranch. But what? She needed time to think and there stood Marvie eying her with strange disfavor.

"Give Ben my regards," she began, with misgivings as to where spoken words might lead her. "Tell him I'm glad about the great catch of wild horses. Tell him Sheriff Strobel is — No, never mind —"

"Gee! is that all?" queried Marvie, as she floundered. "Fine lot of guff!"

"Oh, shut up, you — you little devil!" she cried, wildly, driven to desperation. "Tell Ben I *was* tickled to death when I saw Setter — and knew who'd beaten him. There!" But the momentum and emotion of her words, with the sudden glad light on Marvie's face, proved her utter undoing. "And tell him — to come over."

"Now you're talkin', Sis," replied Marvie, suddenly radiant. "I knew you'd come around. But, gosh! you had me guessin'. I'll leave for Ben's as soon as I can fork a horse."

After Marvie had gone and the reaction from her feelings had set in, Ina was sure she would be unhappy, ill, miserable; but she was nothing of the kind. Indeed, she did not know herself. What burn in her cheeks! She wanted to run, sing, dance. How ridiculous to deny youth, hope, love! She was happy for the first time for days because pride and vanity had fallen down before the truth of her heart — happy because she had asked Ben Ide to come to see her. He might not come, but that did not change the fact of her frank invitation. To be sure, she would rather he did not come very soon — at least until she had gained some control over this incorrigibly strange Ina Blaine.

About the middle of the forenoon she was drawn to her favorite place of outlook, which she seldom frequented until afternoon, and straightway espied a horseman riding up the slope from the west side of the lake. Cowboys never took that course. There was no trail. Ina wondered, grew curious and interested. He was avoiding the ranch, that looked certain. She could not remember ever having seen either rider or horse before.

The horseman surmounted the slope, at a point some distance beyond Ina's position, and then rode directly toward her. There was not the slightest doubt of his having observed her, as she had come out on the edge of the bench in plain sight, and now stood there motionless.

Rapidly he loped his horse to her, halted, and slipped out of the saddle with singular quick grace. His spurs jingled. Ina thought him the most striking rider she had ever seen. Tall, slim, lithe, broad of shoulder, dark as an Indian, with black piercing eyes, he could be none other than Ben's friend. Ina recognized him from Hettie's description. It seemed she would have known him without ever having seen him or heard him described.

"Mawnin', Ina Blaine," he drawled, in the cool easy tone of a Southerner. He removed his sombrero, revealing long raven black hair, and made her a gallant bow. "Shore I'm lucky to meet you heah."

"Nevada!" exclaimed Ina. "You're Ben Ide's friend. I *know* you."

"Reckon we both called the turn, without ever havin' seen each other. Nothin' could be no more natural. Ben's pard an' Ben's girl."

"Oh, I'm glad to meet you," returned Ina, blushing as she extended her hand.

"Shore I'm glad to meet you, Ina," he said, removing his glove to shake hands with her.

"You came to see me?" she queried.

"Yes."

"Did you meet my little brother Marvie? He left for Forlorn River this morning."

"No. But I didn't come by the trail."

"Did — did Ben send you?" she went on, rather hurriedly.

"I should smile not. Why, lady, Ben would murder me if he knew what I was aboot this heah day. He shore would."

"Is — is everything all right — over there at Forlorn River?" queried Ina, haltingly. Her heart began to pound.

"Fine an' dandy. Shore gettin' better every day. Ben an' me are on the rise."

"Did Strobel visit you?"

"Stayed all night with us, an' we'd never have knowed he was a sheriff."

"Did he — mention me?"

"I should smile. Reckon you was aboot all he talked aboot."

From pounding, Ina's oversensitive heart took to sinking.

"What did he say?" Ina forced herself to ask.

"Wal, it was Ben's fault that Strobel talked so much," replied Nevada, with a smile that warmed and somehow reassured Ina. "Strobel wanted to talk hoss an' range to us, but Ben wouldn't give him no peace. Shore all Ben wanted to heah aboot was you. An' all

174

Strobel would tell him was how smart an' pretty you were an' how nice you treated him. Ben kept sayin', 'She knew you was comin' heah an' didn't send no word!' an' then Strobel would say, 'Ben, I don't recollect no word, though she spoke of you casual-like, regardin' the fight an' wild hosses.' Then Ben would groan an' tear his hair. 'That's not like Ina Blaine.'"

Toward the end of this drawling speech, so agreeable in Nevada's cool easy tone, Ina speedily recovered her equanimity, and found herself excited over the purport of the rider's presence.

"Come, let's sit in the shade," she said, cordially. "I'd like to lead your horse. Oh, isn't he wonderful? A sorrel. Of course he was wild once. I see that in his eye. Yet he knows I won't hurt him."

"Lady, wait till you see California Red," replied Nevada. "Talk aboot a grand hoss. An' he's goin' to be yours before this year's out."

"Oh, has Ben been attracted by that extravagant offer of my father's?" inquired Ina.

"Reckon he was first off. But now he swears when we ketch Red that nobody could buy him, an' he's goin' to give him to you."

"That's not good business for a poor wild-horse hunter," said Ina, shaking her head. "You tell Ben to hold Dad to that offer."

Presently Ina found herself sitting in the shade with this friend of Ben's, strangely reveling in the fact, and wholly at ease. She could look at him now without thinking of herself and her secret. He was indeed good to look at. She had never seen a face like his, long and lean, with clear brown skin, beardless and smooth, with a few strange hard lines that vanished when he smiled. His eyes were wonderful in their piercing blackness. Ina feared their penetrating power, yet felt secure under their gaze. She liked him. She trusted him. She felt a something sweet and protective that must have been his loyalty to Ben and his pride in Ben's friend.

His lean head, with the ebony hair brushed back carelessly and curling at his collar, had some resemblance to that of an eagle. His garments, both cloth and leather, showed long service and somehow fitted him the better for that. He wore rough chaps, of a style Ina had not noticed among the cowboys on the ranch. From a pocket on the right leg, low down, protruded the handle of a deadly-looking gun. He had small feet, well booted, and wore enormous spurs.

"I cain't take Ben any messages without givin' myself away," he was saying.

"Nevada, surely you didn't come out of curiosity to see me?" she asked, suddenly recalling the strange fact of his visit.

"No, I shore didn't. But I was awful curious to see you, just the same."

"Perhaps you wanted news of Hettie?" she ventured, shyly.

Then it was Nevada's turn to blush. It became him. It betrayed him, robbed him of that singularly cool and careless assurance.

"Shore I wanted it, but I swear I didn't come purpose for that," he asserted.

176

"Well, I'm glad I won't disappoint you," said Ina, gayly. "I saw Hettie two weeks ago yesterday. We had a long talk. She was well and happy. So glad her mother's improving. She spoke of you. She likes you, believes you are Ben's loyal friend. That you're both honest and will give the lie to this vile gossip. Oh, you'd grow vain if I told you all."

Indeed, Ina had been outspoken enough, to judge by Nevada's agitation. A spasm of agony crossed his face, like a twisting shadow.

"My God! if I could only forget the past an' remember only the present!" he exclaimed, despairingly.

"Nevada, you can live down any past," responded Ina, surprised and touched.

"Even if it was bad?"

"Yes, indeed."

"Could I ever be worthy of Hettie?" he asked, wistfully.

"Surely you could. Be what she wants you — what she asked you to be. That will make you worthy."

"I love her," he said, covering his face with his hands. He remained stiff and tense for a long moment, then his strong brown hands left his face, and he was himself again. "Reckon I didn't intend to talk of myself. But it's no harm. Shore I'm glad you know how I feel. An' shore it won't do no harm for you to know how Ben feels."

"And how's — that?" asked Ina, catching her breath between words. The flash of his black eyes startled her.

"Ben's dyin' of love for you!"

"Ben! . . . Dying? Oh, Nevada, you're — you're —"

"Shore I am. But that's true. Ben's breakin'. He's strong an' hard to kill. But it's begun to knock him. He doesn't eat or sleep or rest. He's crazy aboot you."

Ina had bowed as if under a storm and she leaned against the juniper, quivering under a blow of combined torture and bliss.

"Ina, forgive me for burstin' right out with this," Nevada went on, touching her head with gentle hand. "But we've got to do somethin'. Listen. Hettie told me she thought you loved Ben. That you'd loved him when you were kids an' would never change. She only thought so, but now I know. I've learned it heah. You don't deny it, do you?"

"No, it's — miserable — terrible — truth," faltered Ina.

"It may shore be terrible, but not miserable," he went on in a changed voice, swift, vibrant with strong feeling. "Ben an' you will shore get to each other now. I'm goin' to kill this heah Less Setter —"

"Nevada!" cried Ina, sitting up in frantic haste. "What are you saying? That'd be horrible."

"Killin' Setter may be the only way to save you two. He's no stranger to me, Ina. We crossed in Nevada. He's aboot the most powerful man wherever he goes. Shore he might step in his rope over heah, in which case, mebbe, there'd be no call to throw a gun on him."

"Surely Setter will ruin himself," protested Ina.

"No doubt in the world aboot that," agreed Nevada, "but if he's let alone he'll shore drag us to destruction with him. An' we're concerned with his dealin's right heah an' now . . . Ina, if I'd been at Forlorn River when Setter rode in there —"

"Hettie Ide's heart would have been broken," interrupted Ina, ruthlessly.

That retort pierced Nevada's armor and made him hang his head. But soon he ponderingly shook it erect.

"No, for two reasons. Reckon if she didn't care for me, then it shore wouldn't make no difference what I did. Seemed, if she — Lord it takes nerve even to suppose this — if she loved me — she'd not give me up for killin' Setter. An' I'll tell you, Ina, it'll turn out, an' you'll see that the law an' the people will soon forget Setter. When they find him out they'll welcome some fellow handy with guns. An' that's me, though it's not known in these parts. Setter knows, though. He'd have to get advantage before he'd throw a gun on me as he did on Ben."

"He meant to kill Ben, to get rid of him that way?" asked Ina, shuddering.

"Huh! He shore did, an' it was my tough luck that I wasn't there," rejoined Nevada, shortly. "But we've drifted 'way off the trail. I'm afraid of somethin' worse than fightin' for Ben. He might dodge bullets, but he cain't dodge love. An' love's got him roped, hobbled, down. That's why I came over heah. To tell you what Ben wouldn't unless you surprise or tear it out of him."

Ina blindly held up a hand to this persuasive friend. "Tell him to come to me," she whispered.

"I cain't tell him that," replied Nevada. "Shore he'd know I'd been to you. Find some other way. Reckon it'll take more than Marvie to fetch him. When Hettie

179

comes out, please let me see her. Tell her I love her. Tell her I'll stick to Ben to my last gasp. Tell her we're goin' straight, an' that Less Setter an' all hell cain't make us go crooked. Things are workin' to a climax, Ina, an' it'll shore come by fall. Ben an' I have a trump card to play. This Indian pard of Ben's — Modoc we call him — is aboot the slickest scout an' tracker I ever seen. We're goin' to trail these cattle thieves an' ketch them red-handed. You can tell Hettie. What will your dad an' Ben's dad say *then*? . . . Ina, we're fightin' mad an' we cain't be licked. But you — only you can brace Ben up. Will you?"

"Oh, Nevada, how good you are! Bless you!" whispered Ina, clinging to him. "I will — I will. I'll see Ben if I have to ride to Forlorn River."

CHAPTER
TEN

Ben Ide found himself exceedingly strained and nervous these days, and things that formerly he might have at least endured, now often threw him off balance.

This morning Nevada had mysteriously ridden off somewhere without a word to either him or Modoc. Nevada had a habit of doing that. Ben would not have been upset about it had they been anywhere except at Forlorn River. The Blaine summer camp across the lake had been a catastrophe for Ben.

"Modoc, did he ride off for that camp?" asked Ben, of his Indian helper.

"Me find no track on trail. Look other side lake. No savvy Nevada. He do what he want."

"By golly! you said a lot," growled Ben. "Go hunt all around, Modoc. Find his tracks."

The Indian returned presently to report that he had found Nevada's horse tracks across the river, headed down the west side of the lake.

"That's darned funny. Could he be headed for Hammell?"

"His horse lope. Nevada no start long ride fast."

"Sure he wouldn't. He doesn't care a damn for me, but he loves his horse. Any horse . . . Modoc, he was going to the Blaine camp, but not by the trail."

The Indian corroborated that statement by a vigorous nod of head.

"Son-of-a-gun!" soliloquized Ben, broodingly. "Nevada's going to kill that Less Setter, sure as I'm a miserable wretch. I've raved and cussed, all to no good."

Whereupon he grew exceedingly harassed by worry and dread.

"Somebody on trail," spoke up the Indian, pointing with slow gesture.

Ben espied a cloud of dust far along the left side of the lake, and under it the dark figure of horse and rider. Ben's hope that it might be Nevada was short lived. He went indoors to get his field glass.

With this aid he made out the rider to be a boy on a pony, which fact relieved Ben of anxiety and annoyance. Still, the visitor might be a messenger from Camp Blaine. Ben had to abide the wait in patience, something he was short of these last trying weeks. Before the rider grew close enough for possible recognition or scrutiny he passed out of sight under the ridge of Ben's high promontory. When he reappeared, on the Forlorn River side, Ben recognized the bright freckled face of Marvie Blaine.

"Howdy, Ben!" the lad greeted him, radiantly. "Didn't have no chance to be with you that other day, so I come again."

"Well, boy pard, get down and come in," replied Ben, delighted beyond expression. "I hardly saw you that day. But you didn't lack amusement, did you?"

"I sure didn't," returned Marvie, meaningly, as he fixed Ben with the rapt eyes of hero worship.

182

"Marvie, I'm awful glad to see you. It was darn good of you to come. And I'm going to give you a wild pony for thinking of poor lonely Ben Ide. He's only a colt and but half broke. It'll be best for me to keep him awhile, till you can ride him."

"Ben Ide, you're a-goin' to give me a wild colt?" shouted the lad.

"Sure am," smiled Ben.

"Whoopee! When all I was wantin' was to see you an' go fishin'. Gee! the luck!"

"Well, climb off that cayuse and come see some good horses. Aha! I see you've brought your jointed fish pole. Let's see . . . It's not very strong, Marvie, not for *my* trout."

"Gee!" exclaimed Marvie, with eyes growing round.

"Modoc, you take care of Marvie's pony," said Ben, sitting down on the porch to examine the lad's fishing tackle. "I use a cut pole, Marvie, and as long a line as I can cast. Good and strong. These trout are husky. If you hook a big one he'll bust this outfit all to flinders. Do you want to risk it?"

"Sure. I told Dad it was no good. Got it for Christmas. If I bust it let me use yours."

"Rig it up now your way. Nothing pleases any fisherman so much as his own ways . . . Say, Marvie, did you meet my pardner, Nevada? He rode over that way this morning."

"Didn't meet no one," replied the lad. "An' you bet I had my eyes peeled."

"Well, he was on the other side of the lake from you. Thought maybe he might have cut across round the dry lake bed."

183

"Nevada? Was he goin' to our ranch?" queried Marvie, with interest.

"Modoc thinks so, and I guess I do, too."

"What for? I hear the cowboys talkin' about you an' Nevada. They like you both a heap, since you licked Setter. They're more curious about Nevada, though. He's a stranger. Why'd he go to Dad's ranch?"

"I'm not sure, Marvie, but I'm some worried," replied Ben, looking the lad squarely in the eye. It was a handsome boyish face, with features enough like his sister's to make Ben look and look with possession-taking gladness. Marvie struck him as being a bright youngster, longing for a life just like his and Nevada's, at a most impressionable age, and perhaps not getting along well with his father. Ben sympathized with Marvie. Then it seemed to Ben that he was idealized by this lad. He felt a melancholy happiness. It brought him closer to Ina. Likewise it made him slow to judge how best to meet Marvie's advances.

"Huh! I'll bet you're worried for fear Nevada will do worse to Setter than you did," declared Marvie.

"Son, you're not far wrong," replied Ben, smiling at the boy's acumen.

"Bill Sneed said he'd bet Nevada would never have throwed Setter's gun away. He'd have throwed it *on* him . . . Well, Ben, you needn't worry about Setter gettin' it today, or very soon, 'cause he went to Klamath to get the teeth you knocked out put back."

"Say, I must have bunged Setter up some," laughed Ben. "I was pretty mad. Just had sense enough to fight and not shoot."

184

"Let's talk of someone else. Setter makes me sick. I found out yesterday that his bein' kind to me, givin' me things, lendin' me guns an' horses, was just to get me out of the way."

"Out of the way?" echoed Ben, with a sudden start.

"Sure. He's after Ina," declared the lad, vehemently nodding his head. "He's got Dad buffaloed, so the cowboys say, an' now —"

"After Ina!" flashed Ben, suddenly on fire. "No, Marvie, not that — that —"

"Sure as you're born," said Marvie, interrupting in turn. "It's doggone sickenin'. I wish I was bigger an' older . . . Ben, you needn't look like you was at a funeral. Ina hates Setter. Hates him like my dog hates a skunk. It won't make no difference what Dad says or wants. Look what she did to McAdam. That dude stood in with Dad an' thought he was engaged to Ina. Was he? I should snigger not. Do you know what she did — when he got gay tryin' to kiss her? Ma saw the whole thing. She told me, 'cause she didn't ever want me to be like McAdam. What do you think of that, Ben?"

"Hurry — what'd Ina do?" burst out Ben.

"Huh! She just slapped the stuffin's out of him an' said she'd never speak to him again. He went home red-headed. An' Dad had to hustle off to Klamath to pay money he'd borrowed from old McAdam. I heard Dad tell Ina that an' a lot of other guff. Ina swore she'd go to work waitin' on table in the Hammell hotel before she'd marry McAdam. That's what kind of a sister I got."

"You — don't — say!" replied Ben, in smothered voice, bending over Marvie's tackle. But this attempt to hide his ridiculous state of sudden ecstasy availed him nothing.

"Ben, you're fond of Ina," went on Marvie, seriously now, with the accent of a big-brother guardian.

Looking up, Ben realized that the truth was best, whatever it cost him.

"Boy, I should smile," he replied, but he did not smile.

"Had a hunch you was," continued Marvie, with satisfaction. "Got it that night we met Hettie."

"Yes?" inquired Ben, encouragingly. He wanted to hug the lad. How Marvie reminded him of Ina when she was a youngster.

"Ben, does she know you're fond of her?"

"Why, Marvie — I'm not sure — reckon she doesn't," answered Ben, helplessly.

"It'd be a darn good thing for her to know, Ben," went on the lad, earnestly. "Ina has a rotten time of it, tryin' to brighten Mother up an' keepin' Dad from drivin' her. Say, them Sundays when McAdam was with us all day — gee! they were tough. But he's gone now."

"Marvie, you're old enough to know that I can't go to your sister and — and tell her such a thing," said Ben, striving to be clear. "My dad threw me out. People believe I deserved it — that I'm a no-good horse hunter — and worse."

"Scat!" exploded Marvie, in fine scorn. "Ina has heard all that. I'll bet it's only made her like you more."

186

"Ah, son, you must be wrong," murmured Ben, hanging his head.

"If I'm wrong she acts darn funny. But I've a hunch I'm right," returned Marvie, stoutly. "Would Ina send you messages if she didn't like you?"

"Messages! By whom?" cried Ben, jerking up quickly.

"By nobody but me, Ben Ide," declared Marvie, triumphantly.

"You little son-of-a-gun! You've been here hours without telling me? Hurry, or I'll be Injun giver and take back your wild horse."

"Huh! Thought that would fetch you," said the lad, with a grin. "Well, I'm sorry I got your hopes way up, 'cause Ina didn't really give me much to tell you. She sent her regards —"

"Yes?" cried Ben, eagerly, as Marvie paused to watch impressions.

"An' was glad about your wild-horse catch."

"Yes?" not so eagerly or hopefully.

"An' about your fight with Setter an' the way he looked when he got back she said to tell you —"

Ben could scarcely keep from choking this tantalizing young rascal.

"What?" he demanded.

"She was tickled to death!"

Ben drew a deep breath and glared suspiciously at Marvie. Could this clear-eyed boy be guilty of terrible duplicity?

"Son, if you could lie to me about such a thing! . . . No horse, no fishing, no pardnership with me!"

"Ben, I'm tellin' you true," protested Marvie, with sudden haste. "Ina said that, an' what's more she said somethin' you'll like a darn sight better."

"Then for Heaven's sake, tell me!" said Ben, suddenly weak.

"She said, 'Tell Ben to come over.' . . . Now, Ben Ide, what've you got to say?"

"I'm beyond words, son," rejoined Ben, experiencing the swell of an emotion that would render his reply true. Then for the lack of speech he dragged the boy with him, out of the yard, beyond the barns and corral, to the pasture. There seemed to be a thrumming song in his ears; the sky shone a deeper, intenser blue than ever he had seen; the dry fragrance in his face, a message, a symbol of life; the vast pillared clouds, pearly and golden, gorgeous thrones of gods, hung motionless from the dome of the heavens. He could not explain the transformation in the aspect in nature, nor the ringing, singing self within himself.

He shared Marvie's delight in the whistling, racing wild horses; in the black-and-white pinto colt some day to be the boy's very own.

"Come, son, don't hang here all day," said Ben, finally dragging Marvie off the fence. "We'll likely find some grasshoppers along the river. I like them best as bait for trout. But they're getting scarce. This dry spell has killed them off."

"I've got fishin' worms, if we can't get grasshoppers," replied Marvie, with the confidence of a fisherman.

"Where on earth did you get worms at this dry time?" asked Ben, in surprise.

"Got them at home, in one of the ditches," replied Marvie. "Brought them along with me, packed in wet moss, an' feed them milk. See — look." And Marvie produced a wide flat tin box, full of long fat shiny angleworms.

"Say, son, these big rainbows will break their necks after those worms," exclaimed Ben, enthusiastically. "But let's catch some grasshoppers, anyhow."

They had a hot, merry, exciting chase through the dead grass, which ended in their exhaustion and the capture of a few great yellow grasshoppers.

"Gee! they're dandy big ones. Regular tobacco-chewers," declared Marvie, with the eye of a connoisseur. "I wish Ina had come with me."

Forthwith Ben led his visitor along the river bank to the break where willows and cattails and tule flags were green, in vivid contrast with the sun-seared sage. The river was like a pond thick with green scum, but between the high bank and a jutting cape covered with willow lay a deep swirling pool of clear water. Marvie showed amaze and delight. He heard the babble and tinkle of Ben's priceless spring as it burst from under the bank. This pool was not very wide, though fairly long, extending for some rods before the clear running current slowed and disappeared in the yellow stagnant water of the river. Swamp blackbirds and green-backed frogs and basking turtles were much in evidence.

"Now watch," said Ben, and taking one of the grasshoppers he threw it down into the pool.

Flashes of gold, pink, silver elicited a yell from the lad. Trout appeared swift as light. There was a smash on the surface of the pool, and a trout as long as Marvie's arm beat the others to that grasshopper.

"Oh, Lord!" whooped Marvie, and he sat down as if his legs had buckled under him.

"He was a big one, about eight pounds, but there're some that'll make him a baby," announced Ben. "Say good-bye to your Christmas-gift tackle."

Marvie seemed obsessed with the mystery and beauty in the depths of that pool. They were fascinating, and Ben recalled the days when he was Marvie's age.

"I told Ina I could bank on Ben," Marvie soliloquized impressively. He was manifestly making a most momentous decision.

"Come on," called Ben, gayly, rousing the lad.

"We'll climb down up here, and get on that point. It's the best place, though when I want a trout to eat I just yank him up from here."

"Yank one of those big ones?" queried Marvie, incredulously.

"No, not the biggest," laughed Ben. "But the small ones, say one to two pounds, sometimes more. They're best to eat."

It was necessary for Ben to help Marvie down the high bank and out to the end of the cape. The footing was precarious, and though Marvie was valiant he did not possess length of limb to conquer certain steps without help. The point, however, afforded a comfortable and safe place from which to fish. Ben did not miss the trembling of Marvie's hands or the startled, dreamy, expectant light of his eyes.

"Try a worm bait first," advised Ben. "Then maybe you'll catch a few before some big lunker takes that outfit away from you."

Marvie seemed speechless, but he gazed up at Ben with a fleeting glance of ecstasy. Then he baited his hook and cast it out. Scarcely had it time to sink before a trout seized it and ran. Marvie jerked so hard that he pulled the trout unceremoniously out, to drop flopping on the bank, where he and Ben frantically pounced upon it. Ben secured it, a nice fat rainbow about a pound in weight.

"Gee!" whispered Marvie, very low. "Biggest trout I ever caught!"

"Son, he's a baby," said Ben, stringing the fish on a willow. "His great-great-great-great-granddad is in that hole."

"Oh, why wouldn't Ina come!" cried Marvie, poignantly.

"Wouldn't she?" asked Ben, in apparent innocence.

"No. Girls are queer. Said she couldn't run after you. I'll get her to come yet . . . Now, Ben, here goes again. You've got me scared stiff. But, oh, this's heaven."

Marvie found himself at once attached to another trout, not much larger than the first, but one that got his head and gave the lad some trouble and immense excitement before it was landed.

On a third cast a fish took the wiggling worm right off the surface, exciting Marvie to the extent that he jerked too soon and missed.

"Let them have it a little bit," advised Ben. "You're too nervous. Take time, son, take time."

"Say, if you felt like me!"

Then, in quick succession, Marvie captured three more rainbows, averaging slightly heavier than the others.

"Don't wake me up, Ben. Let me go on dreamin'. What a place to fish! This darned hole is deep an' full of hungry trout . . . Now we'll see . . . There! Wow, Ben — I can't budge him! Am I snagged on a log? Oh no! No!"

"That's a big loggy one," shouted Ben. "Play him easy, Marvie. Don't lift so hard . . . See, you pulled the hook out."

"What'd I do then?" asked Marvie, after a long gaze of realization.

"Too strong. You should have let him run round and round till he was tired. Don't look sick, boy. There's a wagon load of trout like him in that hole. Put on a big grasshopper now, and cast over here under the willows in the shade."

Marvie did as he was bidden, carefully, earnestly, with bated breath and an air of certain calamity. His education had begun. He realized something electrifying and terrible was about to happen.

Ben saw a huge rainbow gleam out of the black depths and smash a hole in the surface on his rush for the grasshopper. He was so savage and fast that he hooked himself. Out he leaped, two feet long, broad and rainbow-hued, glistening in the sun. Sight of him absolutely paralyzed Marvie. He could not lower the rod, and when the big fish surged down the pool there came a snap. The rod broke in the middle. Marvie presented a spectacle for fishermen. The trout again leaped, headed away. Marvie's line whizzed off the reel, overrun, tangled. Crack! The reel came off the rod and fell, to bound and dart like a live thing as the big trout dashed on with more line. Then before Ben could move the reel bounced up from the ground, caught against the guides on Marvie's nodding rod. The line whizzed harder, rasped and twanged. Down jerked the rod. Marvie staggered forward in bewilderment, made a misstep and plunged into the water. Ben leaped to catch his legs and haul him out.

Blinking, disheveled, dazed, the lad got his equilibrium, and gazing from the broken rod and limp line up into Ben's convulsed face he sputtered: "What — come — off?"

"Haw! Haw! Haw!" exploded Ben, shaking with mirth. "Guess the trout come off. And the reel — and line — and you!"

"He got away . . . Was that a fish?" murmured Marvie, wide eyes on the pool.

"Son, he sure was a whopper. Twelve or fifteen pounds, I'd say. He wrecked your outfit, and he'd have drowned you but for me. Didn't you see him?"

"I saw somethin' with jaws open. Must have been a flyin' alligator," returned Marvie, his gaze transfixed on the quiet pool.

"Well, you've got a nice mess for supper. Five, and all together they're heavy enough to lug. Next time fetch a strong outfit or use mine."

The words "next time" recalled the lad to the fact that, dolorous as was the hour, life was still worth living, and future fishing called. By the time Ben got him back to the cabin he was almost cheerful again. Modoc served them with something to eat, and after they had talked awhile it was time for Marvie to leave.

"Ben, I'd rather live here with you than in our big house on Tule Lake," he said, from the back of his pony. "An' I'll bet Ina would, too."

"Pard, it's different with girls — about homes," returned Ben, trying to be natural when he wanted to stand on his head. "We fellows like the open range, you know, horses and outdoor work, hunting, and sure, fishing. But girls like comfort, luxury, people, amusement, and all that."

"Mebbe, some of them. But not Ina. She loves all those things you said, same as you an' me. Besides, she's crazy about you, Ben. Aw, she's a girl an' she can't fool me. I know darned well she is."

He rode away, leaving Ben standing there as still and staring as if lightning had struck him. And that mental fixity, if not the physical, abided with him in the cabin, where he lay on his couch for a long while, staring straight through the rough shingles of the roof. He roused, at length, to the ring of iron-shod hoofs on stone. Going outside, he espied Nevada riding up. He had forgotten Nevada completely, and at sudden sight of him the former anxiety and dread returned tenfold.

"Where you been?" he queried, shortly, as Nevada rode up.

"Howdy, Ben! Heah you had company?" countered Nevada, nonchalantly. He seemed more than usually his virile, cool, and lazy self. Ben groaned inwardly.

194

How he loved this lithe, long-haired, dark-skinned rider!

"Where you been?" repeated Ben, impatiently.

"Me? Oh, I been ridin' around over the lone countree," returned Nevada, as he stepped out of his saddle.

"Where the hell have you been?" shouted Ben. His partner was most irritating to contemplate when he wore this gay, cool, aloof mask.

Nevada turned from uncinching his saddle and gazed with mild amaze at his friend.

"Ben, you're shore powerful curious aboot me."

"Yes, and I'm quite capable of licking you good," declared Ben.

"Wal, reckon you've got the ornery cross-grained disposition too, but, Ben, old pard, you ain't big an' strong enough to lick me."

"For Heaven's sake, don't torment me now with your cowboy gags. I want to know. Did you ride off to find Less Setter?"

"Ben, it wouldn't have done no good if I had. Setter's away gettin' new teeth, so I heah."

"Answer me, did you ride out to meet him? If you went without a word to me, I'm going to take it pretty hard."

"Wal, pard, fact is, if I gotta be honest, I never thought of that pop-eyed rustler boss."

"Nevada, you wouldn't lie to me?"

"No, 'cept for your own good."

"You called Setter rustler boss. Nevada, isn't that just some more cowboy talk?"

"Shore, an' this heah cowboy is talkin' straight. Some day, Ben, if you live out the summer, you'll have the fun of heahing me call Setter that to his damn lyin' face."

In the speech Nevada passed from jest to earnest.

"But you rode over to the new Blaine ranch?" went on Ben, hoping to worm at least something from this exasperating Nevadian.

"Ben, you'd shore make a great scout, figgerin' things so correct."

"What'd you go for?"

"We had a day off, didn't we? An' I had a fresh hoss. I wanted to look over our neighbors. I had a hunch aboot Hart Blaine, an' as usual I was right. He meant to make that ranch the first of a string of ranches, includin' Forlorn River, all the way to his holdin's round Silver Meadow, an' he'll play hob doin' it."

"Who'd you see?" hurried Ben, irresistibly driven.

"Wal, Marvie Blaine for one. Met up with him out heah on the trail. Near talked my head off aboot fish an' hosses. Nice kid, Ben. He shore thinks a heap of you."

"Yes — who else?"

"Wal, I was lucky. Findin' out Setter an' Blaine were away, I scraped acquaintance with some of the hands. Cowboys all gone. Ben, what do you make of Blaine ridin' over heah south of us, with chuck wagon an' outfit?"

"Blaine is just branching out — grasping sounds better."

"Ahuh. Wal, your cute little pardner didn't talk to them hands for nothin'. Blaine took a wagon besides

196

the chuck wagon, an' it was full of tools — shovels, picks, axes, a plow an' scraper, an' some cans of giant powder."

"Well! That means road work."

"I'll hit their trail tomorrow an' see what he's up to. It fussed me some, but after thinkin' aboot it I come to the conclusion roads are shore goin' to make our property twice as valuable."

"That's so. I forgot we owned four ranches . . . Well, who else did you see?"

"Reckon nobody else . . . Oh yes, I did, too. Saw your girl, Ina Blaine. I knowed her, Ben, quick as you could snap your quirt."

"You saw her!" ejaculated Ben, in great excitement. "But not to *speak* to?"

"Shore did, a little bit. She was darned sweet to me. An' if I wasn't plumb crazy aboot Hettie I'd take Ina away from you. She's as pretty as — as — oh, Lord! I never seen anyone or anything as pretty. No wonder you cain't sleep or eat or rest or work, or even be decent to your pard. A girl plays hell with a man, doesn't she?"

Ben stared in impotent agitation at his loquacious and imperturbable friend. Behind all Nevada said and did there hid inscrutable mystery. Ben had to content himself with what little grist he could grind from Nevada's utterances. But recalling the past, and puzzling over former complex situations, he realized that Nevada's motives, strange and obscure as they seemed at first, always turned out to be clear as crystal

197

and pure as gold. Ben had to face the monumental truth that Nevada seemed to think only of him.

"Nevada," he asked, in grave finality, "did you talk with Ina alone?"

"Shore I did, a little."

"About me?"

"Why, of course! You don't suppose the girl would want to heah aboot me? An' you don't suppose I'd lose any chance to boost you?"

"But you and Hettie, and Marvie, too, make her think I'm a million times better than I am," groaned Ben.

"Say, how'n'ell could we do that?" flashed Nevada, showing, as often, how easy it was to strike fire from him.

"I'll bet you-all are driving Ina crazy about me — same as you're driving me crazy about her."

"Nix. You, anyhow, was crazy before. Ben, what you an' Ina need to do is to get off some lonesome place in the moonlight —"

"Hold your tongue," shouted Ben, frantically. "Can't you understand it wouldn't be square or honorable for me to disgrace Ina? I'm an outcast. And they're liable to make me an outlaw yet."

"Shore. Same as your pard, huh?" exclaimed Nevada, bitterly.

"Oh, say, my friend! Don't misconstrue my words. That talk about you never influenced me. I don't care a damn what you were, Nevada. It's what you are to me — and that's the finest and noblest of pards."

"Thanks," replied Nevada, lifting his head. "Shore I take it I am your pard, though I shy on the noble stuff. An' that's why I gotta talk. I was sayin' you an' Ina need to get off in the moonshine somewhere, an' run into each other's arms, an' stick there for some hours more or less — anyhow till you discover you cain't live without each other."

CHAPTER
ELEVEN

The second night after Nevada's return, Ben, sitting up late watching the moon, yielding to dreams hopeless of fulfilment, heard a faint distant clip-clop of trotting horses on the hard trail down by the lake.

Riders were approaching from the direction of the Blaine ranch. As the hour was not one to expect visitors or travelers, Ben rather anxiously picked up his rifle and hurried out through the trees to the edge of the bluff. The night was almost as light as day. A full moon soared high in the rich dark sky; the vast basin appeared boundless, with glistening white bands of sand surrounding the silver lake.

Two horsemen were approaching. They did not, however, keep to the trail that turned the corner of the bluff and climbed the west side to Ben's cabin. Ben decided that he would intercept them, and gliding down the slope he soon reached the zone of huge rocks that had rolled from above. He stole cautiously along, keeping in the shadows, wonderingly curious. Who were these riders? Why did they leave the trail, apparently to approach his cabin from the rear? The sound of hoofbeats gave place to footsteps, light and pattering on the gravelly ground. Presently Ben saw a slight dark form come from out of shadow into the moonlight. A boy! It was no other than Marvie Blaine.

Ben's suppressed excitement changed to amaze and relief. He strode out into the moonlight.

"Hands up!" he ordered, in deep gruff voice.

Marvie jumped like a startled jack rabbit, and his hands shot up above his head.

"Aw — mister!" gasped Marvie. "I — I — won't hurt — you!"

"Meet rustler Bill Hall. Money or your life!" replied Ben, fiercely.

The lad made a grotesque figure, shaking now with horror, his face white in the moonlight.

"Only got — two dollars," he gulped, hoarsely.

Ben lowered the rifle. It would have been fun to continue the deception. But Ben was strung like a whipcord. Who was Marvie's companion?

"Son, you can keep your two dollars," said Ben. "What're you doing out here? *Who* is with you?"

Marvie nearly collapsed. "Aw! . . . Aw! . . . It's Ben! Omilord! how you — scared me! . . . You oughtn't h'done that. I might have shot you."

"Who's with you?" demanded Ben, sternly ignoring Marvie's remarkable exclamation.

"Ina, of course," replied the lad.

"*Your sister?*" whispered Ben.

"Sure. Who'd you think? Ketch me guidin' any cowboys over here after night. An' say, Ben, Ina hired me to fetch her. What you think of that? Sure I'd have fetched her for nothin', but I saw what a chance I had.

Gave me some things she had I wanted bad. An' five dollars for new fishin' tackle!"

"You young scoundrel! Letting her come way out here, alone, in wild country like this!"

"Lettin' her? Say, you wake up," retorted Marvie. "She made me come. Swore she'd come alone if I didn't."

"But — what on earth for?" queried Ben, now in amaze and bewilderment.

"She wanted to see you," replied Marvie. "I've been tryin' to coax her to come over. But, no, she wouldn't. Somethin' changed her mind, Ben. Mebbe 'cause of the two strangers who rode in this mornin'. I didn't like their looks, blusterin' an' pryin' around."

"Where is Ina?" asked Ben.

"Down here sittin' on a rock. She didn't want to go up to your cabin an' be seen by anybody else. So I picked out this place. It was like apple pie, gettin' over here. Cowboys all away. Dad an' Setter away. I got my pony an' Ina's horse an' kept them in the corral. Soon as Ma went to bed we sneaked off, round the ranch, an' hit the trail below. Bet we made the trip in an hour . . . There's Ina. I'll take the horses over here a ways. An', Ben, you needn't be in a hurry."

Ben espied the horses first and then the girl's slender form, dark against the moon-blanched background. His pulses throbbed so violently that they pained him. She was sitting on a high flat rock, and as his step crunched on the ground she turned. Next moment he was gazing up into her face, meeting her outstretched hands. And that moment seemed the sweetest and most compelling of his life.

"Good evening, Ben . . . He found you quickly. I'm glad to see you."

"You shouldn't have come," he returned, breathing deeply.

"Oh, it was easy. Marvie's a brick. You can ride home with us. Dad will never know. So what's there to scold about?"

"You might — be caught," he replied, unsteadily, aware that she was giving his face a scrutiny not in keeping with her light words. Did he read aright her wonderful penetrating eyes, black as the shadows and as mysteriously full?

"I don't think I'd care so much if I were . . . Ben, you're thin, haggard." She withdrew a hand from his and touched his cheek. "Are you quite well?"

"Well? Of course I'm well. Except just now I feel I could drop at your feet . . . I've had six weeks' very hard work, Ina. I've lost weight."

"I don't know whether or not to believe you," she considered sweetly, gravely studying him.

"Did that fool Nevada say I was sick?"

She gave a slight start. "Then he told you he saw me?"

"Yes, of course."

"No. Nevada didn't say you were sick — exactly. He —"

"I don't want to know what he said," interrupted Ben, hastily. He must keep his head. He must impress upon her the madness of risking her father's anger, as well as the peril of such a lonely ride at night. But it was not easy to think of words. She sat bareheaded, her knees level with his shoulder, and she leaned a little down. The cool wind blew strands of her hair across her brow. She was lovely. She seemed different, somehow. He felt something he could not understand.

"I like Nevada," she said. "And if you consent I'll let him come to see Hettie when she visits me."

"You're having Hettie? That's good of you, Ina," he replied, in a warmth of surprise and pleasure.

"Don't thank me. Hettie's a dear girl. You couldn't blame any man for loving her."

"So Nevada loves my sister. I suspected it, even though I thought his talk just cowboy rant. Ina, he has told you."

"Ben, I didn't *say* so," she replied, archly.

"You're strange to me. You take my breath," he returned. "What chance on earth have I against *you*, let alone Nevada and my sister and Marvie, all in league to — to — ?"

"Make my dad and your dad and everybody see you as the man we know you to be," she interposed, with soft directness.

It dawned upon Ben that she was as she had been the last few moments when they were together at Hettie's — only now more formidable by reason of a strange power of confidence, of knowledge that he could not share. He divined it. And she did not make the slightest move to release the hand he held. Whereupon he tried to release it himself, but as he tried, a slight clinging pressure of warm palm irresistibly drove him to grasp it again, closer, tighter.

"Ben, listen," she began, seriously. "I had a good reason to risk coming over here. And if I chose to lie to you I'd let you think that was my excuse. But even before I knew what I found out today, I was going to come, anyway."

"Ina!"

"Yes. Terrible of me. Wouldn't Dad rave? And Mr. Pop-eyes, as Marvie calls Setter. Oh, I shudder to contemplate his jealous rage! But listen, Ben . . . This morning two strangers rode in to the ranch and made themselves at home. I could have avoided them, of course, as our camp is located quite a little way from the ranch. But naturally I was curious, and in the absence of Dad and Mr. Setter and the cowboys, I took advantage of the opportunity to find out who they were. So I went over to the ranch and asked them who they were and what they wanted. They were rather evasive and, well, smart-alec, at first. One was a big heavy man, ruddy-faced and pretty loud. His name was Judd. The other was tall and lanky, with thin face and big nose. He wore a sombrero that hid his eyes, but he didn't inspire me with confidence. His name was Walker. They hailed from Redlands. Well, I asked them the second time, bluntly, what their business was there. Then the big fellow exhibited a silver shield and said he was a sheriff from Redlands. Walker was his deputy. They had come at urgent call from Setter, who claimed to represent the Hammell Stock Association. They had come prepared to arrest certain persons against whom

Setter would produce evidence and charges. That's all I could get out of them. But it was enough to worry me sick. So I got Marvie to come over with me."

"Certain persons must mean Nevada and Modoc and myself," muttered Ben, darkly, in response to the sudden shift of his emotions.

"Of course it means you. But I don't believe Dad had a thing to do with their coming. I tell you, Ben, he has something to think about. He's so deeply mixed up that he doesn't know whether he is riding or walking, as Bill Sneed said . . . Now, Ben, these officers can't arrest you just on Setter's say-so, can they?"

"They wouldn't if they're straight. But the worst of it is that Setter may have hatched up some trick, or found some charge against Modoc, or particularly accused Nevada of something he'd done long ago, before he came here. They could twist it around to involve me. Frankly, Ina, I don't like the looks of it."

"But, Ben, if you're prepared? Forewarned is forearmed, you know," said Ina, in anxious earnestness.

"Ina, it was like you to hurry over here to warn me. Thanks —"

"I told you I didn't come for that reason," she interrupted. "I was coming, anyway."

"Oh, you were — and why?" replied Ben, constrainedly. The change in the direction of his thoughts had helped him toward self-control. But he had not let go of her hand! It seemed that he stood trembling on the edge of a precipice.

"One thing at a time, Benjamin," she retorted. "Or business before — pleasure." She laughed in a way that made him wonder if he heard aright. "What are you going to do?"

"Why, Ina, we can't do anything but go on with our work," replied Ben, in perplexity. "Whatever is bound to happen will happen. I wouldn't mind being arrested. They couldn't prove me guilty of any wrong. But I'd hate the disgrace on account of Mother and Hettie."

"And me!" she added, swiftly.

Ben dared not let his consciousness face that extraordinary implication. His mind seemed about to fly to pieces.

"For myself — I — I wouldn't mind arrest," he went on, hurriedly. "But these sheriffs can't arrest Nevada. If they try it he'll hold them up and escape — or he'll kill them. Oh, he's quicker than eyesight with a gun. Sometimes he throws a gun on me, just for fun. But, Ina, I don't laugh. I grow cold all over. For I love that fellow and I feel that he's been something terrible — somewhere."

"Nevada loves you, Ben," returned Ina, softly. "He will do whatever you ask."

"Yes, he would, mostly. I'll never forget when he rode in on me four years ago. He was wounded, starved, exhausted. I took him in and kept him — nursed him back to health. He stayed with me and we've grown like brothers. But he's never told me who he is."

"It was a fine thing for you to do. And your friendship is beautiful. Surely you can keep him from spilling blood."

"I don't know, but I feel I can't. Not if these officers try to arrest me. And when Nevada finds out Setter got them here —" Ben left off words to whistle.

It was not possible for him to keep his eyes averted all the time. Involuntarily they came back to Ina's face. How sweet — how lovely! She was gazing down upon him. Suddenly Ben had to fight a terrible longing to take her in his arms. He released that warm clinging hand — then instantly had a wild desire to take it back again.

"Ben, did Marvie tell you how this man Setter has hounded me?" queried Ina, as if driven to speak.

"What!" ejaculated Ben, flaring up. "Marvie talked a lot about Setter. But Marvie hates him, and he's only a crazy kid. I didn't take him seriously."

"Oh, I shouldn't have let that slip out," cried the girl, regretfully. "I'm so contrary these days. I don't know myself, Ben. Never mind what I said about Setter."

"You *tell* me," he rejoined, passionately, seizing her arms.

The suddenness and violence of his action startled her. It was only his hold upon her that kept her from falling over in his arms. He realized this and seemed staggered. What avail were resolution and honor? Again the possibility that she might really love him waved over him.

"Ben," she whispered, "don't look like that. I haven't done anything I — you'd —"

"You said Setter had hounded you," interrupted Ben. "How? Tell me. What did you mean?"

208

"Setter's a bad man," hurriedly answered Ina. "He made bold love to me. He hunted me out when I was alone. If I saw him in time I'd run. But when he waylaid me — I — I — Ben, I had to fight."

"My God!" cried Ben, furiously. "Your father let that snake in the house? Gave him opportunities to force himself upon you! That damned money-grubbing cow-hand! I'll horsewhip him."

"Hush such talk!" exclaimed Ina, with emotion. "Can't I tell you things without your flying off the handle? That was weeks ago. Setter has changed his tactics. Now it looks as if he meant to force Dad to marry me to him."

"Ina Blaine!" burst out Ben, hoarsely, in fury and despair. "I'll kill Setter myself!"

"Ben!" she whispered. Her face grew ashen pale in the moonlight. Her eyes seemed to expand and fix in black staring horror. "Oh — what have — I done?" and freeing her arms she clasped them round his neck.

"For God's — sake, Ina! What do you mean?"

"If you killed Setter — they — they would hang you. Then I'd die," she cried, in anguish.

"I won't kill him. I won't even meet him," said Ben, in wild haste to relieve her terror. His heart seemed about to burst.

"Promise me — then?" she begged.

"I promise — anything," he returned, weakening.

She released him, very slowly withdrawing her arms from about his neck. Then as terrible realization dawned upon Ben she smiled, and that was too much for him. Bowing his face upon her knees, he almost sobbed out:

"I knew — I shouldn't see you. What a fool I am! It's all come out . . . I adore you — worship you . . . And it's killing me."

He felt her stroking his head with gentle caressing hand, under which he quivered.

"Well, you needn't let *that* kill you," she said, with something sweetly deep and rich in her voice. "For I love you, Ben!"

"No — no!" he whispered, in mingled despair and ecstasy.

"Oh, but I do! Love you as I did when we were kid sweethearts . . . And more — with the love of a woman who'll stand by you through everything."

Ben lifted his head. His tears seemed burned away. Surrender was upon him. A perilously sweet and glorious joy consumed him like a flame.

"You wonderful girl!" he whispered, huskily.

"Why don't you say, '*my* wonderful girl'?" she whispered in return, leaning to him.

"Because I can't believe — can't accept this — this sacrifice of yours. Ina, for God's sake, think! I'm an outcast — about to be arrested. And you — the sweetest, noblest girl in all the world! I can't disgrace you. I won't . . . Oh, what in Heaven's name can I do?"

"Well, if you're needing advice, Bennie, I'd say meet me in Hammell tomorrow or next day."

"Hammell! Why? For people to see my worship of you — and my cowardice?"

"No — your pride," she flashed.

210

"Ina, I can't savvy you. I'm off my balance. My mind's muddled."

"Yes, poor boy, you are pretty stupid — to let me do it all. But then I understand . . . I meant you should meet me in Hammell — and then — then fetch me back here — to your cabin . . . To take care of you and fight with you!"

"Ina Blaine! You'd *marry* me?" he rang out, with incredulous passion.

"I rather think I would, Ben Ide — if you'd ask me."

"You are mad. We're both out of our heads."

"Speak for yourself, Ben. I'm quite sane — and happy. Happier than I've been since coming home."

"Happy! You'd marry *me*? My God! I never dreamed of such a thing! Hettie wrote me you hadn't changed. Marvie said you were crazy about me. But I couldn't believe. And now you tell me —"

"It's true. Marvie had it right. I do love you. And I glory in it."

"Then, Ina — will you marry me when —"

"Yes, Ben, without whens or ifs," she interposed, radiantly. "I don't purpose to give you a loophole."

"Ina, you'll consent to marry me when I've wiped out this stain upon my name? Your love — your promise will save me — make me rise to anything . . . Darling, it must be this way."

"Very well — my beloved," she returned, with her hands going back to his shoulders, and her lovely flushed face, with its tremulous lips and starry eyes, leaning closer over him. "If you think best — if you won't have me — tomorrow — to help you make this fight, why, I must await your lordship's pleasure. But don't forget I offered."

"You torture me. I can't stand much more."

"Oh — Bennie!" she sighed, and slipped into his arms.

"Sweetheart! — My Ina of the old — kid days," he whispered, brokenly. "I think you've saved my soul, if not my life. God bless you! I pray to be worthy of you."

He kissed her, and the sweet fire of her lips seemed to enter his blood and thrill along his veins. She hid her face upon his breast. Then he stood there wrapping her in a close embrace, while the cool wind blew her silken hair against his cheek. He gazed out across the moon-blanched lake, tranquil and splendid in its solitude. The wandering river gleamed away into the soft silver blur of the sage hills; the dark tree-fringed cape stood out silhouetted against the clear sky. Ever since boyhood this lonely place had called to him. Its nameless promise had been fulfilled.

Ben rode home with Ina and Marvie, bidding them good-bye at the foot of the lake slope not far from the ranch. It was broad daylight when he got back to Forlorn River. As he had expected, Nevada met him in high dudgeon.

"Where'n hell have you been?" he exploded, in as much relief as anger.

"Me? Aw I been ridin' around the lone countree," drawled Ben, who was a capital imitator.

212

"Huh! Shore ridin' all night without any sleep agrees with you," retorted Nevada, shrewdly. "You look powerful bright an' pert."

"Yes, and I'll lick you to get up an appetite for breakfast unless you rustle. Where's Modoc?"

"He's got breakfast ready," rejoined Nevada, studying Ben with narrowed piercing eyes. "Wal, I'll be gol-darned if I haven't got it figgered."

"What?"

"You."

"Me? Why, Nevada, I'm nothing to figure. I'm as clear as spring water. You're the mysterious cuss."

"You've been with Ina Blaine."

Ben uttered a short exultant laugh.

"Wonderful, Nevada. How'd you guess it? . . . You darned slick hypocrite. You know right well what's happened."

"Aw no, I don't, Ben. Honest. Tell me," pleaded Nevada.

"I have been with Ina. We're engaged to be married. Good God! how impossible it sounds . . . Yet it's true. I don't know how much you had to do with my great good fortune and happiness, but I've a hunch it is a lot. Ina wouldn't give you away."

Nevada's face worked convulsively and suddenly shone with a strange glow. He shared Ben's joy.

"Put her thar, pard," he said, in deep voice, and he wrung Ben's hand till it was numb.

"Nevada — friend," said Ben, unsteady for an instant, "we've no time now to talk about how and when and where it happened. We've got a hard job on hand. Now what I want to know is this. We're partners, sure, in this new deal of ours, but you've looked to me for decisions and that sort of thing. Will you do as I say, no matter what I tell you or what comes up?"

"Wal, Ben," replied Nevada, slowly, his mood changing to serious pondering, "I shore will. But understand I'm shy on that in one particular. When I meet up with Less Setter I'm my own boss. Savvy?"

"All right. That's the one condition — the one time I'm not boss. Shake on it . . . Now listen. Setter has had officers come over from Redlands. A sheriff named Judd and his deputy, Walker. They're at the Blaine ranch now. Ina didn't think much of their looks and talk. But she was smart enough to get a line on them. It seems Setter is to return to prefer charges upon somebody they didn't name. Sure that somebody is you and I. No doubt Setter is hatching up some trick. We haven't time to wait. Now my plan is this. I'll send Modoc in to Hammell today with a letter to Frisbie. You know he's keen to take my horses, if he can buy them cheap. Well, I'll instruct him to send his men out here tomorrow to drive in all the horses we leave in the pasture. He can put the money to my credit in the Hammell bank. You and I will pack, and take our best horses, and light out for Silver Canyon and Bill Hall's trail. Modoc can meet us at The Cedars, which is the only water hole this side of Silver Canyon. We'll stay out until we catch Hall red-handed. Now what do you think of my plan?"

214

"Wal, reckon it's the best to be made under the circumstances," replied Nevada, in a brown study. "But it shore has some weak spots."

"What are they?"

"Sellin' the hosses for one hundred dollars a haid when if we kept them an' broke them proper we'd sell for two hundred in Klamath. Second, leavin' heah so sudden. Looks like we was scared off an' takin' to the timber. Third, it'll give Setter a chance to do some dirty trick heah at Forlorn River. Fourth, your dad's new cattle range ain't so darned far from Silver Canyon. He an' Blaine have been buyin' out the homesteaders round Silver Meadow. It'd look damn strange to Ide an' Setter if you was seen up there, 'specially if Hall rustled any stock of your dad's. Perfectly natural for them to think Ben Ide's stealin' cattle from his dad. Reckon you savvy me?"

"Nevada, your mind is like a whip," declared Ben. "I figured a couple of those hitches in my plan. But never thought of my father. Good Lord! Could he be made to believe I'd steal from him?"

"Reckon he could. It's easy for a young rustler to begin on his dad's stock. Fact is, that's common. An' everybody knows you've been treated pretty shabby by your dad. They wouldn't blame you a darn bit."

"But, Nevada, the truth is I haven't stolen from Dad or any man, and I never will. Believe me, pard, the truth is a mighty factor in life. Let's gamble on it. They say murder always comes out. Probably all cattle stealing never does, but just the same we have right and justice on our side. Ina made me see that. She talked a lot about it on our way home. Nevada, she even said she didn't believe God would let the devil win so evil a case as this. Let's gamble on Ina's and Hettie's blind faith in the working out of truth."

"Wal, Ben, there'd have been a heap of sense in that, even if the girls hadn't given us the hunch. Lookin' back, I can see how honesty would have been best, always. But a boy has to live an' learn. Take Setter, for instance. He's got so strong an' rich he thinks he cain't be caught. But his day will come."

"You approve, then?" queried Ben, hurriedly bent on settling the matter. He did not like Nevada's half-meditative talk or the dark set look on his face.

"Shore. It's our only bet. An' if we'd happen to kill Hall, or better, ketch him alive — aw, say, pard! . . . I'd shore like to see this Bill Hall. If he hails from Nevada, then I've got the kibosh on Setter."

"Look here," exclaimed Ben, suddenly, "you don't connect Setter in any way with Bill Hall?"

"Wal, pard, I just do. I kinda dreamed it in my sleep."

"Good Heavens! Wouldn't that be a terrible thing for Ina's dad, and mine? . . . Oh, Nevada, it's too far-fetched! It's ridiculous."

"Ben, you don't know the cattle business in a new country. Setter's work is like the faker's at a circus. But only when you see it straight. What surprises me is the way Setter hangs on heah. He ought to be gone long ago. But mebbe your dad an' Ina's dad, comin' into money so sudden, an' bein' such soft putty-haided marks for Setter, accounts for his hangin' on so long."

"Yes, that and Ina," replied Ben. "It's hard to believe, but she told me. Nevada, if he did marry Ina he'd make himself so solid with Blaine and those Hammell men that he couldn't be held, even if we uncovered his tracks."

"Shore, an' Setter knows it. But, pard, while you're gamblin' you can bet on this heah," drawled Nevada, once again his cool, easy, nonchalant self, "Setter ain't figgerin' none on the uncertainty of life."

"I know. Success and money have gone to his head," said Ben, and then, unable to conquer the weakness of fear and jealous love, he added: "But he might somehow get hold of Ina."

"Not in a million years," flashed Nevada. "Unless he'd kidnap her! Then, with Modoc, I could track him over bare rock. An' he wouldn't live long."

It was next day, toward the waning of the afternoon, that Ben and Nevada finished the thirty-mile ride to The Cedars and made camp under the gray-barked trees which gave the spot its name.

This was considerably higher than Forlorn River, and the cold air after the heat below was welcome to the riders. Their fears that the spring might have gone dry proved to be groundless. Water was still seeping out of the sand, though very slight in volume. It formed a pool below, where green verdure, flocks of birds, deer and other game, attested to the scarcity and preciousness of water.

"No hoss been heah for a long time," observed Nevada, after a bent scrutiny of the cut-up ground

round the pool. "Ben, I'll bet you a hat these rustlers have water holes the cowmen never seen."

"Of course. It's a big wild country. And I'll bet California Red and his band have water holes the rustlers have never seen."

"Say, clean forgot that red son-of-a-gun. Shore now it'd be bothersome as the devil if while we was roundin' up these rustlers we'd run plumb into Red, wouldn't it?"

"Heavens! it'd be terrible! It'd ruin us!" exclaimed Ben, aghast.

"How so? I don't savvy."

"You know I'd quit anything under the sun to chase and catch that wild horse."

"Shore but I forgot. You darned locoed puddin'-haided spineless wild-hoss-chasin' jackass!" ejaculated Nevada, with most consummate wonder and ridicule.

Ben dropped his head in shame. He knew he deserved all Nevada called him and infinitely more. But who could understand him? The very flash of memory of California Red thrilled him to the core.

"Say, Ben Ide," kept on Nevada, mercilessly, "if your girl Ina was hangin' over that precipice there, by one finger an' her eyelash, an' California Red come in heah to drink — you'd run for the hoss, wouldn't you?"

"No, of course not, you idiot," denied Ben, hotly.

"Aw, I'm shore glad you're not *that* bad. But I'll bet a million if you was to marry Ina tomorrow an' you had a chance to ketch that red hoss you'd not be at the church."

Ben pondered for some retort to silence Nevada, and finally spoke up with animation. "Speaking of marriage, Ina and I decided to postpone ours until Hettie and you could be married with us."

Nevada gave a wild start, and then, suddenly beaten, suddenly succumbing to what seemed abject misery, he turned to take up the camp tasks. Ben had his revenge, but was sorry he had taken it that way. Nevada's reception of a remark meant only in fun roused thought-provoking conjectures. If Nevada was so frank about his love for Hettie as Ina had assured Ben, why did the thought of marriage make him mute and miserable? It must be because Nevada could not honestly consider marriage. That worried Ben. Presently, realizing how idly he sat there, thinking, dreaming, worrying, he decided it would be far better for him and the success of his venture to apply all his faculties to that and, so far as was possible, forget his sister and his sweetheart for a while.

Whereupon Ben fell quickly into the primitive joys of work and life in the open. This job on hand was going to be an adventure.

"Modoc ought to get here by day after tomorrow," observed Ben, after supper, as they sat enjoying the warmth of the camp fire.

"Sooner. That Injun can ride when he's alone," replied Nevada.

"He said he saw these rustlers from one of the high ridges back of here and that he can find them again," said Ben, reflectively. "Well now, in case we do find them what's your idea of a plan?"

219

"Easy as pie. The three of us will slip up on them at night when they're asleep, hold 'em up an' rope 'em fast."

"By George! it might be done," declared Ben, slapping his knee.

"Ben, if Modoc finds that rustler outfit, an' they don't see or heah us, why, the job's good as done. You see, I'm figgerin' on this Indian. I've a hunch he'll more than pay you for takin' him home when he was kicked out of that saloon in Hammell. Modoc has eagle eyes an' a nose like a hound. As a tracker he's the best I ever seen, an' shore trackin' has been my job always. The more I think of this trick, Ben, the more I wonder why we didn't get the hunch sooner. Bill Hall's outfit is small — only four or five men. S'pose they are bad men. They gotta sleep, an' shore as you're born Modoc will find them, an' we'll ketch them asleep."

"It'd be rich if we caught them with some stolen stock," mused Ben.

"Say, use your haid. What'd Hall be over heah for unless he had some stock? Modoc seen the outfit. It's a shore bet they've got cattle hid somewheres. An' you know, Ben, all this stolen stock goes south an' west over the ranges. None of your ranchers ever see a brand or a hoof of it again. Shore is a paradise for rustlers."

"Aren't we liable to run into Strobel? Ina told me he had gone to Silver Meadow. Hart Blaine, with a road outfit, is working up that way."

"We won't run into any of them," declared Nevada, significantly. "We got too darn good eyesight. But I reckon we're too far west."

220

"But if Hall drives cattle up into the hills from Silver Meadow he's bound to leave tracks. They could be followed. Strobel might deputize some of Dad's cowboys and hit Hall's trail."

"Shore it's feasible," admitted Nevada, "but it's never been done before. Besides, it wouldn't hurt us none to run ag'in' Strobel. He's a close-mouthed cuss aboot his real meanin', but I had a hunch he likes you."

"Yes, I fished with him when I was a kid," mused Ben. "Well, let's turn in. Tomorrow we'll ride high up and 'look round', as Modoc says. Did you hobble the horses?"

"Nope. No need. They're not goin' to walk two steps from this little wet strip of grass. I tied up the black. Must say, for a wild stallion not long ketched, he's pretty decent. I tell you, Ben, it's the feed that gets any hoss. Blacky likes the grain."

While Nevada took a final look at the horses Ben extinguished the camp fire, and then unrolled his bed and sat upon it to remove his boots. Soon he was snug in his blankets. But he did not feel in the least sleepy. Nevada fell into the deep breathing of slumber almost simultaneously with his stretching out near Ben.

This night Ben seemed to revert to a former state of mind regarding the solitude and wilderness of the ranges. The dread that had weighed upon him for so long had eased and vanished. He found himself more like the boy of old. At any rate the joy of the wilderness returned to him, alluring and satisfying, with the added thrill of strange adventure.

The wind moaned and mourned through the wide-armed cedars. It was cold, with a breath of frost. Ben was reminded of the fact that summer was passing swiftly. The moon rode the waving line of black range like a silver ship. He could hear the munch of the grazing horses. A fox barked from the brush. As Ben rolled over his cheek came in icy contact with the butt of his gun. That reminded him of the quest for an outlaw, some of whose depredations had been laid at Ben's door. It was unjust. It was evil. Ben did not blame Hall, but he was bitter against Setter, and others who had defamed him.

CHAPTER
TWELVE

Ben was up before sunrise, kindling a fire. He had been awakened early by the cold. A thin sheet of ice glistened on the pool.

"Pretty nippy for summer," muttered Ben, spreading his hands to the blaze. "But we're up high and summer's getting on."

Then he gave Nevada a prodigious shove, literally rolling that individual out of his slumbers. Nevada sat up, protesting with vigorous and profane speech.

"Howdy, Nev, old timer! Nice cold morning to pull on boots. Try it . . . Well, you son-of-a-gun! Slept in your boots! You'll never get civilized."

"Got 'em wet last night," explained Nevada as he arose with several motions, like a camel. "Knowed darn shore I'd never get them on if I took them off. Wal, rustle breakfast."

"You fetch in the horses," said Ben.

Nevada cracked the ice to wash, and yelled lustily, "Hey — did you — stick your snoot — in heah?"

"Fine and nippy," replied Ben. "It'll make a man of you."

While Nevada attended to the horses Ben rolled biscuits, cut meat, and filled the coffeepot, and otherwise made preparations for breakfast. When the sun tipped the ridge they were in the saddle, headed up country.

From the lower slopes of the range, where the ridges, mountains in themselves, ran and wound down to the basin, they traveled upward. Between the ridges sank canyons, some shallow, others deep, all of them apparently dry as tinder and seared by the sun. Patches of sage and acres of short bleached grass and clumps of cedar increased toward the black heights.

No living creature, either bird or beast, revealed itself to Ben's roving sight. It was indeed a lonely country. The deer and wild horses were farther up in the hills.

Silver Meadow lay around and below the spur of range, toward the east. Ben and Nevada wanted to look over that valley before taking up a survey of the canyon heads. As they climbed, their command over the country widened. Wild Goose Lake and Forlorn River appeared almost under their position; Tule Lake gleamed yellow with its grain over the sage hills; Mule Deer Lake looked like a dot in a gray waste; beyond it the black lava beds waved to the green forest benches that lifted to the bare mountain ridge. Far away noble Mount Shasta stood up, white and lonely, in the morning sunlight.

At length Ben and Nevada reached their lookout point, several thousand feet above an immense valley, or series of valleys, separated by low foothills. Silver Meadow suited its name. It was an oval valley half a dozen miles long by a couple in width, covered with white sage and bleached grass. Ben took a long survey with his field glass, and then, without comment, handed it to Nevada.

"Wal," said Nevada, after an equally long gaze, "not so much stock as I figgered we'd see. Pretty dry down there. Ben, do you reckon there's cattle an' hosses up the draws, grazin' on trees?"

"They sure are, unless they're dead," replied Ben, shortly.

"Or stolen," supplemented Nevada. "I'll gamble on that. Ben, if the rains don't come this fall all the stock in there will die."

"Don't say if. The rains must come. Nature may be cruel, but not utterly ruthless . . . Nevada, I rather expected we could sight Blaine's outfit or some cowboys."

"Nary a sign. Reckon Blaine is somewheres north of the Meadow. There's some good little homesteads along the river. Shore doesn't look like a river up heah, huh? She's dry, Ben, dry as sand."

"Shall we ride on to Silver Canyon?" queried Ben.

"Hold your hosses, Benjamin," drawled Nevada. "It's pretty far, an' we ought to have the Indian. Let him ride one side of the canyon an' we'll ride the other."

"Couldn't you and I split up and do that?" impatiently asked Ben.

"Reckon we could. But would it be good sense when we're huntin' rustlers? Besides I'll be darned if I know where Silver is from heah."

"I do, but it'll take a climb. Perhaps we'd better go back to camp. Modoc ought to be in tonight."

★ ★ ★

But Ben was mistaken. The Indian did not put in appearance, and when morning came with him still absent, Ben began to worry. All day they watched and waited. By sunset they knew something unusual had happened to their faithful ally. Ben made vain conjectures.

"I lay it to Setter," said Nevada, broodingly.

"Bet you're right," declared Ben, leaping up. "I never thought of Setter. If he met Modoc in Hammell he'd stop him sure."

"Wal, he'd try damn hard. But that Injun ain't so easy to stop. Let's don't give up yet, Ben."

A little after dark Modoc rode into the bright camp fire circle and slipped off a saddleless horse. He had ridden bareback.

"How! Heap hungry," he said, with a grin.

"Plenty grub, Modoc, but let us warm it up. What's happened?"

"Setter lock me up in Hammell jail," replied Modoc. "Me break out, find hoss, come camp."

"Ben, what'd I tell you?" demanded Nevada, ringingly, with fire in his eye.

"Well? Setter arrested you! What for?"

"Me ask jail-man. He laugh. Say long time ago me got drunk — fight in saloon."

Ben felt so relieved to hear the charge that he laughed while Nevada cursed.

"Modoc, did you ever have two fights in Hammell?"

"No; me fight one time. Me no drunk. They drunk. They beat me — throw me out. Same time you found me."

"I remember. Setter — the d — low-down skunk! That's all he could hatch up. Nevada, I'm surprised at Setter. He's clumsy. He must think we *are* outcasts, without a friend in the world. That there's no justice in California."

"Wal, I reckon he just put another nail in his coffin," drawled Nevada. "I'll look after Modoc's hoss. Lucky we fetched an extra saddle."

"Modoc, did you see Frisbie?" queried Ben, suddenly remembering the important mission upon which he had sent the Indian.

"Yes. He glad. Sent lot cowboys."

"Good. That settles that . . . I'm glad you broke jail. I'd have done it myself . . . Now, Modoc, we've got a big job on hand. Tomorrow you guide us to where you saw Hall's outfit. If we find them — well, we will make our plans then."

Ben's first peep over the rim of Silver Canyon was something he felt he would never forget. He had been familiar only with the lower reaches of this wild canyon, where it appeared more like a valley. From this point, to which he and Nevada had been directed by Modoc, he saw into a deep sage and rock-walled gorge with a beautiful broad winding green line of trees at the bottom. A branch of the canyon, opening on the opposite side, appeared even more verdant. It was full of morning haze, like autumn smoke. The main canyon headed up in a notch or saddle, astonishingly accessible, seen now from this point; and over this pass Modoc believed the rustlers drove their stolen stock

227

down into another country. Ben felt convinced the moment he studied the lay of the land. What a wonderful place for thieves to work and hide! It was not clear to him yet how they got the cattle over the rough ridge, if they did so at all. Nevada inclined to the opinion that they boldly drove cattle up the whole length of the canyon. If this theory was correct the cowboys had not, for some strange reason, cared to track them. For that would have been easy for even novices at trailing. The canyon, however, afforded most effective places for ambush, where a few determined men with rifles could hold back ten times their number.

"Pard, I see cattle," whispered Nevada, who was using the glass. "By thunder! ... An' I'm a son-of-a-gun if they aren't wearin' the A1 brand. A number one, the cowboys say. Amos Ide! Your dad."

Ben was so amazed and excited that it took moments for him to verify Nevada's statements. But at length the glass proved these beyond all doubts.

"Heavens!" he gasped, staring at Nevada.

That worthy was smiling at him.

"Shore luck's comin' our way. What do you think of Modoc now?"

"Nevada, let's ride further on, so we can see past this bluff that sticks out."

"Reckon we ought to be careful," warned his companion. "If that Hall outfit sights us, it'll spoil our plan."

But Ben was eager to reconnoiter, believing that because of the distance it would be safe. They rode back off the rim, around rough broken rock, through

228

brush and patches of cedar, to another open stretch. Here they sighted upward of two hundred head of cattle, grazing along a slope and on into the green timber.

"Look!" whispered Nevada, suddenly. "Smoke! . . . Down this way, Ben."

"I see. That's from a camp fire," replied Ben, excitedly.

"Shore is . . . An', Ben, it reminds me that Modoc told us to keep watchin' across the canyon for him. We plumb forgot. Gimme the glass. Shore he could see us when we couldn't see him."

Nevada leveled the glass and took careful survey of the opposite side, beginning well up toward a point above the cattle. Ben watched in a mounting suspense. Suddenly the cowboy steadied the glass, fixed it, and remained motionless.

"I see Modoc . . . Straight across — back from the rim. The darned Injun sees us. Talk aboot eyesight! . . . Ben, he's wavin' us back from the rim — pointin' down . . . Hell! he means Hall's outfit has seen us — or they're goin' to. Let's get back pronto."

Quickly they rode back out of sight from possible gazers in the depths of the canyon. Then, dismounting, they located Modoc again. Ben took the glass and soon satisfied himself that the Indian was trying to communicate important information. Ben watched closely. Modoc's signs were emphatic and picturesque. Most of his gestures indicated something unusual going on down below.

"Nevada, I believe Modoc means they've seen us. He points down — down — then sweeps his arm away. Let's crawl to the rim."

Cautiously they wormed their way to a point behind some brush where, lying flat, they could look over without fear of being seen. But a long keen scrutiny of slopes, weathered rocks, and green groves of trees failed to reward them with any more than the pale column of blue smoke. When again Ben searched the rim opposite for Modoc, he finally caught a glimpse of him riding away into the timber.

"Modoc's riding off, Nevada. What you make of that?"

"Darn if I know what. I'm afraid they seen us. Reckon we'll find out pronto. 'Cause they won't know who or how many men are after them. Shore they wouldn't risk headin' out that canyon pass, an' it's a safe bet they won't stay down there."

"Oh, it's too bad if we let them see us," said Ben, poignantly. "I'm to blame. I was in too big a hurry."

Then they watched in silence for several more moments, which for Ben were fraught with growing bitter regret. What an opportunity! It sickened him to think of failure. They must go on despite this blunder.

"By golly! I see them, Ben!" whispered Nevada, excitedly, stretching a long finger. "Right under us — that thin place — where you can see through the trees . . . Look sharp. One — two — three — four riders . . . An' a pack hoss. They shore throwed that pack quick, unless they was ready . . . Do you see, Ben?"

230

"Yes. I've counted five men, but only one pack. Nevada, they're in a hurry."

"Shore. They seen us an' they're scared. You can always tell men that are runnin' away. Least *I* can, 'cause I've been there myself."

"What's to be done?" sharply rejoined Ben. "Let's head them off."

"Cain't do it from this side. Bet a million they'll go down that branch canyon. If they do, Modoc will sure keep tabs on them."

"Maybe it's not so bad, after all."

"Ben, in a minute they'll pass even with us," returned Nevada, forcibly. "I've an idee. They don't know how many there are of us. Let's empty both our Winchesters, then our guns, fast an' jerky like. It's 'most a thousand yards down there. We cain't hit nothin'. But heahin' a lot of bullets will make them think there's a whole outfit of sheriffs an' cowboys. That'll scare them bad. An' we'll stick to their tracks."

"Come on," replied Ben, cocking his rifle.

When the dark figures of horsemen showed through the thinned-out place in the timber below, Ben and Nevada fired a volley of thirty-two shots in a very few seconds. The walls of the canyon gave the reports a strange thundering volume.

"Look at 'em run!" exulted Nevada, in grim satisfaction, holding aloft his smoking gun. "Out of sight already. Scared. By golly! it worked. Now let's watch. Bet they run down that branch canyon."

"Nevada, wasn't that great?" whispered Ben, huskily, as he laid his gun down to cool. "I swear I hit one of them. He lurched in his saddle."

"Wal, it ain't likely, but you might have. Shore I hope so. Now look sharp."

In a few moments they were rewarded by sight of a string of riders scattered over some distance, entering the mouth of the branch canyon. A pack horse, running wild, furnished proof of the difficulties the rustlers were having.

"Left their beds behind," said Nevada, gleefully. "Reckon Bill Hall has had such an easy time that he forgot what bullets sounded like. Look at 'em go. Some one behind the pack hoss now."

The riders disappeared over a rise in the grassy slope of the canyon mouth, and soon reappeared on an open level into the canyon. Suddenly a heavy rifle report rang out, from the wall above them.

"You heah that? Modoc's forty-five!" cried Nevada, beside himself with delight. "He figgered us, an' he waited till they got by . . . Bow! — Bang! — Spow! Listen to that big gun! Sounds like a cannon. An' say, boy, where's the rustlers?"

"They broke and run," replied Ben, just as excited as Nevada. "Listen to Modoc shoot! . . . Six — seven — eight — nine — ten! And now the echoes in that narrow canyon! Can't tell the difference."

"We shore made a hell of a racket," replied Nevada. "They're runnin' like a lot of scared jack rabbits. Bet they think there's an outfit on each side of the canyon."

"It was fun, by gosh! and maybe it was good," declared Ben. "But what next?"

"Back to camp for us," answered Nevada, rising. "Let's load our guns just for luck. An empty gun ain't much use. It's a long ride back to camp. We cain't do nothin' with these cattle down heah. But, Ben, mebbe we'll have to prove things. Gimme your scarf. It's got your initials on. I'll tie it heah, so if need be we can prove we sighted your dad's cattle from this point. Least we can show we was heah. An' you bet if we was rustlin' them cattle we'd be down there."

"Nevada, they've left some of their outfit in camp, sure and certain. Oughtn't we get it?"

"No time. That'd take a whole day. Shore we want to rustle back to camp an' have light packs ready so when Modoc comes we can leave pronto. Wonder where that branch canyon runs. Might be good for us, an' might be bad. Modoc will know. But one thing shore. Bill an' his gang are makin' for low country where water's scarce. He's goin' to be out of luck."

It took three hours of hard riding to get down to the valley where they had crossed from the other side. Cattle tracks appeared more significant now. Probably Hall had not massed his stolen stock into a herd until he got into the canyon.

Ben and Nevada rode up the far slope, and surmounting it they took the crest of it and went down till they had to cross another canyon and another ridge; and this kind of hard going continued for miles, at last to lead out upon the descent to their camp, which they reached at dark.

Modoc was there, with a warm supper waiting, the horses fed, and part of the outfit packed.

"Injun son-of-a-gun!" was Nevada's lusty encomium.

Ben shook hands with Modoc in a manner that made speech unnecessary. Nevada, however, was seldom deprived of the power to talk.

"Modoc, we shore was a couple of wooden-haided scouts," he said, scornfully. "Ben for givin' us away an' me for lettin' him do it. But it happened so darn quick, soon as we hit that part of the canyon where it haids out to the pass. Wal, I'm damn sorry, for you did a wonderful job."

"No cause for sorry. Heap good," replied Modoc, with his gleaming grin.

"What you mean?" shrilly queried the cowboy, his face lighting.

"Hall take wrong canyon. Best way out down big canyon. He thinks lots men shoot — ride — hold 'em up. So he take little canyon. No way out till Mule Deer Lake. More twenty miles. Rough like lava beds. Hard on hoss. No water. No grass. Hall be more bad off when reach Mule Deer Lake. He be close ranch, but no dare go. Have go Modoc caves for water. We track 'em — ketch 'em like hosses."

That was a very lengthy speech for the Indian, who never used unnecessary words. The importance of it, however, and the satisfaction he evinced, must have been accountable. Ben had never before heard anything from Modoc to compare with this for length and content. He had never known the Indian to make a single blunder in calculations that pertained to matters of the wild country. He had stated he would find the rustlers; now he avowed they would catch them. For lack of suitable expression Ben smacked the Indian's shoulder with a strong hand.

"One Hall man crippled," announced Modoc. "You must shot him. He got behind. Me see 'em look back — yell — make sign he come quick. But he no ride fast long."

At this juncture Nevada nearly knocked the breath out of Ben.

"Had a hunch — this very minnit," he yelled. "We're goin' to get Hall, daid or alive. No matter which. If we kill him we can prove he stole your dad's cattle."

"Let's cool off — eat supper — see what's to do," replied Ben.

"We go quick," said the Indian, quietly. "Take extra hoss — lots grub — lots water — lots grain."

"Modoc, old chief, you an' me belong to the same tribe of trackers," returned Nevada. "An' we're shore goin' to track that outfit day an' night."

"Leave the rest of our horses and outfit here?" queried Ben, dubiously. "I don't like that."

"Neither do I. But we gotta do it, Ben. Reckon we don't run much risk, way up heah. I'll tie Blacky on a long rope on the best bit of grass an' water heah. The other hosses will hang round."

Between them they overruled Ben's reluctance and unaccountable sense of calamity. Finally he analyzed it as a personal and intimate reaction regarding the beautiful wild stallion. When he was persuaded of this he acquiesced readily, wondering at his strange contradictions of nature. Would he not make a terrible blunder some day through his passion for wild horses?

In less than an hour they were in the saddle, Modoc leading the way, with Ben and Nevada attending to pack horses and extra saddle horses. They carried two ten-gallon water bags for the animals and a smaller one for their own needs. Ben felt assured they could make a quick trip to the Modoc caves without grave risk.

During the early part of the night the travel was slow, but as soon as the moon rose they made up for lost time. Modoc had departed from the trails and Ben did not know where he was, except that the stars said westward. The hours passed swiftly like the miles, and before Ben realized either time or distance the stars had faded, the moon was paling in the gray of dawn. When daylight came Ben looked down upon the dreary scene of the drab basin where Mule Deer Lake gleamed with its color like an evil eye.

At the foot of the slope Ben and Nevada halted while the Indian rode out to cross the canyon mouth in search of tracks. He did not get halfway across before he waved his arm, then pointed toward the sheet of green-and-yellow water. Ben and Nevada headed their horses in the direction, soon to become aware of a rank odor of rotting flesh. Presently they espied carcasses scattered here and there around the lake, and upon closer view were amazed to see that they were deer. Driven by terrible thirst, the deer had drunk freely of this poison water and had foundered and died.

Modoc pointed to horses' tracks leading to the edge of the vile pond at one point and another, as if different horses had approached the water only to turn or be dragged away.

"No hoss drink," said Modoc, and he trotted round the lake to find the tracks of Hall's outfit heading north. They had passed the lake not many hours before. Ben argued that it might be as well for them to travel a little slower, so as not to give the outlaws an inkling that they were so closely pursued. Whereupon they rested at the first patch of sage, ate something themselves, gave the horses grain and water, and changed saddles. Soon they were on the move again with the dry fragrant sage and pine-scented wind in their faces and the green-stepping forest rising before them.

At sundown they made camp in the pines.

"Can we trail them over the pumice and the pine needles?" queried Ben, ever anxious.

"Ben, I could do that myself," replied Nevada. "Slow, mebbe, but I shore could. An' Modoc will see their tracks without even gettin' off his hoss. Ben, it's all up with this Hall outfit."

"But Hall might lie in wait for us now. Shoot us from some thicket."

"Shore he might. But it ain't likely. He never would figger anyone this close on his trail. We've done some all-fired ridin', an' made short cuts, too. Nope, he's campin' somewheres within five miles of us now an' never dreamin' we're close. All we gotta do is stick to the Indian. I won't lose a wink of sleep."

"We better stand watch, hadn't we, turn about?"

"Reckon we had, come to think of that. Don't want a hoss to slip a halter at this stage."

Next morning proved that Hall was taking some pains to make his trail less plain, and he would have bothered an ordinary tracker. The Indian, however, lost no time.

"Crippled man no ride like friends," said Modoc, pointing to irregular disturbances of the pine-needle mats. "He no care. He sick. He make tracks."

This tracking was of a nature to swallow up the hours. Ben was set and cool now that the chase appeared to be nearing an end. He knew that Modoc calculated to come upon the rustlers at their first camp in or near one of the caves where water was to be found. This was a wise move, Ben thought, because Hall might start next morning for the high lava mountains where game and water were abundant.

About the middle of the afternoon, Modoc, who had ridden quite far in the lead, waited for his followers, and when they came up he announced: "Me see 'em. Ride slow. Help crippled man. He about ready drop. They stop first cave where water. Me know."

"How far is it, Modoc?" queried Ben, in a tense whisper, gazing round at the waving ridges of timbered pumice, as if to calculate his own estimate of the distance to the outcropping lava. It struck him that this was not far.

"Long walk. Little ride," replied Modoc. "Me walk. You lead hoss. No make noise. Look round good."

Silently Ben and Nevada watched the short squat Indian glide through the forest. He was as much at home here as the wild creatures. He made no more noise than a bird, and always he appeared to be screened by tree trunk or shrub or pine thicket. When he had drawn away some three or four hundred yards, almost out of sight, Ben and Nevada rode slowly on, just fast enough to keep him in view.

Thus they slowly climbed the white green-patched pine-barred ridges of gray pumice, until they reached a point where Modoc turned downhill. Soon Ben saw the black-and-red edges of lava, marring the soft beauty of the forest and revealing its sinister nature. Small pits, full of pine cones and needles, became common, and soon dark apertures showed under outcropping ledges of lava. They had reached the edge of the caves.

"Ben, she's shore gettin' hot," whispered Nevada. "Just look at that Injun! Ain't he grand? I'll bet you a hoss he sees them now. I'm powerful afraid I'm itchin' to throw a gun."

"You shoot when I tell you," ordered Ben.

"But, darn it, pard, you might be a week late! I'm in the habit of throwin' a gun —"

"Sssschh!" whispered Ben, gripping Nevada's arm. "Modoc is making signs."

"Wal, I seen him. What was I talkin' aboot?"

"Nevada, I believe he means for us to tie our horses and come to him."

As Ben spoke Nevada was already off his horse, hitching the halter of his led horse to a sapling. Ben followed suit. Then they tied their saddle horses, and lastly Modoc's. Ben felt a clutch on his arm and he turned to meet eyes like black diamonds on fire.

239

"Pard, this will be new for you," he whispered, hoarsely. "Remember we're after men who'd kill you on sight — shoot you in the back."

"I savvy, Nevada," replied Ben. "But my orders are not to kill if we can hold them up."

"Shore. Reckon they'll be better for us alive than daid. We'll make Bill Hall talk . . . Come on now, easy."

Ben was panting when he reached the side of the crouching Indian. Before them the forest was level, with pines scattered about in stately aloofness. Scarcely a hundred rods out there in the open showed a brush-fringed depression that surely led to a cave. Ben did not recall this one, though there were so many that he might or might not have seen it.

"Good. Cave me know," whispered Modoc, with dark impressiveness. "Little water all time. Cave deep. Other hole far." Here the Indian made signs that the other entrance or end of this cavern was some hundred yards off in the woods, at the edge of that level bench. "Hall no get there quick."

"Did they go down?" asked Ben, with a leap in his blood.

"Yes. Lead hoss an' hold crippled man. They about down now; soon hoss drink — then come up for grass. Modoc think best run quick — hood 'em up."

"Ahuh. Now you're talkin', Injun," ejaculated Nevada, looking to the breech of his rifle.

"How about the other hole?" queried Ben, sharply, tightening his belt.

"Hole far. No get there quick. Me go after little. Roll rock — shut hole up."

240

"Is there only one trail down into this hole? And on this side?"

"Yes, same as wild-hoss trap. Good," replied the Indian.

"Come on, then. Not too fast. Don't get out of breath. If we meet them coming out — hold them up."

Despite his warning, the agile Indian and the long-legged rider covered ground rapidly, so that Ben had to run fast to keep up with them. His skin felt tight and wet, tingling underneath, and his feet seemed to have no weight at all. They reached the brush, and kneeling abreast crawled quickly to peep over into the hole. Ben saw black lava very steep, directly opposite; then to his right a wide shelving cavern, the floor of which slowly descended toward a large dark opening.

"Seen the last hoss go down," whispered Nevada, who had been first to peep over the rim. "An' heah's the trail — pretty darn narrow an' steep. Made to order ... An', Ben, look at that pack. The size of it! Not enough grub there to feed a jack rabbit for a week."

"It is pretty small," whispered Ben, trying to keep the tremble out of his voice. "Maybe they had another pack."

"Nope. Only one. That's it. Aw, how easy! Aw, how slick! Aw, shame to take the money! ... Now, Ben Ide, you listen." He changed, suddenly, to a fierce whisper. "I don't see that crippled fellar. Mebbe he's too far back under this side. 'Cause shore they wouldn't pack him way down to the water. He's layin' heah, somewheres. Now we'll let them get their drink an' come up. We want them hosses to run up out of heah.

Men can eat hoss flesh, you know. I've done it. Wal, it's pretty shore the hosses will come up first. We'll wait an' see how the men foller. Mebbe we can hold them up. But the place ain't good for that. Anyway, we'll begin shootin' pronto, to scare the hosses out. Then we've got Hall absolute-tel-lee."

Ben had no fault to find with Nevada's plan for the finish. It looked perfect. The rustlers were trapped in a place that one wide-awake guard could hold indefinitely. Ben could scarcely choke down his emotion. In the silence of suspense that ensued he heard faint hollow voices from the dark aperture — ring of iron shoe on lava — snort of horse — voice of man. He listened with strained ears, holding his breath. How interminably the moments dragged! Modoc lay as quietly relaxed as if this were rest. Nevada was whispering to himself. At last crack of hoofs rang oftener and louder. Ben saw shadows back in the hole. They emerged. Then six horses clamped over the rough lava floor and out upon the soft pumice, where their hoofs scarcely made a sound.

Ben quivered slightly at sight of another shadow. It merged into a man — short, heavy-bodied, dark-garbed, with face hid by black slouch hat.

"Hey, Bill," called a weak voice, from directly under where the watchers crouched, "I heerd somethin' above."

"What'd ye hear?" demanded Hall, stopping short to whip out a gun. Shadows appeared behind him, growing clear.

"Sounded like footsteps back on top — an' then whisperin'," replied the other.

Suddenly Nevada's body strung as if he meant to leap.

"HANDS UP!" he roared, in stentorian voice.

Hall's answer was to shoot and leap in one swift action. It carried him out of sight behind the shelving edge of the cavern. A bullet hit the branch above Ben's head and, *spang*, it sped off into the forest. Nevada began to fire as rapidly as he could work the lever of his Winchester. Then Modoc chimed in with his heavy gun. Answering shots rang from below. The horses stampeded, and snorting in terror, plunging and pounding, they crowded up the trail, raising a cloud of dust, under which they fled into the forest. Ben reserved his rifle fire. He heard the bullets of his comrades spattering on the walls of the cavern, and the whiz and zip of the bullets from the rustlers. These were coming uncomfortably close. Ben drew back, and hauled Modoc and then Nevada out of danger.

That ended the shooting. Modoc calmly reloaded. Nevada began to take shells from his belt, while he looked with bright eyes at Ben.

"Pard, time of my life!" he said. "You know I hate to shoot for keeps, an' this is fun. Now, I've got a big hunk of lava picked out, a little way past the haid of the trail. I'll crawl round where I can see down an' be safe behind cover. You lay low heah till I call."

"Me go," whispered Modoc, and glided away noiselessly after Nevada, like a snake.

Ben remained where he had last crouched. He could see part of the cavern floor, but nothing of the shelf under which the rustlers were hidden. Turning to look the other way, he watched Nevada and Modoc crawl to positions behind a bulge of lava on the rim. It was a stand that surely commanded the whole situation.

"Hey, Hall," yelled Nevada, in a ringing voice that corroborated just what Ben had decided, "got you daid to rights!"

"Who'n the hell are you?" came in rough hoarse query.

"Me? Aw, I'm only one of a big outfit. Sheriffs, deputies, cowboys, Injuns — an' one gunman I shore know of."

"Wal, what you want?"

"Surrender. Throw your guns out heah where I can see them. An' walk out one at a time, with hands up."

"Ahhaw! An' s'pose we don't?" queried the thick voice.

"Last an' only chance you get," retorted Nevada. "We'll shore shoot on sight."

"Shoot an' be damned," growled the rustler, and low angry hum of voices attested to argument among his men.

"Heah's this crippled pard of yours, right in sight. Shall I bore him?"

"Shoot him an' be damned — if you're that kind of a sheriff."

"Wal, reckon I'll let him off. Once more, now, will you surrender an' save yourselves an' us a lot of trouble? 'Cause we shore can starve you out."

244

The answer to this sally of Nevada's was a medley of cursing that Ben had never heard approached in all his life. It made his heart beat high, his blood run riot, for it was proof of the extremity of the rustlers. It lasted several moments, then gradually died down.

"Wal, how aboot it?" drawled Nevada.

"Wal, Mister Sweet Voice," drawled Hall, in scornful imitation, "we ain't agreed down heah, but I say come down an' git us!"

CHAPTER
THIRTEEN

Nevada accepted the rustler chief's ultimatum as if it was exactly what he had expected, and he wasted no more words in that quarter. Calling Ben over to his side, he said:

"Hall knows, if his men don't, that we've got them corralled. Now let's put our haids together."

"Question of time and close watch," replied Ben, thoughtfully.

"Yep. Some one of us must have an eye on that cave hole day an' night."

"Modoc, you say there's a back door to this cave?"

"Yes. Me shut 'em so Hall no get out."

"Good! When you do that fetch our horses and outfit up. We'll camp right here under the pines. Then take the horses to another cave, water them, and hobble them on the best grass near."

Without a word the Indian crawled away from the rim, and presently rising he glided away through the forest.

"Ben, did we fetch any nails?" asked Nevada.

"Sure. There's a handful of spikes in the horseshoe bag."

"Wal, we'll cut poles an' make some kind of contraption with sharp ends an' jam it tight in the narrow part of the trail. Hall might try to slip out at night or charge us. But we'll block that. Fact is he cain't climb out one darn place but this heah trail. Talk aboot luck! Why, it's smotherin' us!"

"You think he'll surrender?"

"Absolute-tel-lee," replied Nevada, lingering over his best-beloved word. "Reckon, though, he'll take time. He'll work every dodge. Might risk a fight before the grub gives out. But when it does give out he shore won't last long."

"You figure he can get the pack of grub after night?"

"Easy. Though I might heah them. An' I'm pretty shore I seen a stack of firewood when I first peeped over the rim. Reckon we could see it better from heah. But I don't advise playin' giraffe."

"Modoc never made a mistake I can recall," mused Ben, as if trying to assure himself of this phenomenal good fortune.

"Ben, we're gamblin' on the Indian," replied Nevada, with serious certainty. "It's a thousand to one we'll win."

"We must, Nevada. It means all the world to us both."

"Your dad an' Ina's dad are drawin' bad cards this very minnit," declared the cowboy, almost fiercely. "An' Setter — damn him! it's a worse deal for him."

"Even if Judd and his man should track us here — we couldn't lose."

"Hope they do. We'll let them go down an' arrest the rustlers. Haw! Haw!"

"About the other hole to this cave. Could Modoc alone roll stones big enough to hold these men in?"

"Trust that Injun, Ben. But we'll see to satisfy ourselves. I reckon Modoc will cover the other hole with poles or brush, an' then so many chunks of lava that a hundred men couldn't budge them."

Ben's fears one by one were allayed.

"All now depends on our vigilance. We must not be caught napping."

"Huh! I could lay heah twelve hours at a stretch an' never bat an eye. Ben, we'll keep two of us watchin' all the time, while the other fellar sleeps an' gets water an' grub, looks after the hosses, an' so forth. Reckon as soon as Modoc comes with the outfit an' tends to the hosses we'd better take turns on makin' somethin' to close this trail."

The hours of this eventful day passed swiftly, and there was never a moment that two pairs of sharp eyes were not watchful.

Toward sunset Nevada smelled smoke, and as Modoc had not yet started a camp fire for them, the only inference was that the rustlers had one down in the cave. It was Nevada's assumption, presently, that as they would not need or want a camp fire without their supplies, they were burning wood for torches.

The night fell and Ben and Nevada held watch together behind the bulge of lava along the rim. Soon the hole was as black as pitch. Nevada heard something which caused him to touch Ben lightly. Straining his ears, Ben caught a faint scraping sound, which he decided was caused by canvas sliding over a rough surface.

"They're getting their grub, all right," said Ben.

For answer Nevada rose on one knee and rapidly fired several shots down into the black void. Ben, lying flat at the right of the bulge of lava, with his rifle over the rim, saw bright red flashes of answering shots from the vigilant rustlers. Instantly he aimed at the point where he had seen the last flash. A lusty yell attested to the fact that he had come dangerously close to a man if he had not actually hit one. Then silence ensued.

"Say, did you heah them bullets whiz past?" queried Nevada, grimly.

"No."

"Wal, I did. One on each side of me. Hall was watchin' an' he shot quicker'n lightnin'. An' say, mebbe I didn't duck! — Ben, I reckon that sizes Hall up, huh?"

"Don't take any more chances," replied Ben. "We'll play it safe."

At midnight Modoc relieved Ben, and when dawn came Ben cooked and carried breakfast to his watching comrades, then relieved Nevada so he could have his turn at sleep. The rustlers had secured their pack of supplies, and had also removed the crippled one of their number back into the cave. This established the siege. It required infinite vigilance on the part of the besiegers, but the stake was so tremendous that they

249

never lost for a moment their keen zest and mounting hope. The hours passed swiftly. Each man took his turn at camp fire duties, but Modoc attended to the horses and carried water. On the third day he returned to camp with the information that he had caught and hobbled the rustlers' horses.

"Aw-aw-aw!" jubilated Nevada to this good news, and he gave Ben a dig in the ribs that hurt for hours.

On the afternoon of this day, Ben, following careful direction from Modoc, found the place where the Indian had blocked the far outlet to the cave. The aperture must have been small and Modoc had covered it with tons of lava. If there were indeed no other entrances and exits to this particular cavern, Hall and his gang must soon surrender or fight. And in a fight the odds were all against them. Nevada's plan for blocking the trail appeared wholly effective, and if the rustlers rushed it at night they would only get shot for their pains. Ben had only one anxiety and this was that there might be another exit unknown to Modoc. Upon returning to camp he put this forcibly to the Indian.

"Mebbe so," replied Modoc. "But far-way far. No Indian find yet."

"Huh! You can bet your boots it's far," said Nevada. "Reckon they've searched every corner of this cave."

During the first stage of their vigil Ben and his comrades had ample evidence of the presence of their prisoners. The smell of smoke, and often the blue smoke itself, emerged from the cave. Voices sometimes penetrated to the outside, and more rarely the sound of an ax splitting wood. Several times on the darkest nights faint noises down in the hole brought rifle shots from the watchful guard. Indeed, Nevada often fired his rifle by way of assuring the trapped rustlers how keen were their captors. The longer, however, that Hall waited to attempt escape by the trail the keener Nevada bade his allies watch. Hall's apparent inaction and his incredible patience invited extra suspicion.

Two weeks passed by. Ben experienced amaze when he counted up the little sticks he had laid aside, one for each passing day. Yet he might have realized the approach of autumn in the cold mornings and the changing hues of vine and oak leaves. Modoc reported thick ice on the water in the cave from which he supplied their needs. Another proof of the changing season was the fact that deer were coming down from the heights. Modoc shot one from the camp. Ben saw deer often, and heard them every night. They knew the trail to the cave where the rustlers hid.

One afternoon Modoc returned from his daily visit to the horses, and he wore a somber visage.

"Wal, Injun, what's up?" queried Nevada.

Ben gazed at his faithful comrade with a slow sinking of his heart.

"Bad," said the Indian, slowly. "Modoc no want tell."

"Don't keep anything from me," returned Ben.

"Red stallion drink at our trap cave."

"Red stallion! You mean California Red?" shouted Ben, starting up wildly.

"Yes."

"Hey, you darn redskin, what'd you tell him for?" yelled Nevada, furiously.

"Me always tell boss," replied the Indian.

"Aw, Lord! if that ain't hard luck," wailed Nevada, suddenly falling back as if all was over.

Ben leaned on a trembling elbow to stare breathlessly at the Indian. One flash of thought, following his realization of the wonderful truth that California Red had at last been driven to the caves, was sufficient to warn him that if he vacillated a single moment he would be lost. It wrenched him to make a decision that would preclude any weak surrender to growing temptation.

"Modoc, take your ax — destroy that trap gate," he said, hoarsely, and then without a word turned back to his watching task.

"Water 'most gone in hoss cave," returned Modoc. "Soon California Red have go winter range."

Ben did not reply, and strange to see, Nevada for another rare occasion had been rendered speechless. Resolutely Ben forced his mind to dwell upon other things. He knew it was not safe to think of California Red. But nothing except thought of Ina, which he had also prohibited himself, could keep him from longing memory of this noblest of wild horses. Therefore Ben admitted again to his consciousness the sweet face of Ina Blaine, her avowed love, her willing kisses. And then, though he stared at the black cave which held the rustlers, he thought only of this girl who had roused him to significant life.

★　★　★

The day came when neither sound nor smoke emerged from the doorway of Bill Hall's cave refuge.

This stirred Ben and Nevada to conjecture. Had the rustlers used up all their wood? Why did they no longer speak aloud? Could it be possible they had at last found an exit from their hiding place?

"Shore it's a trick," averred Nevada, stoutly. "Bet they'll keep it up till they're starved out. You see, Ben, it's wearin' on our nerves when we don't heah or see them. Hall savvies that. He's smart. Mebbe he thinks we cain't stand uncertainty. I'll agree it's tough."

"It doesn't follow because they're out of wood that they're out of grub," said Ben, ponderingly.

"Nope. An' if Hall had any say with his men he'd shore make them eat light. But that's our weakness. Waitin' without knowin'. Some fellars would have to make shore by slippin' down there. Not us! We'll hang right heah."

Ten more days passed by — days of slow patient watching, with a gradually growing suspense. September had come. The sugar and coffee were gone. Ben and his allies were living on bread and meat and water, some parched corn and dried apples. But they did not suffer from that. Ben got to the point where he ate only once a day.

One morning the sun did not show. A gray pall of cloud had swept down from the heights. The cold air bore a suggestion of snow. Nevada was hopeful that the long drought would be broken. Ben echoed that wish. Modoc, however, said: "Mebbe so — not soon." And toward evening the gray curtain broke and blew away.

253

More days passed, becoming interminable, endless. No sound or sign of the rustlers! It seemed impossible that they could be hidden down there still alive. But Ben, who suffered most under the strain, realized that it was probably easier for the besieged than the besiegers. Hall had no uncertainty. His only chances were for his captors to quit or else risk entering the cave.

Modoc discovered a hole in a lava bank some distance away, and he said it might have connection with the cave they were guarding. Ben had to see it. Leaving Nevada on the lookout, he followed Modoc through the forest, down over a grassy and pine-needle descent of lava to a wide shallow depression, almost a gorge in dimensions. Here Modoc led Ben to a small black hole. A cool wind blew from it, proving that it had another opening somewhere. Ben listened intently beside the hole for a long time. Absolute silence was the fruit of his effort.

"Modoc, you go back to Nevada," he said, finally, and he leaned there until the Indian had disappeared from sight. Then removing his coat and boots, and with gun in hand, he crawled into the cave, careful to be absolutely noiseless.

He felt that the floor consisted of large slabs of lava, too heavy to move with his weight. Therefore he was able to proceed silently. The roughness of lava, however, hurt his hands and knees. When he turned round he found he had progressed only forty or fifty feet from the opening, and it had seemed that he had come a long way. Looking backward enabled him to see the grim walls near the hole. They appeared to open and spread into an enormous cave.

Crawling on very cautiously, he attained at length another fifty feet. Then he crouched in pitch blackness. The air was cold and dank. Behind him the aperture where he had come in looked small and far away. He reasoned that it would never do to go out of sight of this exit. Besides, the floor began to slant downhill, and the rocks of lava to become small enough to stir and grate under him. Still he kept on, intense in his desire to hear, if possible, something of the rustlers. The door at the back shrunk to a pin point.

A few more feet, Ben thought, would be all he could dare. But he did not progress even another yard. Suddenly his free hand reached into a void. He lowered it, and as it found no support he slipped and almost lost his balance. Holding tight with knees and toes and one hand, he moved the other to feel that he had come to an abrupt break in the lava floor. Gradually he worked back a little, then relaxed to pant and tingle. Cold sweat broke out upon him. What a ghastly black pit!

When he recovered he detached a piece of lava from a slab and dropped it over into the abyss. Presently he heard it rattle, far below. That hole was deep, and evidently straight down. Other bits, thrown in different directions, apparently proved a precipice of no small dimensions. One piece of lava alighted in water. Ben assured himself that no human beings could ever have escaped from there without help. This gave him such relief and joy that he thought the risk he had incurred was well worth while.

Then he sat up in more comfortable posture and gave himself over to intense listening. Again he felt the cool wind, coming from somewhere. It was dry. It smelled of lava. The silence was deathly, and the blackness was appalling. Ben endured them for perhaps an hour — surely one of the broadening hours of his life. He might as well have been in the bowels of the earth. He was in a deep lava cave that had existed for perhaps a million years. Nature was most mysterious and inscrutable. How easy there in the terrible solitude and silence, in the impenetrable night, to believe in God!

Laboriously Ben crawled back to the exit and out. When had he ever been so grateful for sunlight, blue sky, green trees? He pitied Hall and his men. They were indeed indomitable.

Ben returned to camp and the unwearied Nevada. "Say," he began, reprovingly, "you stayed away long enough for me to get plugged."

"Pard, I crawled down into a cave. Got my bellyful of caves — don't you forget! But I'm satisfied Hall and his gang are here yet."

"Shore. An' I'll bet we heah from them pronto."

At dawn next morning Ben came on watch to relieve Modoc.

"Pard, I shore heahed a boot down there," whispered Nevada.

Ben had no time to utter a glad reply. From the black depths of the cave pealed a husky voice.

"Hey, up thar!"

"Good mawnin', Bill," yelled Nevada, clutching his rifle and leaning over it.

"You still up thar?"

"Shore as shootin'. Just settlin' down now to real waitin'."

"Wal, damn you — we're starved out. What's your terms?"

"No terms, Bill. Come walkin' out — one of you at a time — an' pitch your guns way ahaid of you on the ground."

"You agree not to shoot?" went on the hoarse voice.

"Shore not, unless you get tricky," replied Nevada, sharply.

"All right . . . Got any grub?"

"Shore have. Venison steak an' hot biscuits an' black coffee with cream an' sugar — mashed potatoes an' gravy — an' apple pie —"

"Shut up, you lyin' Southerner," shouted Hall, huskier than ever. "We surrender an' we're comin'."

Ben's piercing gaze caught a moving shadow that merged into the burly form of the rustler leader. He strode fearlessly into the light of the shelving cavern, carrying his gun by the barrel. When he reached the open he pitched the gun into the middle of the hole. Bareheaded, unkempt, dirty, and haggard, he looked the terrible havoc of those weeks.

"Fine, Bill," shouted Nevada. "Step out an' over to your right. Stick your hands up . . . There. Now call out your men, one at a time."

257

"Come out, Jenks, an' do same as me," called the leader.

A tall ragged ruffian appeared, and flinging his gun with an oath took a stand beside Hall, with gaunt hungry face exposed to the light. The third form in line was a young stalwart man with blond locks and yellow beard. And the fourth was slight of build and as dark as a Mexican. The last came out slowly with a limp, proving manifestly that he was the crippled rustler.

"Where's your rifles?" queried Nevada, whose sharp eye did not miss anything.

"Down thar," replied Hall, wagging his huge head toward the cave.

"Wal, let one fellar go back an' pack them up an' pile them with your other guns."

This order was soon complied with, whereupon Nevada rose, rifle held in readiness, and told Ben and Modoc to remove the obstruction from the trail.

"Now, Hall, come up pronto," continued Nevada. "An', Ben, when he gets up you cover him with a gun, make him set down so Modoc can tie his feet."

It seemed to the exultant and tingling Ben that in a very few moments the five rustlers sat with feet securely bound. What a ghoulish crew! Their ragged garb and unkempt hair and beards, their smoke-blackened weary faces and hungry eyes, attested to the ordeal that had at last driven them to succumb.

"Jest three of you?" queried Hall, gruffly.

258

"Shore. What you want?" drawled Nevada. "But we got some outfits comin'. Ben, heah, is the son of the man whose cattle you had in Silver Canyon."

"Hey, air you Ben Ide?" asked Hall, bending his evil intelligent eyes upon Ben.

Ben nodded, not with any evident enthusiasm. It struck him that Bill Hall had heard of him.

"Wal, now you got us, what're you a-goin' to do?" demanded Hall, turning back to Nevada.

"Bill, you're goin' first to Hart Blaine's ranch. We want you to face a fellar named Less Setter. Ever meet him?"

"Wal, I'm not gabbin' about it now," replied Hall.

"Ahuh. Shore there's no hurry aboot talkin'. I'm a close-mouthed cuss myself."

"All right. Feed us."

"See heah, Hall. You've been out of grub for days?"

"Not more'n five or six. But we're damn hungry."

"Hadn't you better go a little easy on eatin' first off? Stuffin' yourself now might kill you. I've heard of starved men —"

"We'll risk thet. Rustle some of thet grub you sang about."

"Wal, we're not goin' to risk it, you bet," declared Nevada. "But we'll feed you a little — three times today. More tomorrow an' then good square meals."

Nevada's next move was to replenish the camp fire. Ben went to his assistance. Modoc was dispatched to fetch up the rustlers' guns and saddles, after which he was to go for the horses. While Nevada worked he kept close watch upon the five men. Ben caught Hall's curious gaze fixed upon him more than once.

Excitement and strenuous labor, with the unexpected in hazard always impinging, made the ensuing hours like moments to Ben.

Not until he was in the saddle in the rear of a string of bound rustlers did he have leisure to see the actual evidences of this wonderful enterprise and to dwell upon the incredible good they represented to him. Then he soared to the blue skies. Toil and weariness were as if they had never been. He dared again to think of Ina — of the precious reward she would bestow upon him for this deed. To defeat that crafty Setter! To show Ina's father what her lover was made of! To meet his own father and see him shamed and sorry! To keep his promise to his mother! These thoughts were sweet — sweeter than any that had ever engulfed him in irresistible emotion. He lived as many changes of them as he passed trees of the forest. His mind was full while he performed his duty as the rear guard of that cavalcade.

Nevada was leading the way and it was his dominant will in command. Ben felt content to obey orders.

"We'll take a rest an' eat at the edge of the woods," Nevada had decided. "Feed the hosses all the grain left an' empty the water bags. That'll let us travel light. We'll ride all night an' get to Forlorn River by sunup."

Not long after dark they were on the move again and found cool travel by night much preferable to that by day.

260

Hall, the rustler leader, was loquacious and inclined to belittle the capture of his outfit. He did not address Nevada, but it was plain he wanted to talk with Ben. They trotted and walked the horses out across the flat sage country, and as the night wore on the air grew colder. Fortunately there was no wind; if there had been the riders, especially those with hands and feet bound, would have suffered severely. Ben wanted to talk to Hall, but had decided to wait until he had seen the rustler face Setter. Something would come of that.

They rode on and the night grew colder. White frost sparkled under the starlight. The sharp iron shoes of the horses rang with metallic clink on the stones. Modoc was far ahead with the pack-animals. Nevada rode in front of the rustlers, his rifle across his saddle, and every moment or so he would turn to look at them. Ben kept close behind Hall, who was the last in the string of bound riders.

Ben watched for the paling of the stars. When it came he was thrilled anew. Dawn was not far away. Soon he would be home, and then not far from the Blaine ranch and Ina.

Mule Deer Lake shone ghastly white in the wan starlight. It was frozen. The sight augmented Ben's consciousness of cold, and it surprised him, too. But he reflected he had once seen ice on Forlorn River at an earlier date than this. Nature seemed relentless. The drought had been terrible, but now ice had been added. What would become of the deer, the cattle? It hurt him like physical torture to think of wild horses dying of thirst.

261

The stars paled in the gray dome. After a dark hour the east lightened and over the black ranges came the dawn. How bitterly cold!

Progress was very slow, not because of lagging horses, for they were in fine fettle, but owing to the gradual weakening of the injured rustler.

Bright daylight came while the cavalcade drew close to Ben's ranch. They passed between the empty pasture and the frozen river. All the doors of the barn and the gates of the corral were open. Surely Frisbie had not done that. The cabin door, too, was open. Ben was about to declare himself forcibly when he saw Modoc rise in his stirrups as if to peer out across the lake, then duck down quickly. Ben, sensing something most unusual, rode quickly by the rustlers to face Modoc, who had turned. Nevada was peeping over the rise of ground to the lake.

"What do you see?" demanded Ben.

"Wild red stallion — way out on ice," replied the Indian, impressively.

"*California Red!* ... ON THE ICE?" cried Ben, poignantly.

"Shore's you're born, pard," returned Nevada, lowering himself into his saddle. "Only six hosses with him. The lake's frozen 'cept for circle in center. They're takin' a drink. Look!"

"No," whispered Ben, but he had not the will to do what he divined he should. Raising himself in the stirrups, he peered over the edge of the bluff. Wild Goose Lake was white with ice, and everywhere tufts of bleached grass stood up. Far out, perhaps two miles, he

262

espied horses. Wild! He knew the instant his eyes took in the graceful slim shapes, the flowing manes and tails, the wonderful posture of these horses.

California Red stood at the edge of the ice. He was not drinking. Even at that distance Ben saw the noble wild head high.

"Nevada, watch Hall," said Ben, and fumbled at the leather thongs which secured his field glass to the saddle. He loosened it, got it out of the case, leveled it. But his hands shook so he could see only blurred shapes. Fiercely he controlled himself and brought the round magnifying circle of glass to bear upon horse after horse until California Red stood clear and beautiful.

Red as a flame! Wilder than a mountain sheep! Ben saw him clear and close, limned against the white ice, big and strong, yet clean-limbed as any thoroughbred racehorse. While his band drank he watched. To what extremity had he been brought by the drought!

Ben fell limp into his saddle. Any other time in his life but this! What irony of fate! But he knew in another flash that he could not pass by this opportunity, cost what it might.

"Wal, pard, it's shore tougher than any deal we ever got," said Nevada, in distress. "California Red on the ice! We always dreamed we'd ketch him waterin' on a half-froze lake, an' lay a trap for him, or get enough riders to run him down."

"We can catch him!" shouted Ben, hoarsely.

"Nope. We cain't," replied Nevada, tragically.

Ben felt something burst within him — a knot of bound emotion — or riot of blood — or collapse of will — he never knew what. But with the spring of a panther he was out of his saddle, confronting Nevada.

"We've got four men here. With us it makes seven."

"Aw, my Gawd! Ben, you wouldn't —"

"I would," hissed Ben. "I'll have that red horse. Say you'll help me."

"I'm damned if I will!" yelled Nevada, shrilly. His dark face grew dusky red and his eyes dilated.

"I never reminded you of your debt to me," went on Ben, in swift inexorable speech. "I remind you now."

"Hell, yes!" roared Nevada, "if you put it that way. But, you locoed idiot — I'll never forgive you."

"Lighten your horses — untie your lassoes," ordered Ben, and then, drawing his clasp knife, he opened it and strode back to Hall. He knew that he was under the sway of a passion of power of which he had never before been aware. It made him unstable as water. At the same time it strung him to unquenchable spirit and incalculable strength.

"Hall, there's a wild stallion out here on the ice. I've wanted him for years. If I promise to let you and your men go free will you help me catch him?"

Hall bent his shaggy head to peer the closer into Ben's face, as if he needed scrutiny to corroborate hearing.

"Yes, I will," he boomed.

Without more ado Ben cut his bonds and passed on to the next rustler. Soon he had released them all.

"You needn't go," he said to the cripple.

"If it's all the same to you, I will," replied this man, cheerfully. "I can't ride hard, but I can yell an' fill up a hole. I've chased wild horses."

Ben ran back to his mount and with nimble fingers lightened his saddle, tightened the cinch, and untied his rope. The rustlers got off to stretch their legs.

"Cinch up," he panted. "Nevada, take two men — and go around to the left. Keep out of sight. I'll take — Hall and another man — with me. We'll cross — the river. Modoc, you stay here — till we both show on the banks. Then ride in . . . We'll close in on Red slow . . . Soon as he gets to running he'll slip — on the ice . . . He'll fall and slide . . . That'll demoralize him . . . Rest — will be — easy!"

Nevada rode off with two of the men, while Ben, calling Hall and Jenks, wheeled back toward the barn and went down to the river. The ice cracked and swayed, but held the horses. Once across, Ben led the way at a swift gallop round to the west of the lake, keeping out of sight of the wild horses. When he reached a point far enough along the lake he swerved to the height of ground. As he surmounted it he saw Nevada with his two riders come into sight across the lake, and another glance showed Modoc, with his followers emerging by the mouth of the river.

California Red was a mile out on the ice, coming directly toward Ben. His stride was a stilted trot, and he lost it at every other step. His red mane curled up in the wind. The six horses were strung out behind him. Discovering Ben, the stallion let out a piercing whistle and wheeled. Then his feet flew out from under him and he fell. Frantically he tried to rise, but his smooth hoofs on the slippery ice did not catch hold.

"Ah, my beauty!" yelled Ben, wildly, with all his might. "It's no square chase — but you're mine — you're mine."

The other wild horses wheeled without losing their footing, and soon drew away from the slipping, sliding stallion. At last he got up on four feet and turned toward his band. It seemed that he knew he dared not run. At every step one of his hoofs slipped out from under him. Ben caught the yells of his helpers. They were running their horses down the sandy slope toward the ice. Another wild horse went down and then another. It was almost impossible for them to rise. They slid around like tops.

Meanwhile, swift as the wind, Ben was running his fast horse down to the lake, distancing his followers, who came yelling behind. Hall's heavy voice pealed out, full of the wild spirit of the chase. Ben reached the ice. The sharp iron shoes of his horse cut and broke through the first few rods, but reaching solid ice they held. Ben reined in to wait for the men to spread and form a circle. Nevada was far out on the ice now, and he had closed the one wide avenue to the west. Soon the eight riders had closed in to a half-mile arc, with the open lake as an aid.

California Red turned back from the narrowing gap between Nevada and the lake. When he wheeled to the west Modoc's group left a gateway for the wild horses nearest. They plunged and ran and slid and fell — got up to plunge again, and at last earned their freedom.

This left two besides the stallion on the ice. He appeared at terrible disadvantage. Wild and instinct with wonderful speed, he could not exercise it. The riders closed in. Nevada rode between Red and the open water. Another of the horses escaped through a gap.

"Close in, slow now," bawled Ben, swinging the noose of his lasso.

The moment was fraught with a madness of rapture. How sure the outcome! Presently the great stallion would stampede and try to run. That was all Ben wanted. For when Red tried to run on that glassy ice his doom was sealed.

He was trotting, here, there, back again, head erect, mane curled, tail sweeping, a living flame of horse-flesh. Terror would soon master him. His snorts seemed more piercingly acute, as if he protested against the apparent desertion of his band.

"Farther around, Modoc," yelled Ben. "Same for you, Nevada — on other side. Keep him in triangle . . . Now, men, ride in — yell like hell. And block him when he runs."

Suddenly the red horse gathered himself in a knot. How grandly he sprang! And he propelled his magnificent body into a convulsive run, with every hoof sliding from under him. Straight toward Ben he came, his nostrils streaming white, his hoofs cracking like pistol shots. It seemed that his wild spirit enabled him to overcome even this impossible obstacle of ice, for he kept erect until he was shooting with incomparable speed.

At the height of it he slipped, plunged on his side with a snort of terror, turned on his back, and as he slid with swift momentum over the ice, his hoofs in the air, Ben's lasso uncurled like a striking snake. The noose fell over the forelegs and tightened.

Lusty yells from leather lungs! California Red had run into a rope. Ben hauled in his skilful horse. The great stallion flopped back on his side. The rope came taut to straighten out his legs, and stop him short. He could not rise. When he raised his beautiful head the Indian's rope circled his neck. His race was run.

Nevada came trotting up, noose in hand, white of face and fierce of eye.

"Pard, he's ruined us, but he's worth it or I'm a livin' sinner," he shouted.

Ben gazed almost in stupefaction down upon the heaving graceful animal. California Red lay helpless, beaten, robbed of his incomparable speed. Every red line of him spoke to Ben's thrilling soul.

"Wal, Ide," boomed Bill Hall, slapping Ben on the shoulder, "I'm glad you ketched this grand hoss . . . You're a good sport. Put her thar! . . . If I had time I'd tell you somethin'. But I see riders comin' along the lake an' we must rustle."

CHAPTER
FOURTEEN

As day after day passed at the Blaine ranch Ina watched and prayed for the return of her father. She dreaded the thought of Setter coming back to find her alone. She no longer feared him, but he could make the situation there most exasperating, if not actually distressing. Moreover there was always the uncertainty.

Two of Blaine's cowboys rode in with pack horses for another week's supplies. They reported a most unsatisfactory situation at the head of Forlorn River, and that, in consequence, Blaine was in bad temper. Marvie caught a few words not meant for his ears, to the effect that Strobel had conflicted with the cowboys.

Sunday, about noon, Setter arrived. It was Marvie who brought the news to Ina. She and the lad had grown closer than ever in the opposition to Less Setter and the forces that seemed bent upon destroying Ben Ide.

Ina fortified herself against something inevitable and disastrous. Her mother and Marvie were adequate protectors in a way, but she could not be with either all the time. Marvie had his work and his play, and to have been deprived of his fishing would have broken his heart. Twice he had returned from Forlorn River with smashed fishing tackle and most extraordinary tales.

From the camp Ina kept pretty close watch on the ranch. She possessed a field glass, which she brought to bear upon other places than Forlorn River. Setter passed under her sight several times that day, manifestly in serious council with the sheriff, Judd, and his deputy, Walker. From her tent Ina watched them, and after each look her resentment augmented. How she hated this sleek coarse man of intrigue!

Naturally she expected Setter to approach her sometime that afternoon or early evening. When he did not, she experienced relief, yet a sense of calamity. Marvie, who played eavesdropper outside Setter's cabin an hour after dark, rather added to the complications of the case. He reported that Setter and the two officers talked endlessly, but too low for him to get at the drift of their conversation. Marvie protested however that they must be hatching some plot.

Next morning he tapped on Ina's tent door while she was dressing. She peeped out. "Hello, early fisher bird! Are you after worms?"

"Naw, they're snakes," he retorted, with his bright smile. "Look, Sis. There goes Judd an' Walker, with pack outfits. On the Forlorn River trail!"

After a moment's survey of the gray waste beyond the ranch Ina made out four horses headed down toward the lake.

"Wonder what they're up to?" she mused.

"After Ben," muttered Marvie, darkly. "An' they're goin' to ransack Ben's ranch before huntin' him . . .

Ina, if you'll lie to Dad for me, case it's necessary, I'll ride around the other side of the lake an' see what Judd is up to."

"I'll say I sent you and fight for you, Marvie. Go. Take my field glass and keep out of sight," she replied, resolutely.

An hour after breakfast, as had been her custom since her father's absence, Ina went down to the ranch office. She had completed the small tasks he had grudgingly permitted her to undertake, but she did not let that keep her from going. Indeed, she needed to precipitate whatever it was that seemed inevitable.

As some of the ranch hands were always within call, the office was perhaps the safest place for Ina. Ina was sitting at her father's desk with open record book before her and pen in hand when Setter's frame filled the doorway.

"Mornin', sweetheart," he said, blandly.

Ina did not look up or reply, and went on writing.

Setter laughed and there was something in his laugh that rankled deep in Ina, dissipating indifference if not self-control. He advanced slowly and sat upon the desk near her.

"Ina, aren't you goin' to say good mornin'?" he went on, pleasantly.

"Not to you," she replied, and rose to face him, outwardly composed. His appearance had vastly improved since she last saw him, though his features still bore the marks of the beating Ben had given him. There was visible, too, more of that strange confidence

in his utter mastery of this situation. It inflamed Ina —
baffled her — roused her to battle.

"Mr. Setter, will you please leave the office?" she
requested, coldly. "I've work, and I can't do it with you
here."

"Why not get used to me?" he retorted, subtly.

"Nothing could induce me to."

"Sharp of tongue this mornin'," he muttered, eying
her speculatively with his bold gaze. "What's come over
you?"

"My feelings are none of your business," flashed Ina.
"Will you get out of here?"

"No. An' you can't put me out," he returned,
insolently. "If you've got to be told, this office belongs
more to me than to Hart Blaine."

Ina betrayed no surprise. This was precisely what she
had expected and wanted to hear. Affronting this man
might lead her into an embarrassing if not hazardous
situation, but it certainly was productive of information.

"Indeed? But I think you're a liar," she said, just as
insolently.

"It's no lie," he returned, louder, and his
olive-skinned face began to take on a heated tinge. "I've
got your father's paper. The McAdam deal fell through.
Amos Ide finally refuses the backing he promised. The
Hammell bank holds Blaine notes for two hundred
thousand. An' when *I* say so they shut down on him.
That'll take his ranch, an' I've got his cattle."

"Well, assuming all this is true — what then?"
queried Ina.

"You marry me or I'll ruin him," snapped Setter, leaning toward her.

"Mr. Setter, do you still harp on that?" asked Ina, in pretended amaze.

"On what?" he rasped.

"Marriage. It's too ridiculous. Even if I didn't despise you I wouldn't marry you."

"I tell you I'll ruin your father," shouted Setter, angrily. "I can make him a pauper."

"Do it, then," flashed Ina, passionately. "Who'd care? My mother and I would welcome poverty. We hate this sudden wealth. *That* has ruined Father, as much as crooked men like you."

"Bah! I don't swaller that, Miss Ina Blaine," said Setter. But it was plain that her unexpected repudiation of his offer and indifference to her father's ruin staggered him, and therefore made him furious.

"I don't care what you 'swaller'," rejoined Ina. "But get out of here or let me out."

"Just you wait till I'm through talkin'," he went on, with calculating eyes. "I didn't tell you I can put your father in jail for hirin' rustlers. Wal, I can."

Ina saw in his face that he was telling the truth, if not all the truth. This then had been the secret of his veiled power; and he unmasked himself before her because he believed she dared not betray him. Indeed, the thought of disgrace and imprisonment for her father filled her with exceeding bitterness, but she did not weaken under it. After a momentary faltering she was again strong, with keen mind revolving and grasping the possibilities Setter's brutal candor laid open.

"Oh, I see!" she spoke up, mockingly. "A while back it was poor Ben Ide who was an accomplice of rustlers. Now it's my dad . . . I suppose you mean that Dad and Ben Ide are partners in crime."

"I'll run Ben Ide out of the country or put him in jail," hissed Setter.

"You will not!"

"Oh-ho! You flare up about Ben, eh? More than about your father. I begin to see a nigger in the woodpile."

"If my father has been such a fool — such a greedy fool as to let you make him dishonest — he deserves disgrace, and jail too," declared Ina, hotly. "But Ben Ide is as good as gold. He's been driven away from home and friends. He's honest. He's true. And the truth will prevail. Your vile insinuations, your lying evidences, can be torn to tatters by any honest magistrate . . . It's *you*, Less Setter, who'd better run out of the country. For I'll stand by Ben Ide until he's vindicated."

"The hell you say!" ejaculated Setter, stridently, and with swift movement he grasped her arm. "What's Ben Ide to you?"

"Let go of me! That's none of your business, either, but you're welcome to know," cried Ina, suddenly ceasing her effort to get away from him. "I love Ben Ide . . . I'm engaged to him . . . I intend to marry him."

"Ben Ide! . . . You white-faced cat!" he returned, hoarsely, in a rage of defeat and amaze. Livid, savage, he dragged her to him. "Then Ben Ide will get what I leave!"

274

Instead of weakening under his rude clutch and vile kisses, Ina became endowed with almost superhuman strength. Clenching her fists she pounded his face, aiming at his sore and discolored eye. Her aim went true. She hurt him terribly, for he uttered a kind of hoarse bawl and momentarily lost his equilibrium. Then Ina wrestled away from him and pushed him with all the violence she could summon. Setter tripped on a chair and fell heavily. Ina darted out at the open door, and hurrying toward camp, panting and hot, shaking in every muscle, she swore that if Setter attacked her again she would kill him.

Marvie did not return until after dark. He said he had watched Judd and Walker through the glass, and had been able to gather that they pretty well took possession of Ben's cabin and were not going to leave soon. Marvie had seen them carry what looked like a sack out into the barn and then reappear empty-handed. They left barn doors and corral gates open.

"Likely they'll stay there until Ben returns," said Marvie.

"Ben won't come soon," rejoined Ina, broodingly.

"Where'd he go?"

"Marvie, you mustn't breathe it. Ben went away to catch the very rustlers he's supposed to work secretly with."

"Bill Hall's outfit? The cowboys say Ben is in cahoots with Hall . . . It looks funny — Ben goin' off *now* just when they're lookin' for him. An', Ina, how'n earth could Ben with only two pardners ketch a whole rustler gang? Dang it!"

And evidently Marvie went away laboring under a doubt. What he had said found lodgment in the fertile seeking soil of Ina's mind. Despite her uttermost faith in Ben, she could not but admit that even a boy's logic was incontestable. Loyally and prayerfully she tried not to ponder and brood over things she could not understand. Her duty was clear.

Next morning, to Ina's extreme surprise Setter rode away from the ranch alone, leading a pack horse. He, too, took the direction of Forlorn River. Was he going to join the officers from Redlands or her father? Ina calculated that Setter would do both. Thus the plot revolving around Ben Ide thickened and lengthened its ramifications.

Camp life during the August days was delightful, except perhaps in the very early morning, when at this altitude the air was too cold. The days passed, and Ina accommodated herself to the best obtainable from them. As before, she found work and play preferable to idle moments. These were conducive to the dominance of the hydra-headed dread that would not stay quiet. It was well, she thought, that Hettie Ide had postponed her visit. She could not have kept the truth from Hettie, either the love of Nevada or Ben's terrible predicament.

Not until the wild geese came honking back did Ina realize the end of summer was at hand. By day and by night the honkers passed, some alighting on the shores of the lake, but most of them holding their flight to the south. Their melodious cries haunted Ina; and in the

276

blackness of night, when sleep would not come, she covered up her head so she could not hear.

Early in September her father arrived at the ranch, with his cowboys and Setter.

Ina was dismayed at sight of him. If business troubles had begun to worry him before he left, they now weighted him down. Rather than add to them, Ina held her tongue, sure in her intuitive feeling that revelations would come soon enough. She scarcely saw her father, not even at meals, and certainly did not go out of her way to meet him. Most of all she was curious about what Less Setter had told him. It was conceivable that her father's difficulties precluded serious attention to her.

With the arrival of this party at the ranch there flourished much gossip, which Marvie heard among the cowboys and carried to Ina.

Judd and his deputy had found proofs at Ben Ide's ranch of his guilt, so far as the rustling of cattle was concerned. They had taken his trail for the hills. Amos Ide's stock at Silver Meadow had been sadly depleted in a July raid. Strobel, the Hammell sheriff, had approached Blaine at a rancher's homestead, and had locked horns with him about something that was not clear. The cowboys thought Strobel was calling Blaine to some accounting. Certain it appeared that this interview upset Blaine and changed his plans. Lastly the arrival of Setter had thrown the old man into a fit of spleen that amounted almost to a serious illness. Bill

Sneed avowed that Setter pestered the life out of Blaine.

At this juncture Mrs. Blaine, perhaps through sympathy and worry, became indisposed, so that Ina and Dall had to nurse her, besides do all the other work.

"Dad, let's go home," begged Ina, the first opportunity that offered. "It's too cold for Mother. These nights are growing a little too wintry for tents."

"Ina, I'd gone back to Tule Lake long ago," he replied, somberly. "But mebbe it's not mine any more. So Setter says. This ranch is all I've got without a lien on it."

"Dad, it isn't possible?" exclaimed Ina.

"I don't know. I'm muddled. But I balked on Setter. He's naggin' me now to make you marry him. He's like a bulldog. Reckon I wouldn't want you to marry him if you was willin'."

"Thank you, Dad," she replied, in gladness. "Now don't you give up one more single inch. Not for anything. Just you wait."

"Wait? . . . Wal, daughter, I was weakenin' over a final deal, but, by thunder! now I'll wait."

September brought a skim of ice round the edges of the lake, and daily it whitened and lengthened. The autumn days were glorious with blue skies, fleecy clouds, coloring hills, and a bracing sage-scented wind.

Then one morning, which was so beautiful that Ina forgot the shadow which hovered over the ranch, Marvie rushed in on her.

278

"Judd an' — Walker's back," he burst out, breathlessly. "They're waitin' for Dad before — holdin' a regular court."

Ina hurried to the tent of her mother, who was well again but not very active, and found her father there. She had observed that he spent a good deal of time with her mother.

"Dad, those officers from Redlands are back and want you," announced Ina.

"Wal, I'm glad," he said, wearily. "If they'll only help to clear up this mess."

She held to his arm and walked with him, studying what was best to say.

"Dad, will you listen to me?" she appealed, earnestly.

"'Course I will, child."

"I mean really listen," she went on, suddenly seized by impulse. "It can't do harm. It may do good."

"Wal, I've come to a sad pass if I can't listen serious to the lass I wanted educated."

"Then take what I've worked out in my mind," she rejoined, swiftly. "Setter means to ruin you, and poor Ben Ide along with you. For I'll not marry Setter, even if you or Ben would let me . . . But, Dad, evil as Setter is, he can't accomplish all this. Something will happen. I can't explain. It's what I feel — here! . . . No matter what apparent facts these officers show, don't act upon them. Don't do anything. Just wait!"

"Lass, I've drunk in Setter's honey words an' listened to everyone 'cept Mother an' you," he replied, with pathos. "It's high time I remembered that."

They approached the office cabin together. Cowboys lounged around lazily. Saddle horses stood, heads down, dusty and weary, waiting to be led away. Bill Sneed sat on the steps and Ina thought he meant her to catch the glint of his eye. Setter stood inside, conversing intently with Judd and Walker. Ina entered beside her father and she did not miss Setter's dark conjecturing glance.

"Mornin', men," said Blaine, stiffly. "What you wantin' of me?"

"Good mornin', Mr. Blaine," replied Judd, in his loud voice. "We've got results, I'm glad to report. We found proofs in Ben Ide's barn that he's been stealin' cattle. Also we took his tracks an' found his camp up in the hills. He got wind of us some way, mebbe with a glass, an' left his camp the night before we got there. Left supplies, clothes, hosses, an' a black wild stallion he'd just broke. We lost his tracks then, but we kept ridin' all over, an' one day we hit upon cattle tracks in a deep canyon. We trailed them, an' come on a herd of two hundred an' fifty head. Most of these had Amos Ide's A1 brand. But there were some steers belongin' to you. Fine stock that you got in the deal for Welch's homestead, near Silver Meadow."

"You rounded up some missin' stock, hey? Wal, how're you goin' to fix it on Ben Ide?" rejoined Blaine.

"I just informed you," replied Judd, testily. "We found his camp with things that identify him near a canyon full of your stolen cattle."

"Wouldn't amount to shucks in court," said Blaine. "Sure he might be guilty an' mebbe he is, but leavin' a

280

camp sudden means nothin'. He's a wild-hoss hunter. What's your other charge?"

Here Setter intervened with step forward and authoritative mien.

"We're withholdin' that till Ide is arrested. I expect you to appear against him."

"Wal, I won't do it," declared Blaine, bluntly.

"I can force you to. I'm your partner. He stole our cattle."

"Setter, when I go to court it'll be to recover more than a few head of steers," returned Blaine, with enigmatic stubbornness.

"I'll make Ide's own father appear against him," shouted Setter, paling with passion.

"Wal, that'd be a low-down trick," observed Blaine, in weary amaze.

Setter cursed behind his teeth. Ina, watching him closer, felt that his case against her father and Ben was not as perfect as he wanted it. There seemed a flaw somewhere.

One thing and another, in the way of camp articles and a rider's apparel, were brought in to exhibit to Blaine. Ina could not doubt her eyes when she was confronted with Ben's initials burned in leather. Her heart misgave her somewhat. It was hard to be brave in the face of all this incredible animosity toward Ben Ide. Still her father's gruff antagonism to Judd's arguments and Setter's plans surprised her. It was a hopeful sign. She was not the only one surprised. Setter chafed under a restriction that he could not afford to disregard for fear he might lose prestige in the eyes of these officers.

"Mr. Blaine, will you send cowboys to Silver Canyon to drive out the stolen cattle?" inquired Judd.

"How're the grass an' water there?"

"Best we've seen in all this country."

"Wal, better leave the stock there, anyways till Amos Ide has his say," decided Blaine.

"We'll send a messenger to notify Mr. Ide an' advise him to come over here," added Judd, with an interrogating glance at Setter.

"Good idea," spoke up that individual. "Ide's deep in this, too."

For the time being then there appeared to be a deadlock. Ina left the office, to wander campward, divided between a mounting emotion of hope for her father and again that strange insidious question as to the apparent contradictions in her defense of Ben. The instant it entered her consciousness she passionately repudiated it, as if she could be so low as to doubt him. She did not.

The day endured as if minutes were hours, every one of which wore on Ina's nerves. She had waited almost to the limit of her reserve. Something must happen any moment. She worried over the strained situation between her father and Setter. But at last the day ended and she found much-needed oblivion in sleep. Toward dawn she awoke, almost freezing. Dall had appropriated more than her share of the blankets. She dropped into slumber again, to be awakened by Marvie at her door.

"Ina, wake up, for goodness' sake!" he called.

"Hel-lo, Marv! What's up?" she answered, rousing.

"Not you, by gosh! I'm sorry, Ina, but I just had to wake you. Sun ain't up yet, either. Gee! it's colder than blue blazes."

"Don't I know how cold it is? Why'd you wake me? Is Dad — has anyone — What — ?"

"Nope. Everythin' peaceful so far as I know, 'cause they're all asleep. I had to wake you, Sis, 'cause if I was a gurl in love with a wild-hoss wrangler I'd sure want to see what I'm seein' now."

"Marv Blaine! I'll — I'll —" burst out Ina, half angry and half curious.

"Ina, the lake's 'most froze over this mornin' an' wild horses are walkin' out on the ice. Seven of them. Pretty close to Ben's place."

"Honest, Marv?" queried Ina, with a thrill.

"Cross my heart."

"I'll get up, cold or no cold. Fetch me some hot water and I'll let you use my field glass."

Ina had scarcely had time to get into some warm clothes when Marvie came with the water. She handed him the field glass in exchange and heard him plump down on her steps. Then she forgot him, to be reminded presently that he was still there.

"Omilord! Omilord!" he was uttering in ecstasy.

"Marvie, what ails you?" she called, halting in her ablutions.

"Omilord! Omilord!" he ejaculated in tones of most intense awe and joy.

This was too much for Ina, and hastening with her toilet, and throwing on a heavy coat, she rushed out. Marvie sat hunched on her step with the glass leveled out over the lake. Ina's gaze followed the direction thus indicated. How beautiful the white frost-coated ice! Far across the open circle of water she saw a number of horses, black against the background. They looked small, but she saw them move.

"So they're wild horses," she mused. "Too bad Ben's away."

"Omilord!" moaned Marvie.

"You goose! Are you getting as wild as Ben?"

"Ina, look — look at that leader in front!" cried the boy, leaping up to put the glass to her eyes.

It took a little time for Ina to readjust the glasses and to find anything but muddy water and white level expanse of ice. Suddenly into the clear circle walked a magnificent horse, red as fire, wild as nothing Ina had ever seen.

"Oh! — Marvie! A red horse! . . . Is that what you saw? No wonder! . . . Oh, how beautiful!"

"Is that all you see?" scornfully and agitatedly queried Marvie. "He's red — he's a stallion."

"Yes, I see that, Marv."

"Well?"

"Well what, you queer boy?"

"That's California Red — the wild stallion Ben loves," declared Marvie, impressively.

Ina nearly dropped the glass, lost direction and object, fumbled with fingers all thumbs, laughed at her blurred eyes — and then, controlling herself, she soon found the horse again and brought him distinctly into her sight. She saw him differently now. She reveled in his color, grace, wildness. Long she gazed.

"Now — I don't blame Ben," she whispered, as if in judgment on herself.

"What the dickens!" muttered Marvie, turning away. "Who's yellin'?"

"It's the cowboys," declared Ina. "See, in the bunk-house door . . . Marvie, they see the wild horses. That's what they're yelling at."

"Funny. Darn. I'm sorry they seen California Red on the ice. He could be ketched easy. Nobody but Ben oughta ever own Red," declared Marvie, turning again to the lake. "By gosh! More wild horses . . . I dunno, though. Sis, gimme the glass?"

The instant Marvie got the glass leveled to suit him he yelled: "Riders pilin' down on the ice. Ina, they're goin' to chase Red."

"Oh, let me see, Marvie — please!"

"Just a minnit . . . Three riders on this side — two comin' out from the river — three more on other side . . . Who'n the dickens are they? I'll bet Ben has got some fellars to help him . . . Omilord! it *is* Ben. He's on his gray . . . Gee! look at him go! Out on the ice!"

Ina snatched the glass away from her brother, and even as she brought it to bear she heard the wild yells of the cowboys and hoarser deeper cries following. Like Marvie, they had at once connected these horsemen with Ben. She grew tremendously excited and thrilled.

The wild horses were moving to and fro, haltingly, it seemed. Perhaps the distance caused their movements to look slow and awkward. All of them except the red stallion showed black against the white. It was difficult for her to hold the glass steady; she trembled so that she had to sit down on the steps and rest her elbows on her knees. Then she got the circle of action under clear vision and watched with palpitating heart.

California Red pranced forward and back, then moved swiftly and fell on the ice. His efforts to rise were those of a horse with crippled hind quarters. He appeared left alone. The horsemen drew closer. Ina made out the gray horse mentioned by Marvie, and though she did not recognize it she believed she recognized its rider. She strained her eyes. The lithe form and wide shoulders belonged to Ben Ide. She was unable to hold the glass so as to inclose him and the wild stallion at one and the same time. When she changed the direction it took a moment for her to find anything. Then she found California Red again and decided to keep the glass on him.

For a wild horse he acted strangely. Why did he not flee? If he was the king of all swift horses, he could escape. She wanted him to have freedom, yet contrarily she hoped Ben would gain the desire of his heart. The stallion appeared moving with mixed gait that was very ungraceful. Horsemen appeared beyond him, drawing closer. He wheeled this way, then that, and his actions were expressive of uncertainty. He was hemmed in.

All at once he seemed to lower himself, then plunged into a run. How his red mane and tail flew in the wind! Swift — he was like an arrow from a bow. Ina screamed in joy of his freedom. Suddenly he went headlong. Had he been shot? He slid over the ice. The gray horse flashed into Ina's field of vision. His rider swayed in the saddle. Other horsemen entered the circle. From under the hoofs of the gray horse flashed white puffs, probably ice cut by the sharp iron shoes. Suddenly he plunged back on his haunches. Ina saw California Red slide to a quick stop.

"Oh, Marvie, Ben has caught him!" exclaimed Ina, in a transport.

"Gimme the glass!" shouted Marvie. "Yes — he's down — he's down. Ben's horse holdin' back . . . There's another rider close. Ropin'. Gee! I know that swing . . . Ina, your California Red is a gone goslin'! . . . Whoopee!"

Marvie's yell of conquest and exultation appeared strangled before full utterance. Ina saw him look and start. Then she discovered that horsemen were galloping away from the ranch.

"Aw, hell!" groaned the lad, and that was the first profane word Ina had ever heard him use. "Look! . . . Judd an' Walker goin' over to arrest Ben."

CHAPTER
FIFTEEN

The remainder of that morning, so thrillingly started, was a long-drawn-out hateful period of suspense for Ina. She spent the last of it in her tent with a coverlet over her eyes to shut out the light of day.

A little before noon, Marvie, acting under her instructions, returned for her, rapping at her door.

"Ina — they're comin'," he said, reluctantly.

"Have — have they got Ben?" she asked, uncovering her face.

"Yes. They're a good ways down the road yet. But I seen with the glass. They've got Ben an' the Indian."

"I'll come. I must — be there," faltered Ina, rising.

"I should smile you will," retorted Marvie, more like his real self. "We just gotta get mad, Ina. Wait till you see Setter down there — big cigar — swellin' out his chest — an' rubbin' his hands when he thinks he ain't seen. But I was spottin' him."

Marvie's resolute passion and the content of his words held strange power to inspirit Ina. She felt the shock of suddenly released blood, with its accompanying heat and accelerated pulse. She brushed her scarf, and went out to join Marvie.

He met her with a quick, intent look of pride and confidence.

"Come on; we mustn't miss nothin' now," he said, taking her hand. "Mother is down at the office. Setter an' Dad wanted her to sign papers. She wouldn't. Then Setter got ugly an' that made Dad mad. He an' Setter were havin' it hot an' heavy when Mr. Ide come in."

"Ben's father!" exclaimed Ina.

"Yes. Gee! he looked like an owl. But his comin' stopped the row. Setter took Mr. Ide to his cabin, where they are now. Dad fired me out of his office, but I peeped in a winder. Heard him tell Mother he was glad she wouldn't sign the papers. An' Dad cussed Setter awful. 'Somethin' wrong about that man.' . . . An' then Ma said, 'It oughtn't be new to you.' . . . Then Dad: 'Wal, it's too late. I'll not give in. I'll go to jail with Ben Ide. That's what sticks in my craw — the way Setter is houndin' this poor boy. It's come to have a queer look.'"

"Oh, Marv, did Dad say that?" whispered Ina, squeezing her brother's hand. "Did you hear any more?"

"No. Some cowboy yelled that Judd was in sight, so I made sure, then hustled up to get you."

"Then — is Ben in sight?"

"Yes. Down the road. Take a look with the glass."

"No." Ina pushed the glass away. She would put off as long as possible the spectacle of her lover riding in under arrest.

Soon she and Marvie crossed the sage field to enter the ranch. The square between the cabins contained a dozen or more saddled horses, and groups of cowboys, all with heads together. The usual lazy languor of a Blaine ranch was not in evidence.

"Cowboys been in row," whispered Marvie. "Bill Sneed on Ben's side, an' that split the outfit. I tell you, Sis, there's a-goin' to be a hot time here."

As Ina drew closer she saw that her father's entire force of employees was present, and whatever the direction of their sympathies, it was plain that excitement ran high. The nearest cowboy group left off their whispering as Ina walked by to the cabin. She did not espy either Mr. Ide or Setter. Her father was in the office alone with her mother.

"Ina, Mr. Setter says dreadful things about your father," spoke up Mrs. Blaine, almost tearfully. "If I don't sign papers an' if you won't marry him —"

"Mother dear, don't be distressed," interrupted Ina. "I've heard Mr. Setter's threats. We'll stick together if we *all* go to jail."

"But that'd be terrible!"

"Indeed it would. But it'll never happen," declared Ina, earnestly.

"Daughter, the sheriff is comin' with Ben Ide," said her father.

"I know. Marvie told me."

"An' Amos Ide is here. It's toughest for him. That damned Setter has got him in a corner now."

Ina ran to her father, and slipping an arm round his shoulders, as he sat stooping, she whispered: "Dad, once in your life — now — think, and boss this affair, whatever it's to be. You're on your own property. Don't let Setter dominate things. Don't let him do all the talking. Be fair an' square to Ben Ide — for I — I love him, Dad."

Ina expected her father to be shocked and furious. He was neither, yet she saw that her poignant speech had penetrated deeply. He rose to his tall height and looked down upon her with a softer light in his gray eyes than she had ever seen there. Trouble, realization, defeat had begun their broadening work upon Hart Blaine.

"Lass, I'm sorry I didn't wake up to this long ago," he said, with regret. "Marvie gave me a hunch, but I didn't take it . . . So you love Ben Ide?"

"Yes, Dad," she replied, proudly.

"Wal, an' I reckon you take yourself to be a Blaine?"

"Did you ever boss me, Dad?" she laughed.

"Huh! I should smile not . . . But you should have told me. It'd make a difference, even if I was bullheaded . . . Now it's too late. They'll make Ben out a rustler even if he ain't. But —"

"Dad," yelled Marvie, at the door, "they're here!"

Blaine strode out of the office, and Ina, with her mother, followed. Four horsemen had ridden into the square. Blaine advanced, with the cowboys crowding behind. Ina felt Marvie holding her and whispering fast, but she could not distinguish his words. Her mother appeared nervous and excited, and Ina thought it was as well that she had her to look after. In another moment further advance was checked by the halting crowd, and Ina with staring eyes looked over the shoulder of a cowboy.

Judd had just reined in his horse. His florid face beamed; he waved a big gloved hand, with gesture that suited his look.

Ina saw a gray mettlesome horse, wet with sweat — then its rider, Ben Ide. His face was white. He seemed dazed. His unnatural posture was owing to handcuffs. Beside him rode a somber, dark-faced Indian, also handcuffed. Walker, the deputy, sat his horse a little behind the others. Ina's gaze, rushing back to Ben, fastened on his face. Her heart swelled to the bursting point. Why did he look like that? His eyes had a terrible haunting shadow. Was he hopeless? Had he no defense?

"Here's your man, Mr. Blaine," called out Judd, pompously. "I told you we'd fetch him. An' we sure got him dead to rights, ketched red-handed —"

"Say, Mr. Judd," broke in Blaine, almost roughly. "I'm lettin' you understand he's not my man. I had nothin' to do with this arrest."

"But your partner, Mr. Setter, he did. Same thing," expostulated Judd, nonplussed and affronted.

"No, it ain't the same. Setter an' me are *not* partners. Do you understand?"

"I'll be darned if I do," shouted Judd, beginning to fume. "Setter said he represented you — that you offered a thousand reward —"

"Shut up!" called Blaine, in a voice that Ina well remembered. "I aim to do some talkin' here myself . . . I offered no reward an' I'll pay none."

Judd's heavy jowl dropped. He was silenced, and in bewilderment and rousing resentment he gazed about, manifestly for Setter.

292

Blaine strode up beside Ben's horse and laid a hand on his knee.

"Ide, I'm sorry to see you here," he said, gruffly, but not unkindly.

Ben showed instant surprise and a fleeting look of gratitude.

"Thanks, Mr. Blaine. You can't guess how sorry I am," he said.

"Your dad is here with Setter."

Ben's haggard face burned duskily red.

"Yes, sir — I — expected that," he replied, huskily.

"Boy, are you guilty?" went on Blaine, gravely.

"Yes, I am — guilty as hell," confessed Ben, in a passion of shame and remorse. "But I was crazy — out of my head. I never thought — I never thought how it would look."

Ina sustained a terrible shock. For a moment she seemed frozen within — clamped round a knot of agony. She almost fainted. The deathly spasm passed, and sight, thought, emotion became inextricably mixed. She stared at Ben Ide. She saw the torture in his working face. The words of his confession thundered in her ears, stirring wild and whirling thoughts. Guilty as hell! He had betrayed himself. And worse — he had betrayed to her his deceit, his weakness. The damning truth almost broke her heart then and there. But she longed to fly to him, to stand by him even in his guilt.

"Wal — Ide," she heard her father speak in sorrow and amaze, "I reckon I can't help you none."

There was a commotion outside the circle of cowboys to Ina's left. Someone crowded through — made a lane. Setter strode into view, pale, with burning eyes. Amos Ide entered the space, but kept back, half hidden by the other.

"Aha, Judd — you've only two of them here. Ide an' the Indian. Where's the third man? That one they call Nevada," demanded Setter, loud voiced, authoritatively.

"He got away," replied Judd.

"What! You let that one escape? You're a fine sheriff," ejaculated Setter, furiously.

"Wal, listen to facts in the case before you go to rakin' me," returned Judd, sullenly. "This Nevada fellar acted tractable enough. But when he seen the handcuffs Walker had, why, he said, 'Have you the gall to try puttin' them on *me*?' . . . Walker tried it an' got knocked flat. Then Nevada jumped his hoss an' got away. I shot three times at him. Missed. He rode off after Bill Hall an' his outfit."

Ina, in her piercing intensity of gaze, felt as if she saw the sudden check to Setter's thoughts, under a blank mask.

"Bill Hall! . . . What do you mean? This Nevada rode off after Bill Hall?"

"I mean what I say," retorted Judd, more testily. His temper had been ruffled. His great coup had not earned him anticipated adulation. "Bill Hall an' outfit was with Ide. They was chasin' this wild stallion California Red. They ketched him, too."

"Bill Hall with Ide — chasin' wild hosses?" ejaculated Setter, as if he had not heard aright. His olive tan showed a shade of gray, his prominent eyes a questioning furtive glint.

"Say, Mr. Setter," returned Judd, with a sneer, "didn't *you* expect Bill Hall to be with Ben Ide?"

"No — not at this stage of the game," returned Setter, with effort. "He — I — But no matter . . . If Hall was there why didn't you arrest him, too?"

"Haw! Haw! Haw!" guffawed the sheriff. His mirth might have been ridicule of such hazardous enterprise or it might have meant something else. Ina thought she caught a subtle double meaning. How complex the circumstances! She had to fight to keep her faculties keen. At this juncture Marvie squeezed her hand, and letting it go he slipped between the cowboys into the circle. Ina's last glimpse of his tow-colored head showed him edging toward his father.

"Blaine," spoke up Setter, turning, "we've got two of the rustlers, an' conviction will help break up as slick a gang as I ever heard of. Will you appear in Hammell court against them?"

"No, Setter, I won't," replied Blaine, curtly.

"All right, you'll appear there in another capacity," harshly rejoined Setter.

The tall form of Amos Ide stalked past Setter. His lined and craggy face was set in stern bitterness. He strode out to confront his son. The whispering cowboys grew silent. No one moved. Even the horses seemed to sense catastrophe.

"Benjamin, you've come to what I predicted," said the father.

"Yes, with your help," replied Ben.

295

"Prodigal son! Wild-horse hunter! Associate of low outcasts! . . . A prisoner to be tried an' sentenced in your home town! Rustler!"

"That last is a damn lie!" cried Ben, passionately.

"Rantin' will do no good. You'd better turn state's evidence an' get off. You might spare your family the shame of havin' a son an' brother in jail."

Ben's white face worked convulsively in a spasm of pain, and he tried to speak and raise his manacled hands in protest.

"I've done nothing I can turn state's evidence for," he finally managed to say. And with the words he attained a bitter cold grimness.

"Don't perjure your soul. Don't lie to your father."

"I wouldn't lie to you to save my life," replied Ben, sitting erect with ashen lips.

"You've already confessed your guilt. Why now do you deny? I tell you a clean breast of it will save you much. All of us."

"God knows I'm guilty, but not of what you think."

"Do you deny you've stolen cattle?"

"Deny! Do I *have* to deny that to my own father?" flashed Ben, with eyes like flames.

"I'm afraid you will. But do you deny it?"

"YES!" thundered Ben, his face swelling black for an instant. His terrible force checked the ruthless father, who shrank, momentarily, as if baffled. But passion, deeply controlled, began to rise in him also, and he returned to the attack.

"Do you deny you harbored an Indian outcast?"

"No. But I made him an honest man."

"Do you deny you made a partner of a Nevada outlaw?"

"I can't deny because I don't know. He never told me. But I made a friend who has helped me more than *you*."

"What do you say to the findin' of a sack of steers' ears up in the loft of your barn?"

Ben stared at his father in blank mute consternation.

"They found them. I've seen them," went on Ide, remorselessly. He seemed to be obsessed by the passion to prove something to himself. "These ears were slit, an' some nicked. We know from such marks who owned the stock they came from. So did you. You killed cattle to eat an' kept tally on numbers! An old trick of rustlers."

"*You* say I did?" questioned Ben, hoarsely and low.

"Yes. I saw the ears found in your loft."

Suddenly Marvie leaped out from the edge of the circle to confront Ide. He was pale, bristling, bursting with a fury of passionate conviction.

"Mr. Ide, there wasn't any sack in Ben's loft," he cried, shrilly. "I've hid my fishin' pole up in that loft all summer. It was empty."

Setter aimed a kick at Marvie and all but reached him. "Get out!" he growled, menacingly, forgetting the crowd.

"Come here, lad," spoke up Blaine. "If you know anythin' you can tell me."

"But, Dad," burst out Marvie, "now's the time to tell *them*."

"Blaine, keep that brat's mouth shut," ordered Setter, and he spoke so fiercely that Marvie slunk behind his father.

"Yes, Setter, for the present," grimly answered Blaine.

Setter's frame jerked with the loosening of restrained passion. His face was sweating and no longer olive tan.

"Mr. Ide," he said, "that Marvin Blaine is a little liar an' smart Alec. He doesn't mind his father. He steals hosses to ride out alone. He's a wild kid."

"Startin' in the steps of my son," returned Ide, bitterly. "Hart Blaine, you better not spare the rod on that boy, or you'll suffer some day as I do now. He'll likely become a wild-horse hunter an' rustler."

"Wal, whatever he becomes I'll stick by him," declared Blaine, in dry sarcasm.

Ide turned again, slowly and ponderously, to the bitter task of catechism. The momentary by-play of Marvie's had released the tension, which now tightened. Ben Ide's big eyes were black with pain. He seemed to see in his father a heartless Nemesis.

"You drove cattle into Silver Canyon?" he demanded.

"No."

"These officers found your camp in Silver Canyon."

"That's another lie. It was half a day's hard ride."

"Ho! Ho! Ho!" roared Judd, reeling in his saddle. "Mr. Ide, you seen some of his things we fetched. But we left others at his camp in Silver. The cattle are there an' his camp. If you need more proof, ride over with us."

"You black-hearted devils!" shouted Ben, in a hoarseness of realization. He rose in his stirrups. Then he sank as if near collapse.

Amos Ide raised a shaking hand — a long finger of accusation.

"You stole from ME!"

"Oh, my God! Father, you don't believe that?"

"You must indeed be wild. Mad is the word. Look at the proofs. If you'd come out like a man — tell the truth — I'd try to —"

"Proofs? They're not proofs — but lies — lies," cried Ben, brokenly. He was as white as death and his eyes streamed. He wrung his fettered hands. All seemed forgotten save this accusing father. "Listen — please — for God's sake listen! *Dad!* Don't turn away! Hear me! . . . I'm innocent of what you think! I *never* stole! Never! Never! I'm guilty enough. I don't care what they do with me. But don't believe I stole from you! That's horrible! Do you believe me a hardened vile criminal? . . . I'm innocent. Listen . . . Nevada and I and Modoc here — we went out to catch Bill Hall and his gang. Modoc had struck his trail. We found the cattle in Silver Canyon. We chased Hall out. Trailed him clear to the lava beds. Holed him in one of the caves! And we camped there — kept watch days, weeks — we starved Hall and his men out. We tied them up and started on our way to this ranch. I wanted Hart Blaine to see the proof of my honesty . . . But at Forlorn River the Indian saw California Red out on the ice . . . My God! it was terrible for me! . . . I've loved that wild stallion for years. I *had* to have him. You can't understand, but believe me, I had to catch him . . . There were only three of us. We couldn't corner him — run him down alone. So I thought of Hall and his men . . . I offered them freedom if they'd help me . . . They agreed. We caught him . . . *California Red!* It was like a dream . . . Then Hall saw these officers coming — and dragging one of my pack horses. He and his men left — without even their guns . . . That's all, Father — and it's — the honest — God's — truth!"

Amos Ide stood shaken, incredulous, terribly agitated by Ben's poignant narrative.

"My son, what would you make of these officers — and Less Setter?" he queried, in husky voice.

"For Mother's sake — for Hettie's — say you believe me?" entreated Ben. "Let them jail me. I can stand — anything — if you'll only say you believe — I couldn't steal from you."

Amos Ide's heart might have been convinced, but it could not in such hour of stress pierce the armor of his long disappointment in this son, of his stubborn positiveness.

"You tell a wild tale. It's like your life," he replied, with bitter repudiation.

Ina saw Ben's anguished face set and his head fall. He had asked only a last faith — that an unforgivable sin should not have his father's seal. He was scorned, ruined, damned. If Ina had possessed the strength she would have sprung to him, to reveal her love, her fidelity. But she was unable to move. She had doubted Ben; she had believed his self-accusation; and she hated herself for her miserable weakness. Too late! The moment passed. Even if she could walk out now, to his side, to bid him lift his head, it would be too late for her own consciousness of unfaith. She had not been big enough in his hour of great trial. And she was growing spent with the agony of the moment when she felt herself clutched from behind. Marvie was there, trembling, unable to speak. He pointed down the road. Ina's startled gaze caught a horse and rider approaching with the swift even celerity that characterized a racing cowboy. Who could this be? How swiftly he came! Through the gate, past the corrals! The rythmic beats of hoofs seemed one rapid patter. She saw long black hair streaming in the wind. Nevada!

As she stood, paralyzed, clinging to Marvie, the horse bore down on the circle of men. With loud cries they broke the lines, just escaping the sliding hoofs.

Ina saw Nevada in the air. He lit on his feet, almost within reach of her. As he passed, the unearthly whiteness of him, the terrible eyes, seemed to flash on her.

A thundering shot — and another — burst in front of Nevada.

Judd lurched out of his saddle and fell soddenly, face in the dust. His horse plunged. Walker screamed horribly. His face was half blown away. His horse, leaping, threw him to the ground, where he beat and wrestled like a decapitated fowl.

Bill Sneed, securing the bridle of Ben's plunging horse, dragged it down and aside.

"DON'T MOVE!" called Nevada, in a voice that whipped.

His black smoking gun, held low, quivered in his lean hand.

"*You!*" gasped Setter, his eyes popping out.

Nevada's hawklike head nodded in a terrible significance.

"All the time — you've been — Ben Ide's pard?" queried Setter, as if strangling.

"Pard? I reckon. Take a look at Judd an' Walker."

Setter's face flashed a greenish white.

"God Almighty!"

"Setter, look down the road," shouted Nevada. "See who's comin'. Bunch of riders, huh? Too far away, yes? . . . That's Strobel an' his deputies comin' with Bill Hall. I helped Strobel ketch that outfit. I made Bill Hall give you away to Strobel. An' I steered them heah! . . . Shore now it'll be great when Hall tells Mr. Blaine an' Mr. Ide just who you are."

Panic seemed to clutch Setter. But he did not appear to be concerned with Nevada's denouncement. There was a more vital and intimate thing. His changed face betrayed the malignant soul of a man of tremendous passions, betrayed, defeated, overwhelmed. His eyes stood out like round black balls. About him there was a suggestion of terrific need for hurry without the power. He knew what Nevada knew.

Then spasmodically he jerked at his gun.

Crash — crash! Nevada's gun spoke twice, so swiftly that the two shots were almost as one. The bullets whipped up dust far behind Setter. They had passed through his body. He seemed to stop — action — glare — meaning. Then he sank like an empty dropped sack.

Nevada strode over, holding the smoking gun up, and looked down.

"Ahuh!" he exclaimed, in strange cold finality.

Then wheeling, he made long strides for his horse. He did not see Ina, who could have touched him. Leaping astride, he bent a piercing gaze upon the stunned and sagging Ben. A wonderful smile lightened the corded marble of his lean face. He spurred the horse.

"So long, pard. We're square," he called. "I'll stop over home long enough to get a pack — an' take a good-bye look at old California Red."

The last words came as he was speeding away. Through the gate he passed swift as a flash and swung off to avoid the group of horsemen riding up the road. The dust trailed from under the fleet horse. Nevada did not look back. Soon he disappeared in a hollow.

CHAPTER
SIXTEEN

Ben sat his horse, eyes riveted on the gray slope where Nevada's wild pace had soon taken him out of sight. *So long, pard. We're square!* That farewell would ring in Ben's ears and heart until he died. Nevada had saved him. But deliverance at the cost of his friend seemed on the moment pale and worthless. Ben's varying emotions had clamped into a wrenching, insupportable pang. His one instinct was to fly in pursuit of this friend who had loved him.

Other sensations tore Ben from the fixity of his gaze down the sage slope, from consciousness of the havoc in his heart. There was a pulling at his leg. Marvie, wild with rapture, the brown freckles standing out on his white face! On Ben's other side someone was taking his manacled hands. Ina! She was sobbing, clinging to him. Her eyes were pools of transport, anguish, of unutterable thought.

Bill Sneed, too, was there, bareheaded, with wrinkled brow and stern lips.

"Miss Ina, let go his hands," he said, tersely. "Darn keys got Judd's blood all over them. They was in his breast pocket . . . There, Ben."

"Thanks, cowboy," rejoined Ben, spreading his arms with a strange sense of the significance of freedom. It rushed over him, sweet as life in its sweetest moments. Then he lowered a hand to Ina, beginning to feel a release from shock. She seized it in both hers, carried it to her lips, her wet face. The crowd pressed close, staring, clamoring. Ina was drawn away by a woman, perhaps her mother. Marvie was tugging at him. In the babble of hoarse and excited voices Ben could not hear him. Then the hubbub quieted.

"Clear the way! Get back, you cow-punchin' *hombres*!" That was Strobel's voice.

Ben saw the sheriff, on foot, gun in hand, come into sight with a group of riders. The widening circle revealed the prostrate bodies of the three men, lying in grotesque laxity.

"Damn me!" ejaculated Strobel, raising a hand in awe.

"Wal, Sheriff," replied Blaine, advancing, "we couldn't have done anythin' if we'd wanted to. He rode down on us like a whirlwind, an' it 'peared to me he shot Judd an' Walker before he hit the ground. Then he razzed Setter to pull a gun . . . An', you see!"

Strobel stood over Setter, curiously, without compassion, and then with his foot shoved the inert body over on its back.

"Two bullet holes — inch apart — over that left vest pocket! By gum! who was thet fellar Nevada?"

"We don't know. Young Ide said he didn't, either," returned Blaine. "But Setter knew him — that's as sure as death."

"Wal, sir, Nevada was so amiable on the way over I never suspected him of any deep game," said Strobel. "But when he lit out down the road a ways I shore was afraid he was up to somethin' bad."

"Reckon it's somethin' bad to you, Sheriff, but it has another kind of a look to *me*," responded Blaine, feelingly.

"These other two fellars, Judd an' Walker, who're they?" queried Strobel.

"Sheriff an' deputy from Redlands."

"Humph! Never heard of them. Must be new appointed. I was in Redlands last winter. By gum!"

"Strobel, is it true you've got Bill Hall?"

"Look at him, thar! . . . The heavy fellar with the big bushy head. That's Hall. An' there's his outfit . . . Hart, I don't mind tellin' you it was the darnedest piece of fool luck I ever seen."

"Wal, wal, so say I," returned Blaine, with loud breath. "Let's clear up this muddle right now."

Blaine gave orders to his cowboys to cover up the dead men.

"Mr. Ide, go into my office, please," he went on. "Strobel, bring in Hall, an' anybody else you want. Marvie, you come with me . . . Ben, I reckon you're needed."

The strangest hour of that terrible day, and as sad as full of joy, was this in which Ben found himself in Blaine's office. One look at his father's face had been enough for Ben. His bitterness, his almost hate, suffered a violent check.

Blaine proved a wonderful contrast to Amos Ide. Havoc, indeed, showed in his worn visage, but it could not dim the light, the unutterable relief, the return of will strengthened by the grief and wisdom of experience.

"Men," he said, sitting on his desk, with his arm around his wide-eyed son, "I'll have my say first, an' be short an' sweet about it. Setter was responsible for all the deals I went into. I won't lay the blame of greed at his door. To my shame I confess I was greedy. But I'd been poor so many years that when money came, with the power it brings, I lost my head. I never meant to be dishonest. I always hated buyin' out these homesteaders. If I've been drawn into somethin' crooked — an' lately I've feared I have been — it was because of my ignorance an' blindness. I can an' will be square by every rancher I've ever dealt with. I reckon I can save Tule Lake Ranch out of the wreck. But that's all, unless the paper of mine Setter held can't be taken over by banks or men he dealt with."

"Mr. Blaine, I'm shore glad to tell you that any paper dealin's of Setter's are null an' void," spoke up Strobel.

"Wal, then, I'm luckier than I deserve to be," rejoined Blaine, fervently. "Amos, where do you stand in this deal?"

"Nothin' but Setter's death could have ever saved me from ruin — maybe worse," replied Amos Ide, solemnly.

"Wal! Reckon I thought I was the only fool round Tule Lake," responded Blaine, bluntly. "Amos, mebbe some of our differences can be laid to the door of Less Setter."

"That's dawnin' on me," said Ide, ponderingly.

"Now, Strobel, will you tell us your side of these doin's?" asked Blaine, turning to the sheriff. "Just pass over our quarrel at Welch's ranch. I was wrong an' you was right."

"As to that, Mr. Blaine, I'm bound to tell you I'm a good deal better informed now than I was then," replied the sheriff, frankly. "But as you say, I was on the right track. All losses of stock for the last two years can be summed up in one word. Bill Hall! We have him here, an' he vouches for that. So I can get down to today ... I was ridin' some miles up Forlorn River when this cowboy Nevada met me. He whooped an' threw up his hat in the strangest way. I reckoned the darn fool was drunk. But shore he wasn't. 'Heah's Bill Hall an' outfit, over heah a ways, on spent hosses, an' without guns!' ... Wal, then I thought Nevada was crazy. But he wasn't. I let him guide us an' soon we caught up with Hall. He surrendered without a fight. That's all, an' I reckon Hall can clear up a good deal."

Blaine's face was now a study. "Hall, come here," he called to the handcuffed rustler, who stood in the background.

The burly Hall strode with heavy step to confront Blaine. He smelled of sweat and tobacco, and he made a dusty, ragged, sordid figure. But there was frankness in his mien and fearlessness in his eyes.

"Hall, would promise of light sentence persuade you to turn state's evidence in court an' talk straight to us here?" demanded Blaine.

"Reckon it would," replied the rustler.

"Wal, you have my promise. An' if Amos Ide an' Strobel agree you'll sure get off easy."

"Strikes me all right," said Strobel.

They turned to interrogate Amos Ide. He stood erect, in exactly the same posture that he had assumed on entrance, and his features attested to grave conflict of soul. Blaine had to repeat the question at issue.

"I'll not prosecute Hall. I'll not appear in court," answered Ide.

"There, Hall — you're as lucky as — as the rest of us," went on Blaine. "What's your idee of this talk of Ben Ide rustlin' cattle — especially his father's?"

"Damn nonsense!" replied Hall, with gruff bluntness. "You fellars must have been locoed. Setter filled your heads full. It was plain business with him."

"Setter! Business? . . . Then he was a rustler?" ejaculated Blaine.

"Reckon he was, if you split hairs over it. We worked together. I rustled the cattle an' he sold them. Five years ago we worked in Arizona. It got hot for him thar. He went to Nevada. An' then he come to Californy an' sent fer me."

"How long ago?"

"Reckon about three years."

"Are there any other rustler outfits around Silver Meadow?"

"No. Mine is the only one. But we worked so it'd look like thar was other outfits. Thet was Setter's idee. We drove most stock up over Silver Canyon Pass. Down on the south side thar was homesteaders who knowed cattle was bein' rustled. The reason they never squealed was because Setter had us leave a good many unbranded calves an' heifers on their range. Thet was another of his idees. So we got the cattle across the Nevada line."

"Who're Judd an' Walker?"

"Reckon I don't know," rejoined Hall. "Thet's straight. But the last time I seen Setter, more'n a month ago, he was full of his biggest an' last deal. He didn't say what. But thet's plain now as the nose on your face. He was keen to fix rustlin' on young Ide hyar, fer reasons I couldn't see then. So we planned to drive some of the Ide stock into Silver an' hold it thar. Judd an' Walker fitted in hyar somewhars. Reckon I had their deal pat soon as I seen them lyin' dead out thar. Mebbe Judd was a bonyfide sheriff. But if you'll go to the county he represents you'll find he hasn't been thar long. Thet he had lots of money, spent it free, an' got himself appointed sheriff. Another old trick of Setter's."

Hart Blaine cast a look of mingled pity and scorn at his rancher rival, Amos Ide. Then he bent to the wide-eyed Marvie.

"Lad, I reckon you can speak up now," he said, kindly. "You didn't get much chance out there. But your daddy was sure ready to hear what you had to say."

"I stole a hoss an' run off to watch Judd an' Walker," began Marvie, and hesitated fearfully.

"Ahuh! Wal, reckon it's the first time any good ever come of your runnin' off, an' you'll escape a lickin' *this* time. Go on."

"I took Ina's field glass, an' rode round the west side of the lake, an' got off, an' crawled behind sage bushes till I could see Ben's cabin. Then I watched. An' I saw Judd an' Walker carry a heavy sack from Ben's cabin to the barn. When they came out they didn't have it. An' —"

"Strobel," spoke up Blaine, interrupting the lad, "Judd fetched over a few of the split an' nicked steers' ears that he swore he'd got out of a sack up in Ben's loft. Said he'd left the sack there to show us."

"Well, Dad, it *never* was there before Judd went over," burst out Marvie, "'cause I hid my fishin' tackle up in Ben's loft, an' I went up there 'most a dozen times. Never was no sack there — *never!*"

Blaine regarded the youngster with a grave smile.

"Marvin, among other things cleared up," he said, seriously, "there seems to be the fact of your stealin' a horse an' runnin' off to Forlorn River — say 'most a dozen times."

"Y-ye-yes — sir," faltered Marvie, suddenly appalled.

Blaine drew the lad to him and actually hugged him, while his gray hard eyes glistened.

"My boy, I'll give you your hoss to ride when you like," he said, "an' as for fishin' an' chasin' wild hosses — wal, mebbe me an' my friend there — Amos Ide —

mebbe we missed somethin' that might have made us better men — an' fathers."

Then he arose with dignity.

"Strobel, I guess our little private confab is over," he said. "You can have the boys an' buckboards to drive to Hammell . . . Good day, Bill Hall. I wonder what made you a rustler. Wal, wal! go mend your ways, as all of us need to."

With that he turned to Ben and offered his horny hand.

"Reckon you'll stay for dinner before ridin' back to Forlorn River an' that red hoss."

Ben met the outstretched hand and found other response difficult.

"Thank you, Mr. Blaine. I'll grab a bite an' rustle back. I clear forgot California Red."

"You remember my ten-thousand-dollar offer for him?"

"No. I'd forgotten. But I — now — it — Oh, Mr. Blaine, I can never take the money."

"Why not? You earned it, an' if you didn't surely then — Nevada —"

"No — no!" broke in Ben, hastily, checking the rancher. "I can't part with Red."

"Wal, you'll have to take the money, anyhow," he replied, slyly. "I expect it an' you an' California Red will all be in the family."

Then he stalked out of the open door.

Ben, suddenly ecstatic, torn by thrills and heartbeats that were dazing him, hastened to follow. And he caught a glimpse of his father still standing motionless,

312

like a statue, riveted to the spot. Ben wheeled — passed on.

"*Benjamin!*" called his father, in a tone Ben had never heard. Nevertheless he rushed on.

"*Ben!*"

But Ben went out, deaf to that voice.

Hurriedly Ben swung around the cabin toward the Blaine camp. Marvie made a dive for him.

"Can I ride over with you an' see California Red?" pleaded the lad.

"Sure, if your dad lets you," replied Ben.

"Gee! Dad took my breath. I was scared stiff when I gave myself away. But now I know you an' me together, an' mebbe Ina, too, have got Dad licked."

"It looks that way, Marvie," said Ben, as he strode swiftly on, with the lad running at his side.

"Ben, we worse than licked *your* dad," babbled Marvie, in high glee. "Did you see how he looked — after my dad got through spoutin'?"

"No — Marvie — I didn't," returned Ben, huskily.

"By golly! you should have seen him. He looked somethin' terrible . . . But you spoke to him, didn't you?"

"No, Marvie. I just run."

"Ben, you will, won't you?" queried Marvie, earnestly. "After all, he's your dad. We've sure had hard nuts to crack in our dads, huh? . . . Ben, what my dad said about fishin' an' chasin' wild hosses was an eye-openin', wasn't it? Gosh! I'd have liked Ina to hear that. Sort of a dig at your dad, too."

313

"Indeed it — was," returned Ben, with a deep-throated laugh.

"Here's Ina in the hammock," said Marvie. "Aw, she's cryin', Ben."

They approached the juniper tree and the swaying hammock. Ben thought Marvie's eyes were sharper than his, or at least clearer at the moment. Ben saw a lovely face and woebegone eyes.

"Ina!"

Marvie gave the hammock a tug. "Say, I'll turn my back for a minnit," he said, mischievously.

Ben heard, but could not take advantage of Marvie's fine appreciation of the moment. He drew the box seat closer to Ina, and took her hands in his.

"Oh — Ben!" she faltered.

"Ina, how terrible for you!" he ejaculated. "All the worry — and suspense — and then — Nevada! . . . My God! he was terrible! . . . I see it all, now, dear. It was written from the first! . . . But you must forget — you must think —"

"Ben, you — you misunderstand," sobbed Ina, wildly. "It's not the worry — or suspense — or Nevada! . . . Oh! He was grand! . . . I'm down in the dust — because — because — I — believed — you guilty!"

Ben's heart froze. He leaped to his feet.

Marvie shied away from the hammock, suddenly panic-stricken. "Ben, this ain't no place for me. I'll rustle the hosses."

"What?" whispered Ben, almost inaudibly, with transfixed gaze on those beautiful, darkly dilating eyes.

" 'Guilty as hell,' you said," wailed Ina. "I believed it
. . . I thought you meant — guilty of stealing. How
could I — know — about California Red?"

"But you loved me!" burst out Ben, who seemed to
be laboring under a horrible dread.

"It didn't look — as if I did," cried Ina.

"You love me *now?*"

"Ben Ide! — you — you . . . I love you so . . . If you
don't stop looking like that — and forgive me — I'll —
I'll die right here — at your feet."

Ben fell upon his knees and gathered her in his arms,
hammock and all. An interval followed, devoid of clear
sight, and reason, and consciousness of emotion, except
for something exalting and unutterably sweet. And then
it was Ina who brought him back to his senses.

"Dad said that ten thousand dollars — and you — and
California Red — would all be in the family?" asked
Ina, rapturously, after Ben had narrated the proceed-
ings in her father's office.

"Yes. You could have knocked me down with a
feather . . . Asked me to dinner, too! But I can't stay.
Modoc and I will have to hurry back to California Red.
We've got him tied down in the corral."

"Oh, it's all too good to be true!" murmured Ina.
"This will teach Dad some sense. And your dad, too."

Ben hung his head.

"You let him make up with you, of course?"

"I did not . . . Never looked when he called," replied
Ben, hoarsely.

"He called you? Oh, Ben, you should have gone to him! He's old, and it was his very love for you that hurt him so — made him hard . . . You forgave me. Now forgive him."

"I'm afraid I never will."

"Ben! That's not like you. It's cruel, bitter. It's not Christian. Be magnanimous. Be big like Nevada!"

"Don't speak of him," whispered Ben.

"Oh, dearest, forgive me," entreated Ina. "It's too soon to think of him — and your father . . . Now, Ben, take up your work — the life you love — before you were forced to fight . . . What you do I will do — what you love I will love."

"It's settled, then? Ina, you will marry me?"

"Yes," she answered, softly.

"When?"

"Whenever you come for me. Dad said he would pack up at once for Tule Lake Ranch. That means work . . . As soon as I get home I'll go at once to see your mother and Hettie. Imagine their joy! Oh, it will be happiness to tell them . . . You will find me at home — waiting."

"You — you angel," whispered Ben, unsteadily. Then with a tender touch on her flushed cheek he stood up again, with decision and renewed energy. "I'll hurry back to California Red. I'm the richest man in the world with you and him . . . Ina, that reminds me, I must have ten or twelve thousand dollars in the Hammell bank. For wild horses! Poor Dad, I'd like to show him that bank account. So you'll not be marrying a poor man, exactly . . . As soon as I break Red I'll

come to you, Ina. I want to ride Red into Hammell —
to Tule Lake Ranch . . . Yes, I want my father to see that
horse . . . But, Ina, I couldn't sell him."

"I should think not. He belongs to *me*," replied Ina,
archly.

"Of course he does, but *you* belong to me," returned
Ben, with happy significance. "And now I must go, Ina.
I see Marvie and Modoc waiting with the horses. By
George! there's my black stallion — one we caught in
the caves. Judd found him, brought him in. Luck! luck!
. . . And now, if it'll only rain!"

"It will, Ben. I know. An old wild goose honked it
down to me not long ago."

Of all the wild horses Ben had ever broken — and they
numbered hundreds — California Red turned out to be
the easiest to handle, the most intelligent, the most
responsive. Considering the spirit of the great stallion
and his years of absolute mastery of the wild range, Ben
thought his capitulation most remarkable. And he put a
good deal of it down to the treachery of the ice, making
the capture of Red so quick and easy. Ben made a
mental reservation, growing out of his experience with
wild horses, that Red would never again, in all his life,
trust himself on ice.

With infinite patience and kindness, yet with arm of
iron and inflexible will, Ben broke the stallion after a
method of his own.

One sunset, in early October, when the day's work was
done and Ben allowed himself to dream of his

triumphal ride into town, he observed Modoc most attentively watching the last flight of wild geese toward the south. The familiar honk, honk, honk seemed singularly full and significant of the beauty and strangeness of nature.

"What do they say, Modoc?" he queried.

The Indian turned his gaze on the darkly sinister, red-and-purple sunset, and from that to the wonderful panoply of clouds over the gray sage hills.

"Heap storm soon. Heap rain — snow — big winter," replied Modoc, with his inscrutable mystic gleam of eye, and his slow majestic gesture toward the horizon.

Then into Ben's heart full of thanksgiving and joy there crept a cruel recurrence of a new pang. Nevada! His friend would not be there to revel in the rain, to share his gratitude that the stock of the ranges and the wild creatures would be saved. Nevada was gone, surely to some unknown range, never back to his old life, whatever that had been. Setter's recognition of Nevada had been illuminating with its terrible significance.

Morning brought a leaden, swiftly moving canopy of clouds, and a fine drizzle. All day the storm gathered, slowly, as if the forces of nature moved ponderously to this long-neglected task.

Night brought the bursting of the floodgates of the heavens. Such a deluge poured down upon the little cabin that Ben feared the roof would cave in. How he reveled in the roar and patter and gust and ceaseless drip, drip, drip.

It rained all night, and all the next day, and for six succeeding days and nights there were only few intervals when rain was not roaring over the land.

Muddy streams poured off the hills; raging torrents tore down the canyon beds; the sage flats around Mule Deer Lake were submerged with water; Forlorn River emptied a wide turgid yellow flood into the swelling lake.

When at length the black pall of cloud broke, and the sun burst through, it shone down upon a brightened and freshened land. The clouds lifted, dispersed, and blew away on a bracing October wind. After seven years of unparalleled drought Northern California was saved.

On an Indian-summer day, when the golds and crimsons and purples of autumn flamed on the hills, Ben rode California Red into the village of his boyhood, from which he had been an outcast, and where he discovered he had become a hero.

The great stallion created more of a sensation than any circus that had ever visited Hammell.

Quite by accident, or incredible good fortune, or through fate — Ben could not decide which — he met Ina and Marvie and Hettie on the main street of Hammell. They drove up in a new shiny buckboard just as Ben mounted Red to ride out to Tule Lake Ranch. Marvie yelled and Hettie screamed, while Ina clasped both hands to her breast and gazed at Ben's horse in such mute rapture that it seemed she never saw Ben at all.

Ben's star was in the ascendant that day. The surprise of meeting him shocked Ina from her balance; the manifest change of public opinion about him quite overwhelmed her. He never knew what prompted him to importune her, when they had a moment alone, to marry him then and there.

Ina had no resistance. Her eyes hung upon his, fascinated, in a mute transport.

"Dearest, I didn't intend this," he went on, swiftly. "It's just happened. This is my day. Make it perfect . . . Marry me *now*. We've Marvie and Hettie to go with us to the minister's."

"Oh, Ben — it's so sudden," she gasped. "I know I promised — I should — I must keep it . . . But, oh! — Why, I'm not dressed to — to — and what will they say at home?"

"Just think what it'd mean to me to ride up to Hart Blaine and say, 'Meet my wife'! . . . I hope I'm above revenge, Ina, but that thought stampedes me."

"It'd — it'd — make you very — very happy?" she faltered.

"Such a question! I can't tell you. Please, Ina, please — darling! What difference does a day or a week matter?"

She was pale now, with a pallor that made her eyes dark purple gulfs. She was earnest, grave — and Ben trembled at what he saw.

"If I consent — when we've told Mother and Dad — will you let me take you home to your father?" she flashed.

"*Ina!*" he cried, in poignant distress. The thought pierced his happy ardor. He had forgotten the hard old man who had never understood him, never believed in him. A wrenching pang brought back the old trouble and the new conflict. This time it seemed to rend his soul.

"I've seen your dad," went on Ina. "His heart is breaking. At last he sees that he should have let you choose your own life . . . Ben, say you will forgive him."

Her hand was on his; her eyes were shining with divination of her victory.

"Yes — yes, I will," burst out Ben, and it seemed that with those words rancor and bitterness passed out of his heart.

So they were married, and Ben rode California Red alongside the buckboard, from which Marvie shot naïve remarks, and where Ina sat as one in a dream, and Hettie smiled mysteriously, as if she was in possession of vast love secrets herself.

Ben rode up the lane ahead of the buckboard and into Tule Lake Ranch, finding at the sunset hour a horde of noisy cowboys home from work. With Bill Sneed at their head they ringed the great stallion, raising a clamor that filled a long empty void in Ben's heart.

In the midst of the excitement Hart Blaine strode out, his gray hair standing, his ruddy face wreathed in a smile of welcome and wonder.

"My land! I seen him from the house. So this is California Red? . . . Reckon at last I understand you, Ben . . . Ride over an' show him to Amos Ide."

Marvie drove the buckboard in with a grand flourish and he stood up to yell: "Ben, have you told Dad yet?"

321

Ben vibrated to that, as if he had been suddenly galvanized, but he was panic-stricken. Ina made the situation worse by blushing scarlet at Marvie's words and beating a precipitous retreat to the house.

"What's up, Ben?" queried Blaine, with his characteristic bluntness, but he was grinning. "You look sort of white round the gills."

"I forgot to tell you," blurted out Ben, "Ina and I got married in town . . . I — I should have spoken out at once, sir, but I forgot."

"Haw! Haw! Haw!" roared Blaine, slapping his leg with a broad hand. "Wal, reckon it's a wild-hoss hunter's way to be sudden . . . Come in an' tell Mother . . . An' that check for California Red squares me for a weddin' present."

The afterglow of sunset kept the day lingering as Ina led California Red across the intervening fields, with Ben walking between her and Hettie. The wire fences had gates where the old path used to cross and a new path showed well trodden. It led into the yard, where at the wood pile Amos Ide in his shirt sleeves was wielding an ax. He did not hear until they were quite close. Then, springing erect, he dropped his ax and became riveted.

One glance filled Ben's heart with remorse, but he clung to his preconceived plan of a meeting with his father.

"Hello, Dad," he said, cheerfully, as if they had not been separated for more than a few days, as if no dark obstacle had ever loomed between them.

"My son!" exclaimed Ide, huskily.

"Brought my wife and California Red home," went on Ben, with extended hand.

The old man fought valiantly to rise to Ben's idea of reconciliation — to realize his astounding statements without being utterly overcome.

"Ben? — Your wife! Daughter of Hart Blaine! . . . You've come home — back to the old man?"

"Sure, Dad. Back to you and Mother, for a visit, anyhow. I always was coming . . . Take a peep at my bank book, Dad, and at this check Hart Blaine just gave me! . . . And look at this girl! . . . All in one day, Dad! . . . Now what do you think of your wild-horse hunter?"